Secrets of the Devil Vine

Faith Kaiser

ISBN 13: 978-1-60489-194-2, trade paper
ISBN 13: 978-1-60489-195-9, hardcover
ISBN: 1-60489-194-7, trade paper
ISBN: 1-60489-195-5, hardcover
Library of Congress Control Number 2017948556
Printed on acid-free paper
by Publishers Graphics
Printed in the United States of America

Hardcover binding by: Heckman Bindery
Typesetting and page layout: Joe Taylor, Teresa Boykin
Proofreading: Shelby Parrish
Cover design: Teresa Boykin

Cover drawing: Damaris Anderson
Photo of Faith Kaiser: Demaris Anderson

This is a work of fiction:
any resemblance
to persons living or dead is coincidental.

Livingston Press is part of The University of West Alabama,
and thereby has non-profit status.
Donations are tax-deductible:
brothers and sisters, we need 'em.

first edition
6 5 4 3 3 2 1

Secrets
of the
Devil Vine

Lovingly dedicated to "Tut" Altman Riddick,
whose daily call for another chapter helped a pile of paper
become a book.

Pearl, 2009

Pearl was trapped between her garden, God, and good manners. She argued continuously with herself, or anyone who would engage, as to whether God was a woman or a man. She had plenty of examples to win either side of that argument and after eighty-some-odd years, had not yet come to a conclusion.

She sat in a loose cotton shift working in her garden, pleased that even at her age, she could still sit cross legged and get up with grace. She yanked weeds out of the well-turned soil and occasionally found a late vegetable which she placed in her basket. Her glory days, now long gone, nibbled relentlessly at the edge of her mind. Though she now sat in dirt, the memories of the world she had created for herself back then continuously flew around her head, a swarm of aggravating gnats that simply would not allow her to forget. In those days, it had been hard to tell where her physical beauty stopped and her grace and charm began. Yes, she admitted, she had been cunning, even beguiling, when necessary. Perhaps bordering on what some would consider evil. She had done some things that she shouldn't have. But it was so long ago, she no longer cared, if she ever had. Her lips were pulled tight into a thin line, switching from side to side, thinking on recently heard gossip. It seems her youngest child had shown up, like the bad penny Pearl considered her to be. How many years had it been since she had even gotten a card from the girl, much less a call? Yet, Abby was back, digging up all that Pearl had so carefully buried, hidden and forgotten.

From her spot in the garden, Pearl studied the small, four-square building. It balanced on wobbly looking four-foot high pilings, tall enough to keep it high and dry should the piddling little creek rise above the normal ebb and flow of a tidal creek. It had never been a proud house, though at some point someone had tried to add a bit of dignity by attaching a small porch. As porches go though, it was pretty much useless, inaccessible from the inside, and now even the steps had given in to rot and termites. The whole thing just leaned along with the leaning house.

Pearl's little house by the creek was certainly not the cottage she had envisioned it would become when she bought it so many years ago. Pearl looked at the place and shook her head. How long ago now it seemed that she had been the Grand Dame of her home that drew the envy of all the neighbors. The big white house sat high atop clay cliffs overlooking the bay. In those days, she drank sweet tea from silver goblets and watched sail boat regattas and sunsets from her own front porch. It seemed so long ago she wondered if she had ever lived that life.

Once there had been Ecor Rouge, and now there was this, this *shack*. It was nestled deep under large live oak trees at the end of a long, sandy drive, invisible to the outside world. That much, at least, was just the way she liked it. Out of sight and out of mind.

Pearl specialized in concealment, secrecy really, spattered with a bit of paranoia. She had no intentions of ever letting anyone know any of her business, past or present, and offered only a vacant face if anyone was rude enough to pry. She lived like a pauper but had amassed rights in more oil wells than she could count and owned more land than anyone could guess. She knew she couldn't take it with her, but she'd be damned if she would sell one single thing she owned. She'd eat dirt and wear rags first.

Pearl bought this little place years ago when her husband developed an allergy to the pecan sap that leaked out of the trees in the yard atop the clay cliffs. Every fall when the trees started oozing, they would escape the sticky mist by coming down to the little cabin on the creek. That's the story she told, anyway. Only she knew the real reason. It was her never-ending need to own as much real estate as possible. Plus, the creek ran north and south, a sure sign that gas or oil was in the area. It wasn't long after she purchased the house that she was making a deal for twenty-five acres across the creek. Now she owned both sides. Pearl's elegant and elderly husband, long since passed, found this quirk of his wife's peculiar personality to be quite charming and gladly brought out the check book whenever some land caught her attention. After all, he had been the one of many suitors who finally caught the beautiful woman and anything she wanted was his joy to provide.

Pearl trudged up the sandy drive, making her way to the door of the cabin, her slippers dragging in the dirt. She shook off her canvas hat, flapped her gloves together and dropped them all on the stoop at the door. It was time to sit in her green chair and have a hot cup of coffee.

Pearl went inside, passing her palm lovingly over the antique Portuguese paned doors as she entered. These doors were one of few changes she had managed to make long ago when she first bought the little house. Her plan had been to turn the hut into a darling cottage. She looked around almost as if something might have changed while she was out gardening. Out there, all the green and growing things changed constantly. Even the soil was sculpted and reshaped after a washing rain. No such luck in here. Walls were papered in thick brown butcher paper, something she had done during the first fall down here trying to cover the slits between the wallboards. Her original plan had been to cover the brown paper in some rich and luscious Southern wallpaper design. Like most of her plans, that never materialized.

The inside, aside from the brown-papered walls, was a stark contrast from the outside. When they first came down from Ecor Rouge, she managed to stuff the little house with fine art and antiques. Shining wood glimmered and sparkling silver candlesticks stood at attention. Bouquets of fresh flowers were artfully stuffed into anything that could serve as a vase.

The living room, dining room and kitchen were all in one open space. The bedrooms were on the backside of the house, each with a window view of the porch, but no doors that accessed it. In the one small bathroom there was a claw foot tub, toilet, sink, and a good sized chest freezer that held forgotten things from seasons past. Atop the mass of frozen mysteries lay birds. Beaks, feathers, feet and all. Pearl thought she might someday buy a good hound and train it to retrieve the frozen birds. As was the fate of her many passions, this one had not come to pass either.

She shuffled over to the kitchen sink and picked up the coffee pot off the stove as she passed. The phone rang and she counted the rings. If she counted nine, and there was a quick call back, she'd answer. She counted to herself, but said aloud, "Nine." Then the call came again. Pearl picked up the black receiver and stretched out the coiled cord over to the sink while she filled her coffee cup.

"Pearl? Is that you?" Doesie asked in her usual breathless tone.

"Who the hell else would be answering my phone, Doesie?" Pearl snapped.

Doesie was Pearl's oldest and dearest friend since they had attended the state teacher's college together. God, how many years ago now? Sixty? Doesie knew, or thought she knew, everything there was to know about Pearl. She knew that Pearl could mesmerize a snake charmer and he wouldn't see it coming until a pair of fangs needled him.

Some thought Pearl was crazy, or at the very least eccentric, but Doesie knew otherwise. She knew her friend was much smarter than most of those who fell for her charms. Once Pearl fixed her eye on a prize, the price of the toll was not important if she decided to cross that bridge to stake her claim. Doesie had heard some horrible things about Pearl, most of which she chose to ignore as her mother taught her. Keeping a good friend is worth looking away sometimes, and especially when the years settle in with a measure of loneliness.

"She's back, Pearl! She's in town. Well, at least in the county. Betty Lou saw her at the Old Tyme Feed and Seed."

"Yes," Pearl sighed. "I know. I may live in the woods, but I don't live in the dark, you know."

"Well, you never answer your phone so how would I know that you know? And how do you know, by the way? You never come out of those damned woods."

"Word travels fast. I heard she bought herself a fancy-pants house up on the bluff. She and that damn Yankee husband of hers."

"Has she called? Have you seen her?" Doesie asked. "What is she doing back down here?"

"No. No. And who knows?" Pearl answered. "That child can't say a kind word to me. I gave those children everything

I had. I worked my fingers to the bone. Hell, I didn't have decent underwear and they went to private schools. But can she call and say 'Hey Mom. I'm home'? Hell no. Ungrateful brat."

Pearl grew silent. She looked at the Frigidaire, taking note for the umpteenth time at the drooping freezer edging. Years ago, she had come up with the bright idea of defrosting the ice box with a blowtorch. It had been a hot day and all she wanted was some ice cubes, frozen solid and stuck deep in the back of the freezer under aluminum foil packets of unknown contents. The blowtorch melted the rubber trim around the freezer compartment, igniting a small piece and filling the room with the smell of burning tires. Pearl clapped out the blaze with both hands and a dishtowel, but the melted gasket still hung down the front of the refrigerator door, stretched and sagging. The freezer now seeped out mushy water every time she opened the door. The ice trays remained frozen solid and trapped.

"Pearl? Are you still there?" Doesie asked.

"Where the hell else would I be, Doesie? Are you drinking already today?"

"Are you worried at all? I mean about all that stuff that went on down at the fort? What if she tries to dig up all that mess?" Doesie sounded worried.

"I have absolutely no idea what you are talking about, Doesie Mayfield. I have told you before, do not ring this phone or darken my door when your snout has been in the hooch."

Pearl slammed down the receiver and poured another cup of coffee, closed her eyes and tried to settle her breathing. The dense aroma of fresh brewed coffee enveloped her. She lifted the cup from the saucer and poured coffee into the dainty plate and gently blew. She sipped warm coffee from her saucer just as she had seen her mother do a million times.

After her coffee, standing at her bathroom mirror, she looked at her image. She always kept in mind that real ladies never look like they *have* to work a garden, so she made a practice of wearing long sleeved shirts and a brimmed hat. Pearl had no interest in scrutinizing her skin so tanned, weathered, and wrinkled. She failed to notice the frown etched onto her forehead, the white and thinning hair, her stooping spine, or her once dazzling green eyes now a cloudy, faded hazel underneath eyebrows that no longer existed. Pearl smoothed her cotton shirt down with bony hands and unkempt nails. With a passing glance she looked back at the glass, noting she had maintained her girlish figure. After that last look, she picked up her garden basket and shuffled out of her antique doors, retrieving her hat and gloves, passing the bloody carcass of a rabbit she had beat to death just this morning with her shovel.

As she walked back out to the garden, she wondered why Abigail was back down here. She never had understood children, especially her own. She already had three too many when Abigail happened along. Quite by surprise. Pearl resented her the most, that fourth pregnancy making it clear to the outside world she'd had an affair. It wasn't the embarrassment of being found out in an affair that offended her. Shame was not a feeling Pearl knew. But the interruption and scrutiny of her private life was not acceptable.

Pearl made a point of being delightful, downright captivating, to any stranger she met, especially if there might be something in it for her. Her own children had never enjoyed the affection she poured on a distant nephew, or the warmth and loving praise she concocted on the spot for a neighbor's child. Regarding her own brood, in Pearl's opinion, all of that sweet stuff was hocus-pocus Hollywood bullshit. She had no remorse or regret for anything she had ever done. Hell, she didn't even know what those emotions felt like. What she knew was that her secrets were simply her business and Abigail was not clever enough to get to the bottom of them. Determination set on her pursed lips as she vowed to herself Abby would get no information. She had hoped that at least one of her children had inherited her street sense, her sense of survival, but it seemed to her they were all gooey and soft. She shook her head. Such a disappointment, her children.

Abigail: 2009

She shed houses like a snake shed its skin. Abigail Whitney Stewart inherited her mother's penchant for buying real estate. However, unlike her mother, Abby sold hers, typically after the last box was unpacked and the last improvement had been made. Like a dog that continues to circle and scratch in an attempt to get his sleeping spot just right, Abby never found a house in which she could be at home. With each new house, she was sure that *this* time she had found the ideal home, one where her spirit might settle and be at ease.

Her husband transferred frequently and they had agreed years ago that if she was to drop her jobs and her friends to traipse around the country after him, she got to choose and buy all houses. Joe really didn't care where they lived, as long as Abby was happy, and he trusted her explicitly when it came to real estate. He recognized her uncanny ability to buy and sell at just the right time.

Abby dashed to this newly purchased house ahead of Joe, to open doors, turn on lights and get everything just right before he saw the house for the first time. She left him in the hotel with a hand-drawn map to the house and a kiss on his lips. Now she stood on the front porch waiting for him to arrive. As she waited, she admired the heavily wooded yard with magnolia trees whose scent would knock her socks off, giant crepe myrtles, and old, established azaleas. She sighed as she looked at the vines that crawled all over her bushes.

"Oh, Joe," Abby spoke into her cell phone, pacing on the porch. "Wait until you see this house! She is a real southern beauty. It's very private, set well back from the road and right down the street from the bay. She reminds me so much of Ecor Rouge!" Her nostrils flared as she stuck her nose in the air. The breeze was right and the sweet scent of the bay sailed up the bluff that was just at the end of the street. "God, it's good to be home" she said.

Joe listened to her enthusiastic description. He had heard it all the night before and the week before and the month before. He sighed and she heard his deep exhale. Abby stopped talking. This was not the first time she had spoken the words "home at last" to him and she could feel him dismiss her.

Joe turned the wheel of his car and glanced down on the passenger seat at the map she had given him earlier. It seemed he was still headed in the right direction. As he made the last turn into the drive, he saw his wife, barefoot and dancing on the front porch of their new home in a skirt much too short for a woman of her age. He shook his head at the sight of her. She looked like some aging hippie dancing by herself on a porch, a scene from a movie with an imaginary full blown band playing in the background, the actress swirling and turning in time to the music, dancing with a partner only she could see.

When she saw him coming up the drive she stopped dancing and waved excitedly. She heard the engine switch off, but still he sat there in the car, his arms draped over the steering wheel, his fingers laced together. Abby tried to smile, but it didn't work. She walked toward his car. She knew by heart the scowl on his face.

"Are you going to get out or just keep driving?" she asked, adding a hollow laugh.

He rolled down the window. "Abby, what in the hell were you thinking?" he asked as he glanced up at the house. "This place looks like it's falling down and you know I don't know a hammer from a screw driver."

"Honey, please keep your voice down," she said, looking around in hopes no neighbors were about. "It's a really lovely house and there is not as much to do as you think. It's minor, really. Just cosmetic. It's been vacant for a while, that's all. Look, just look at the porch. The split brick on the porch floor is so old it looks like it's been polished. It just begs for a rocker and a glass of tea, don't you think? And the bay is at the end of the street!"

Her husband still sat frozen in the car. She watched him look at the pale yellow house through the driver's side window. Dread crept into her chest, rose and stuck in her throat.

"Could you have a found a yard with more trees? That

could need more maintenance?" he asked. "What landscaping? A few old bushes covered in vines?"

"But, Joe. I love how the driveway swoops around and through and under all these beautiful old trees," she replied. "It won't take any time at all to get this front yard whipped into shape. The back yard, I admit, is a complete ferny, shadowy, hopeless mess. But I promise, I'll do all that work myself. You won't have to lift a finger."

"What's with the big pile of bricks back there? Something fall down?"

"It's the rest of the brick from the porch floor. We can make pathways with them ... at our leisure, of course."

"Do you think we are some kind of hippie gardeners," he grumbled.

His car door swung open with a loud squeak. Joe climbed out of the familiar and comfortable car, the seat sunken in to fit his rump. He ambled toward the front door that she had left open for him.

Abby tried to switch gears. "Do you smell the bay?" she asked.

Joe snorted. "Smells like stagnant water to me."

"Oh, it's just low tide," she offered in defense of their new home. Then, to lighten things up, "It's the smell of the sea. Our place at the sandy beach!"

She knew Joe was aware that the Mobile Bay, at least this far from the mouth of the Gulf of Mexico, was brown, shallow and brackish. Sand was also an overstatement. A number of hurricanes over the last few years had washed away much of the beach. Joe was accustomed to the embellishments of "her south." He listened briefly then started up the porch steps.

Jamison Joseph Stewart was raised in an upstate New York mill town by a blue collar family. He was proud to be his family's first college graduate. Joe's father still lived in the shingled house that he had built with his own hands, and Joe did not share Abby's fondness for moving. He wondered, sometimes, how they had come together at all, and more, how they'd lasted these many years as a husband and wife.

Abby had spent her childhood being raised right on these bay waters. But she was not tomboyish, no fishing pole in her hands, nor a net over her shoulder. She liked correct table settings and proper etiquette. She had no wish, however, to be

9

the silly and pretentious southern belle. Though Joe characterized her as impulsive, Abby liked to think she was spontaneous. She was tall and lanky and had aged with grace, just a few streaks of gray showing through her short blond hair.

"Joe," she smiled, trying to get through his surly air, "we can put our toes in the sand, catch a crab or two and watch sunsets right at the end of our very own street."

Joe ignored her. As he ascended the steps, he grabbed the stair rail. When he clutched the white wooden railing, the whole shaky thing came off right in his hand. Joe stood there holding a big section of handrail and spindles, snapped and splintery on the ends. He looked first at the rail and then at her. Abby looked at him and then at the rail. She was shocked when he chunked the broken rail down on the ground, as if it were a spent piece of junk. She picked it up and lovingly leaned it against the house on the porch.

"Just minor cosmetics?" he asked with a snarl.

She didn't answer but ushered him in through the double front doors into the wide, front-to-back entrance foyer. Old timers would call it a dogtrot. She showed him the small living room, which, she explained, would be a perfect office for him. Joe was quiet and did not look at Abby. She showed him the ample dining room and her favorite features, the wall-to-wall china cabinet and the swinging door into the kitchen. She admired for him the wide plank heart pine floors, mentioned how the boards were aged to a glossy patina. She pointed up to the high ceilings, over to the fireplaces. "The kitchen has at least been updated," she said. When they walked into the master bedroom, she stood still, not moving an inch. She studied the look on his face as he took it in.

"Abby," Joe said, this time his voice defeated and quiet, "why is the bathtub in the bedroom instead of the bathroom where it belongs?"

"I'm not really sure," she responded. "I wondered the same thing myself. I guess the old girl who built this house liked bathing and looking at the fireplace at the same time. Moving the tub back into the bathroom is on my do-*first* list." Abby's voice, too, was quiet.

Joe turned to look at the fireplace. He saw there, over the fireplace, a shadow-boxed and perfectly hung frame showing off his high school letter sweater. The sleeves were folded over the front just right so that you could read the school name, his number, and the year the championship had been won. Joe turned slowly to face her, smiling. "That's a nice, manly touch," he said. Abby did special things just for him and he recognized this sweater as one of those things. It was a sweet but brief moment. He then turned toward the French doors that led from the master bedroom outside.

The doors opened onto the rear deck and the back yard that was a looming jungle. The deck had been built around two large magnolia trees and a fountain stood at a tilt on a small brick patio off the deck. The fountain held still, green water where mosquito larvae twisted and grew. Joe stepped out onto the deck, covered in huge magnolia leaves.

"These leaves are like shoe leather," Joe said. "I'd bet they never disintegrate. And look, Abby, they even hold water. That should make the little mosquitoes happy. Their very own little breeding boats." Joe's lips were pulled tight. "And what's that vine-covered mystery?" he asked. "Oh, never mind, I see. More bricks. More picturesque pathways." His voice was filled with vinegar.

Abby rubbed her eyebrows. Her own doubt was surfacing. She wondered what plans she could come up with for this back yard. It was covered in every kind of vine known to man, including one called the devil vine. She looked at the invading popcorn trees, proliferating at will, at the bamboo engulfing the side yard, at the few Christmas ferns surviving all the overgrowth. The enormity of the work in and outside the house and the opposition from Joe struck her, and all at once she wondered what the hell *was* she doing back down here? Insanity can be genetic and she questioned herself.

"I'm gonna cut half of these trees down," Joe declared, interrupting her daydreaming.

"You can't cut down trees in this town that have a diameter of three inches or more," she said. "That's why it's called the City of Trees. That and something to do with some laurel leaves."

"Are there tree police?" Joe was incredulous.

As they walked back inside, Joe motioned toward the second set of French doors that opened off the den. "Great," Joe said. "That backyard will never leave my sight, even while I'm *inside*."

He followed as she took him upstairs to see the guest bed-rooms, and finally, back out the front door. Without a word, Joe climbed into the sanctuary of his car. He started the engine and was rolling backward when his window slid down. "I'll meet you back at the hotel," he said as he drove through thick leaves layered on the circular drive.

Abby sat down on the front steps of their new home, watching the tail lights of his car as he pulled onto the main street. She leaned back, her palms to the smooth, old bricks on the porch floor. She closed her eyes, listening to the leaves rustle. She had hoped he would have seen the potential of the house. A sound nearby caused her to look across the yard. She heard the creak and groan of metal on metal and looked to her right. There between some bushes she spied an old iron post with a sign hanging down beneath the scrolling ivy ironwork. The breeze had picked up and as the sign swung, it creaked.

Abby walked through the undergrowth, out to the old sign swinging on the post, realizing it had once been a mailbox support. IDO, the sign said, and she remembered a family by that name.

Abby touched the letters and smiled. "I do, too. I do, in-deed," she said and gave the sign a playful swing.

She wandered back up to the house and thought about the day she had ridden out of Alabama on the back of a motorcy-cle with a man-boy she hardly knew. It had not been the first time she had been rescued by a motorcycle. She had sworn she would never return. Yet, here she was, soothing her simple desire to hear the sound of the gentle southern tongue but dreading finding the truth she had come here to find. She had not seen her mother in years. A knot grew in her stomach and she swatted the thought away. She glanced up at the pretty dormered house, now one hand rail short, and vowed that this would be the best home they had ever owned.

The Sky Blue Truck, 1954

The first house Abby could remember was a small white ranch perched precariously on the lip of a deep red clay gully. Climbing, curly kudzu vines engulfed the crevasse. A huge drainage pipe ran under North Border Drive and emptied into the gigantic ditch. After a hard rain, it gushed cascades of water that whooshed through the ravine, stirring up frothy, elfin shaped hats, meringue that happily bounced atop the rushing water. It was a short lived show, the water receding as quickly as it had come, but one Abby loved watching.

Pearl did not describe this house as the circa 1947 plain little ranch it actually was, but rather with her predictable aggrandizement, it was a darling cottage in a perfect neighborhood. Pearl paid more than she could afford for the house, but the address was desirable and that was all that counted. Pearl wanted to ensure that her children were raised in the proper part of town and be exposed to all the finer things she could imagine and afford. She played small red records of waltzes on a record player she had splurged on and large art books decorated the living room tables.

Pearl had four children. Matt, the eldest, was approaching fifteen. Margaret had just turned fourteen and went by Mags. Mary was barely thirteen. Abby was the youngest, a love child that could not have come at a worse time in Pearl's life, eight years after Mary. Pearl had planned on leaving her abusive husband but only on her terms and time table. Her pregnancy resulted in the last brutal beating and threw Pearl into a man's work world for which she was barely prepared. Pearl's resentment for the child lived on her lips. She never missed a chance to tell Abby she had been an accident. Abby's sisters always came to her rescue, reminding Abby that the beauty spot on her left lower eyelid made her look like Marilyn Monroe.

"Children" Pearl called every day when she came home from work. "Line up and confess."

On command, all four children stood in front of her like soldiers, chins up, shoulders back, while their mother switched their legs with a willow branch she picked right outside the front door. Matt was far too old for this and told his mother so on a regular basis. The older girls agreed. After the punishment, the children were called out from oldest to youngest to tell Pearl anything and everything they had done that day. She sat in a straight back chair right in front of them and listened to each in turn tell things that happened, things they did. The three older children were determined not to cry and there was not a tear between them, but rather a stance of defiance that Pearl appreciated. Abby tried to emulate her older siblings, but the switch's sting was more than she could bear, tears running down her face.

"Line up and confess is best idea I've ever had," Pearl was known to tell her sisters over coffee. "My little darlings are always doing something they shouldn't be doing. Didn't we all?" She laughed. "I'd rather beat the information out of them than listen to Mrs. Briggs, that busy body next door, tell me all about it before I even have a chance to get inside after work."

"Pearl," one of her sisters asked. "Aren't you encouraging them to go out and get into mischief? I mean, if they are going to get a whipping anyway, why wouldn't they go out and get into all kinds of trouble?"

Abby, hanging around the corner listening in, smiled at this new idea. What a clever aunt she had! 'All kinds of trouble' sounded like all kinds of fun. Abby scurried off to find her sisters and run the new plan by them.

When not in school or working at the gas station, Matt spent his time rebuilding car engines and digging shot out of the ribs of the gully, the remnants of local men and boys who shot their manhood into the red clay walls. Matt melted the things down and poured the hot molten metal into a cupcake pan, making large and heavy metal cupcakes. The first batch was such a success he had put them on a tray to show his mother. The metal muffins slid off the tray and onto Pearl's foot, almost breaking it. The metal muffin business was brought to a halt.

One afternoon after school, Matt decided to bring the dismantled pieces of the car engine into the living room. "Come on, Abby," Matt said. "You and Mags grab a rag and help me clean these parts. I've got a can of gasoline on the porch. I'll get it."

"Are you crazy?" Mary cried. "Mamma will kill us!"

"Gasoline?" Mags said. "Something sparks and we'll burn down the house!"

"We're gonna get our legs striped anyway. Might as well have some fun." Matt grunted at the thought of a man of his age getting a switching.

"This is not fun," Abby said. "Who wants to smell like gasoline?"

"You're just chicken," Matt dared. "What about you, Mags? You scared of Mamma, too?" That did it. Rags came out, the gas can inside, and a family garage was opened on the dining room table. The grease did not go well with Pearl's bright yellow couch in the adjoining living room where the girls had taken a seat to do their work.

Pearl came in after her final day of training for a new job for a local oil company. She grabbed the switch on her way up the three steps that led to the front door. When she entered the living room she heard waltzes playing on the little record player. The children, who normally greeted her with a cup of coffee, were nowhere to be seen. She looked around and saw blobs of thick, heavy black grease all over her couch, the one that she had saved for by skimping on groceries and the one that caused her former husband to beat the stew out of her. She couldn't believe what she was seeing. She looked at the dining room table, the mahogany one her father had built as a wedding present. More thick globs of black grease. Bleached spots were all over the table, the result of someone trying to clean up the mess.

"Children! What the hell has happened in here? Matt, get your ass out here, now!" Pearl screamed at the top of her lungs. She snatched the little red record off the turntable and broke it over her knee, flinging pieces around the room. All four children crept into the room, the three older ones defiant and proud. Abby hung back, standing behind Mags. Pearl glared at all of them then stomped into her bedroom and grabbed one of her ex-husband's long, thick leather belts. She wadded the little switch up and threw it on the floor at Matt's feet.

"Strip!" Pearl ordered. "Every damned one of you. Down to bare skin."

"Mamma," Mags cried. "It's that time of the month for me. I can't strip in front of Matt."

"I said STRIP, goddammit, and I mean NOW!"

The children started slowly unbuttoning and unzipping. "Don't you dare fool around with me. Get those clothes off, RIGHT THIS MINUTE!" screamed Pearl.

The children stripped quickly and didn't have a chance to see the belt in Pearl's hand as it swung down onto their legs, their backs, their heads. Each dodge of the belt they attempted meant that it hit another spot on their body. Pearl swung the belt at all four, in no particular order, until she had no energy left. Large red welts had already risen as she stormed out of the living room, slamming her bedroom door so hard the house rattled. All four of the children were squalling, even the eldest. They huddled with each other and just cried, no longer aware that they stood there naked.

After an hour or so, the children had dressed and Mags started a pot of soup for supper. Pearl came out of her bedroom as if nothing had happened. The children remained quiet.

"I have to be both Mother and Father in this household. It is not an easy task, keeping a roof over your heads and food in your stomachs." Pearl's tone of voice was neutral and matter-of-fact. Once everyone was seated at the table, a table cloth covering its new scars, Pearl began the expected dinner table conversation. "My training is over and I will be out in the field a good bit of the time. I will be an independent contractor and have to take jobs as they come up. That means my hours will be long and irregular. I expect the four of you to take care of yourselves and not pull any more shenanigans. Crazy Ruby will come from time to time to look after Abby."

Pearl worked hard to make ends meet. She said she was the only lady wildcatter in the state, a land-man, the person who hunts down lost family members for people who wanted to buy mineral rights that lay under the land. After only a short time in her new 'land-man' job, Pearl was out late most nights. Monday or Sunday, it didn't matter. She was gone so much, she often felt as if she really didn't live in the cottage by the gully.

Soon, Pearl earned quite a reputation in the land-man business. Attorneys from all over Mobile called for her services. She could get signatures from people that other more experienced land-men had been unsuccessful in even finding. She would come away with signatures for mineral rights when others had left empty-handed. Word spread through the oil business rapidly.

Pearl slid up and down dirt roads in North Mobile County, her green Studebaker splattered with red mud. "I am a hard-working and God-fearing woman," Pearl told her children, coming in the door. She carried a fat stack of papers. "That's why these people sign my papers. They trust a fellow Christian." She plopped down on the couch, taking off her shoes. "But I tell you right now, children, when you are older, remember to never sell your mineral rights. You never know where you might strike oil. Don't trust anybody. Church or no church."

"Abby, the Watchie Bird is watching you," Pearl would say each morning before leaving. *The Watchie Bird* was a children's book about a bird that was always looking in on kids, keeping up with their every move. How many times had Pearl sat Abby down for a re-reading of the book? Abby was always on the look-out for that bird.

Abby stood on the stoop in the early morning dew. Her mother backed out of the driveway and sped away, black smoke puffing from the tailpipe of the car. Matt, Mags and Mary walked off to catch the school bus. The sun blocked all but their silhouettes from Abby's view as they walked up the hill to the bus stop. Abby waited to see if Crazy Ruby would come or not, eating the azalea flowers while she waited. She couldn't wait until she was old enough to go to school.

Some mornings Abby went across the street to her friend's house. The father in that house yelled and Abby was glad there was no father in her house. At Brenda's house she could watch Captain Kangaroo, always fun as Pearl didn't own a television. But they might give her powdered milk to drink and powdered eggs to eat. They had a lot of powdered stuff in that house and

Abby hated the taste. She did not dare refuse it, however, lest she be whipped for having bad manners.

"Hi, Abby" said Crazy Ruby, walking up to the stoop where Abby waited. "I'll be your company today."

Pearl told Abby that Crazy Ruby was as crazy as a bed bug but was down on her luck. According to Pearl, you always had to help people who were down on their luck. Abby thought Crazy Ruby was probably an albino, like the ones she had seen in her mother's *National Geographic*. Ruby's hair and eyelashes were baby chick yellow-white, her skin was whipped egg white, and she always dressed like a nurse. White dress, white stockings and white shoes. Crazy Ruby endlessly sang one song, "You Are My Sunshine." Ruby's voice rang out in the house all day long.

"You gonna be a good girl for me today?" Ruby wanted to know.

"Yes Ma'am. Will you help me get some pennies out of my bank so I can get something from the Ice Cream Truck this afternoon?"

"I shore will. Long as any extra that comes out, I get to keep,"

"In that case, I don't need your help," sassed Abby.

"You know you the devil's seed, doncha?" Ruby asked Abby.

"I am not a seed, Miss Crazy Ruby," Abby stuck out her lips and stomped off to the bedroom she shared with her mother. She didn't know what a devil seed was, but she knew the devil was bad and she didn't want to have anything to do with him. Abby grabbed her piggy bank and started shaking it, now and then carefully looking up into the slot. She was getting nowhere and was still mad at Crazy Ruby. Finally, she shook it so hard, the pig's butt with the curly tail shook right off, her pennies scattering around the floor. She scooped up the change and put it into her sock drawer. Then she took the ceramic pig to Ruby to fix. Ruby walked straight to the back door, opened it and chunked the thing into the deep gully.

"That bank breaking is just another sign you are from the devil seed," Ruby said, smiling, batting her yellow eyelashes. "That's what you get for being stingy."

"My mamma coulda fixed it," Abby whined.

"But you mamma ain't here, now is she? You mamma

woulda called that natural punishment." Ruby laughed.

Abby stomped her foot. "Mamma is going to be mad at you!" She heard Crazy Ruby call out behind her, "Look out for that Watchie Bird! He's gonna tell the devil on you!"

The next day Abby was relieved when Crazy Ruby did not show up. She went down into the gully exploring and searching for the remains of her piggy bank. She picked up a stick and whacked this and that bush. She found a weed whose leaves smelled like grapefruit. She squeezed the juice out of it and dabbed some behind her ears, like she had seen her mother do with perfume. Her mother would be really happy that she had found this great new fragrance and it was free, right here in the gully. She searched and found a dirty bottle and squeezed a tiny bit of juice into it, having forgotten all about her bank. By evening, Abby's face, neck and shoulders were covered in watery blisters.

"You idiot child," Pearl screamed at her. "Anything with three pointed leaves is poisonous and I am sure I have told you a hundred times, if it's got three, let it be," she continued. Pearl dabbed calamine lotion on Abby's blisters. "You better not wind up in the damned hospital. I don't have time or money for that. Squeezing juice out of poison sumac—only you, Abby!"

The next day, more of Abby's body was covered in hives and she was itching all over. She was in too much pain to move. The sores were oozing. She hoped her agony would get her out of the day's switching.

It was late afternoon, her brother and sisters home from school, when the man in the sky blue pick-up truck arrived. He parked on the sidewalk, right in front of the cottage. Matt peeped out of the living room window, the flash of pale blue having drawn his attention. Matt was surprised and slightly scared, a reaction Abby noticed immediately. Abby wondered if this may be the devil from which her seed had sprung. Mags came running into the living room and stood with Matt at the window. Mary walked in the room, noting the look of worry on Matt's face. No one moved.

"You kids going to invite your daddy inside?" the man yelled as he walked up the stone sidewalk.

Mags grabbed Abby and steered her to the closet in Pearl's bedroom. Abby hid deep in the closet while Mags and Matt darted out the back door. Mary stood by the front door and, sure enough, the man came up on the stoop. "Don't just stand there. Mary, open the door."

Mary let the man inside, backing away from him. She fixed coffee as he commanded. When he told her, "Come and sit in my lap," Mary did as he told her. It was all part of a well rehearsed play that Pearl and the older children had been over should this day ever come.

Abby, way back in the closet, did not know the man or why her siblings were acting like maniacs, but as Mags had instructed, she pushed as far back in the closet as she could. She squeezed her eyes shut and smelled her mother's clothes, then moth balls in the very back when she slid down into a ball in the corner. She wondered where that Watchie Bird was when you needed him. Abby could hear herself breathing. Then she heard a man's voice outside of the bedroom window.

"There's another child in the bedroom closet," Abby heard a deep voice say. She wondered if the man with the voice could see through walls and tucked herself even deeper. She waited. One of the men's voices came inside her house. Then she heard her mother's voice, at last, and she scrambled out of the closet.

Pearl was in the small center hall with the phone to her ear. Abby overheard her mother whisper something about going to a safe place, but her mother's voice was so quiet Abby didn't hear most of what she was saying. A police officer milled about the living room while two more handcuffed the man in the front yard.

Abby's mother got off the phone and went over and talked to the policemen. Pearl walked to the door with the policemen and said something as they walked out. She turned around and said firmly, but in a quiet voice to Abby, "Go get your brother and sisters, Right now! Get them in here."

The children gathered behind their mother who was bent over, dragging suitcases from beneath the bed. She put two suitcases on the bed, reached back under and stood up with another. Standing there with the empty suitcase in her hand, she ordered the children to start packing.

"Where are we going?" Matt mewled, his voice the sound of a rabbit in a trap.

"Now's not the time for questions. It's a safe bet, wherever

I'm going, you four are going with me. So get it moving!"

Within the hour, the Studebaker's trunk was packed and the car was stuffed. The children barely fit, surrounded with clothes, books, the record player and anything else Pearl had deemed necessary. Pearl backed the muddy car out of the drive and waved at Mrs. Briggs next door, who was putting her cat out. "Convenient timing," said Pearl as she drove off into the night. Abby quietly cried, suspecting her life in the white cottage next to the gully had come to an end. She wondered where in the world they were going on this moonless, windy night.

A Long Dark Road: 1954

"Stop worrying," Pearl said. "That man has been put under the jail and the key thrown away. You saw them haul him off with your own eyes." She continued to lecture the huddled children in the dark car. The soft yellow glow from the dashboard was the only solace offered on this night. "He is in jail. Now just be quiet!" Pearl's fists were clinched around the steering wheel as she drove. Abby was feigning sleep atop a pile of clothes, books, pillows and blankets on the shelf in the rear window of the Studebaker. Her sister's cat shared the pile with her. Abby strained her ears to hear the conversation in the front seat. Pearl drove quietly for a while and added, "And remember, Little Pitchers have big ears," she turned her head slightly in Abby's direction, crooking her right eyebrow upward. Pearl was careful what she said in front of Abby. She knew her sisters would interrogate the child at every opportunity. Pearl wanted her life to remain mysterious, hidden, secret. Especially from her sisters.

Abby wondered if her mother had told Crazy Ruby where to come for work. Abby wanted to ask, but didn't dare get caught not sleeping.

"Besides," Pearl continued, "we are not leaving because he came. I have had this move planned for some time now. I have met some very, very important people working with these oil folks. You children are about to live the life you deserve. You will learn a lot and love our new home."

"But where will I go to school?" Matt whined. "I haven't even seen a school and we've been driving for hours!"

Abby heard the terror in her brother's voice and could almost feel the tears trapped in her brother's throat. This was new territory. Matt had always been the man of the house. As far as Abby could tell, he never worried about anything. Abby peeped over the edge of her little shelf and watched as her sisters looked at each other, their ears practically pointed as they tried to hear the front seat conversation.

"Don't you get sassy with me, young man! I have always put food in your stomach, a roof over your head and made damn sure you were in a good school!"

"But I'm almost in high school now, Mamma. Where I go really counts, if I want to go to college."

"I am not a complete idiot, Matt! I have kept you children safe and I did it alone. We will have help. Now, this conversation is over."

He hoped there was a gas station nearby, wherever they were going, and that one of his mother's friends could get him a job.

The wind had picked up and howled when Pearl stopped the car. Abby saw the bay on one side of the car, separated from the narrow black-top lane by a rocky seawall. None of the children had slept during the entire trip and to them it seemed they had arrived at the darkest place on earth. There were no street lights or traffic lights. The dashboard lights were the only lights they saw.

Abby pretended she was waking up, stretched and yawned, and looked around. Looking like giant boxcars that had derailed, she saw three very large and very dark buildings. The buildings had full length porches, front and back, upstairs and down. Abby watched the clouds scuttle past quickly, making a hasty retreat. The wind smelled of salt. Abby hoped this was just a stop on the way to wherever they were going.

Pearl rushed the children from the warmth of the old car and drug them up a short flight of stairs to the building on the right. The wind spit and hissed, as if daring them to take one more step. Pearl dug around in her purse finally coming up with a ring of keys. After fumbling for a bit, she swung open the door to Room 23. A bare light bulb hung down a wire and Pearl pulled the string. Warm light spread its welcome glow around the otherwise dingy little room. With her normal flourish, she whipped off the sheets covering the furniture, revealing two twin beds and a nightstand. She flapped the sheets for good measure, dust sprinkling down on her four dazed children.

"This is going to be wonderful, children," Pearl said with her usual enthusiasm. Her children were not persuaded. "Just look! You have your own bathroom! Now, get yourselves ready for bed and I will see you first thing in the morning. Matt be the man of the…" Pearl paused and gestured around the motel room, "house. You are in charge!"

Pearl promptly abandoned her disoriented children. They stood bewildered in Room 23. Matt seemed to be figuring out how to be the man here. "I guess we have to share a bed," he said. "You brats better never breathe a word of this sissy shit. I call the bed on the right. Abby, you're the smallest so you pile up with me."

Pearl's sheet shaking seemed to have stirred up endless dust that continued to rain down on them. The girls choked and coughed on the musty odor. Mags checked out the bathroom and declared it a moldy mess. The room was cold. They stopped talking. They turned in but no one slept. Abby said, "I can barely breathe!"

"I wonder if Mamma will come back in the morning," Mags said. "I feel like we are at the end of the earth. Where is *she* sleeping?"

They nestled, two by two, in each of the twin beds in the dusty old room. They were so quiet they could hear each other's breaths. Each knew the other was still awake, yet no one said a thing.

A New Life, A New Year: January, 1955

Abby squeezed her eyelids tight, not wanting to open them at all. She heard her brother and sisters stirring about in the dank bedroom. It was cold in the room and Abby remembered they were far from the white house on the gully. She pulled the covers up under her chin and grimaced when she smelled them. Cold was better than stinky, and she pushed the sheet and blanket down away from her face.

"This shower is disgusting," Mary complained. "It's downright slimy. She doesn't expect us to shower in that thing, does she? These towels are stiff and rough. They're brown at the fold, they've been hanging here so long. God, what are we doing here?"

Mary studied the teal and yellow tiles in the bath, covered in a dense green-black mold in the corners of the shower. The tiles matched the once colorful curtains on the two windows in the bedroom. The bedspreads were a mix of some teal and yellow with a green bamboo pattern. The carpet was slick and flat from years of use. Between the twin beds was a cheap nightstand, the front of the drawer missing. A copy of the Bible was in the slot that was once a drawer.

"Yesterday was my birthday," Abby said to her siblings. "I'm six years old now."

"You know how Mamma feels about that," Mary said. "Being born to her is present enough and the only birthday we celebrate is that of our Lord, Jesus Christ."

"Mamma never forgets Christmas," Abby agreed. "How long is it until Christmas?"

"Technically, it just passed. But in our house, it's when

Mamma decides it is and puts up the Christmas tree," Mags said. "Mamma says the Bible doesn't know when Christ was born because there could not be new lambs in the winter. So, we celebrate when she decides it's time. She says that is all we need to know about religion."

"Besides," Matt added. "Our grandmother is full enough of religion for all of us."

Her sixth birthday would be one Abby would never forget. Her birthday was on the night they had driven down the darkest road to the darkest place on earth. She hoped, at least, she would start growing into her Cherokee nose, she the only child who had inherited that feature from their mother.

"I hate my nose," Abby said. No one heard her.

The door to Room 23 suddenly opened and brilliant morning sunlight invaded the dark little room, dust mites visible and floating through the air. Pearl's body was silhouetted by the light. When she came inside and Abby could see her clearly, she was surprised at how dressed up her mamma was. Cool air rushed in, stirring the dust. Mary sneezed.

"Chop, chop, little soldiers. It's a grand new day and I have much to show you." Pearl was very cheerful this morning.

"Mother," Mary said. "There is only a shower and it's black and slimy. I cannot and will not bathe in there."

"You can and will bathe wherever I tell you to and you'd best not take that tone with me. Be damned grateful there is a shower at all. You will shower in there and do it quickly. You have running water. A lot of people do not." Pearl would raise cultured and polished children, not ungrateful brats.

"Mom, you look really nice," Mags said. "I don't think I've ever seen that dress before."

Abby took in the sight of her mother in a black dress with while polka dots, a snow-white collar and snow white cuffs. Pearl turned, modeling her ensemble. She wore dark hose, the seam down the back of her curvaceous legs as straight as a ruler, and red high heels to match the red belt around her tiny waist. Abby saw a tiny smudge of dirt on one of her cuffs, but was not about to mention it. Pearl appeared to her children as though she had just walked out of the pages of a fashion magazine.

Abby wondered who this mamma was. She wasn't the Bad Mamma who had spells and threw fits. And she wasn't the Good Mamma who took them on magical walks in the woods. Somehow this Mamma was different. A whole new Mamma that Abby had not seen before. Her hair was combed and styled. Her lips were slathered in ruby red lipstick. Abby thought maybe something in the night, when Mamma was missing, had changed her for good. Abby wondered if she'd had a magic potion of some kind. Abby watched this woman who graciously smiled and moved around the room in high gear.

Pearl disappeared into the bathroom and wrinkled her nose. "For now, just pretend we're camping. I need you all to shower and dress and make sure Abby is presentable. We have important people to meet today. I brought shampoo and I splurged on cream rinse. It's in the train case and any feminine products you may need, too, God forbid. Further proof that God is not a woman. That's why we women get cramps and cycles and the joy of birthing babies. Yes, He is definitely a man." Pearl would unexpectedly go off on tirades, arguing first one side, then the other, as to the gender of God.

Pearl paused and looked about the room, to make sure she hadn't forgotten to tell the children anything important. "Girls, I am telling you. Do not ever, and I mean ever, let a man lay a hand on your lady parts unless you want to go through childbirth. See, more proof. God is not a woman. Now, everything you need is here. Get ready." Pearl had the door open and the sunlight cascaded through her final instructions and the dancing dust mites.

Pearl, the new version, sashayed out of the room on the way to meet the anticipated guests. Polka dots flew from side to side of the full skirt. She knew how to make those skirts dance, a loose jib flapping in the wind. Abby made a mental note to herself that she would practice that sway.

"Well, let's get started," Matt ordered. He had been the stand-in man for so long, he took responsibility for Pearl's orders. "Mary, you go first, then Mags because you damned girls take so long to get dressed. Then, if there is any hot water left, I'll get in. Just put on some old tennie shoes or flip flops for the shower, if you have them. I'll get the water started and see if we really have hot water."

The water was icy cold and they had no shoes for protection from the shower floor. Slime, cold water, dirty towels and all, they soon emerged out onto the long porch in front of Room 23. Abby had been wiped down, but still looked like she could use a bath. From the porch, the narrow black top lane was visible with the rip-rap rock wall keeping back the bay. The mouth of the Mobile Bay, where it emptied into the Gulf of Mexico, was visible from where they stood. They heard waves slap the shore. The wind had abandoned the lonesome landscape and the morning was only slightly chilly, even though it was January.

"Those are the tallest damned oleander trees I have ever seen," Matt commented. His sisters looked and nodded agreement. In the oyster shelled parking lot sat their mother's battered Studebaker, fenders still covered with red mud. It looked bad enough, but worse compared to the sleek, long shiny black car that was parked next to it.

"Never mind the oleanders," Mags said. "I've never seen a car that long and shiny,"

"I guess we are about to meet Mamma's very-very important friends from North Mobile County," Mary said, straightening her skirt, making sure the seams were exactly where they should be on each side.

Mags fluffed her hair and spat in her hand, rubbing down a cowlick on top of Abby's head with the spit. They walked down the steps, all wet, clean and slick, to meet someone who sat in the big black car.

Pearl's New Friends

The doors on the black limousine swung open without a sound. First out of the car was a portly older man, his cheeks red like a man who'd spent years of hard drinking. Next out came a tall and slender man, dark haired with olive skin. His eyebrows were utterly straight. He looked important, and his manner suggested that he agreed.

"Children, these are our new friends," Pearl announced. "This is Uncle Jim," she said as she pointed to the taller of the two. His eyelids were narrow slits and the children couldn't make out what he was looking at, but he seemed to be carefully observing everything around the place. "And this is Uncle Boyd," she said with a flourish, her hand pointing toward the shorter, rounder man.

Abby thought that her mother's new friends seemed to make her a bit jumpy. Pearl spat in her hand and rubbed down the cowlick still sticking up from Abby's dirty hair. Abby wished people would stop spitting on her. Pearl added a little more spit to her fingers and wiped away something on Abby's face.

"Uncle Boyd," Pearl continued, "owns this fine piece of property and is the seated congressman for our state! Uncle Jim is our governor!" Pearl was breathless. "Did you ever think you would meet such fine and important gentlemen, children? These are men of stature!"

Both shiny men bristled with pleasure as Pearl gushed over their importance, both heads nodding and bobbing, both smiling, both appreciating that Pearl knew and appreciated their status. Uncle Boyd was the first to speak.

"Your charming and beautiful mother has leased this piece of property from me. And she's gonna turn it into a fine resort. A very fine resort. The State needs a fine resort and this

29

is gonna be the best. You children can be mighty proud of your mamma. Yes, indeed. Proud."

Uncle Boyd sounded deep and serious but his twinkling blue eyes and booming voice gave the impression that he was just kidding. He reminded Abby of the ringmaster at the circus her aunt had once taken her to. The Governor just stood, smiling and nodding. Abby thought he seemed to be taking more than a lot of notice of Mary and Margaret. His black eyes glistened under his straight, hooded eyebrows. Abby stood in the back ground. Abby was tall for her age, wily, cautious, and curious. She listened and watched, wondering and waiting.

Matt crossed his arms over his puffed out chest, his back straight. He wanted it to be clear that he was a man. He shook the men's hands firmly, looking them dead in the eye.

Mags was shy and demure by nature. Compliments made her blush. Still, she stood there an attractive young woman, whose caramel colored hair blew in the wind. To her side, standing for these men to admire, Mary was small and elfish. She had a cute turned up nose, lively eyes, and was Pearl's favorite and Pearl made no secret of it.

Uncle Boyd boomed again. "See that fine yacht out there?" He pointed to the biggest boat Abby had ever seen and she wondered how she could have missed seeing it when they first stepped out on the porch. "Well, that's the Governor's fine yacht and I suspect you'll be seeing a lot of it. Yep, seeing a lot of it, I suspect."

"Now that everybody knows everybody," Pearl said in her most professional voice, "why don't we take the tour and decide what we need to do to pull this place together?"

What had looked to Abby like box cars by night turned out to be three quite large buildings by day. Each was long and narrow and each had a long porch. The paint had mostly peeled away. There were some random places where white still remained on the weathered wood. The windows and doors were intact with only an occasional glass missing.

"These were the barracks of our fine service men," Uncle Boyd thundered. "These barracks have held hundreds, hell I bet thousands, of our troops. Children, you'll notice the steps sag in the middle. Well that's from hundreds, hell I bet thousands, of soldiers storming up and down them. Yes, indeed. Our fine fighting forces. That building," he said pointing to the one that housed Room 23, "was a fine motel at one time. A fine motel. But the manager just did not have the wherewithal to make a go of it. No, he did not. Can you imagine? Right here next to this old fort and these fine beaches? Can you imagine? I do not understand at all. At all."

His voice grew louder and louder. Abby thought it was funny how he repeated his words. Plus, he cursed in front of her just like she was one of the big girls.

"I mean, that fort, that grand ol' fort has seen Civil War battles and has tracked U-Boats right here in our Gulf of Mexico," Uncle Boyd said. "If those walls could talk. If they could talk. Yes, tourists will want to see that big ol', five-star fort. With new and improved management, with your mamma at the helm, this ship is gonna sail. Yes, sir, she's gonna sail. This fine ol' fort will finally get the recognition it deserves," he said, his voice loud, his gaze going often to Pearl's cleavage that peeped through the top of her dress. "All with our fine Governor's help, of course."

The Governor smiled and took out a pipe. After a few tries and several spent matches, he finally got the thing to puff out smoke stacks. As the smoke dissipated and danced in the breeze, it created a smoky coil that seemed to wrap around Mary's neck as if she had been lassoed. She stifled a cough, while the governor's black eyes stared at her, his thin lips pulled into a smile. He rocked up on his toes, his fine black leather shoes creasing with the movement. He rocked back on his heels and his smugness was palpable.

"Let's start with the main building," Pearl said, as she led them to the center building. "The main restaurant, ball room, bar, and convention center will be on the first floor. But, I think there's room upstairs for a few retail shops. Tourists love their trinkets and souvenirs," Pearl said, smiling at Uncle Boyd. She hoped he was pleased with her ideas, and was eager to tell him more.

Pearl and Uncle Boyd continued the tour, discussing this and that, things that would have to be done. The governor and the four children tagged behind, the children amazed at the high ceilings and shear enormity of the building. The governor stopped and lit his pipe every few steps, and Abby decided pipes didn't work very well.

"Now, the motel building is fine," Pearl continued on. "It

just needs some freshening up. New carpet, paint, curtains and the likes. No construction. Maybe a little plumbing or electric, but nothing too expensive. I believe, however, that last building is utterly hopeless. It would take more money that the State of Alabama has in its coffers to bring that one back to life."

"It is in complete shambles, Miss Pearl," Uncle Boyd agreed. "Complete shambles. I think we can get done what we need to get done with these two fine barracks. We'll leave the last one for later. I'm sure the place will outgrow itself in no time, and there'll be money to remodel. Don't you worry your pretty little head."

"Now, children," he said. "There are three small houses just up the road. They were the officer's quarters, back in the day, and they are fine houses. Fine houses, indeed. Once y'all get this hotel and restaurant ready to go, y'all can move on down to the Officer's Row. They are fine houses, fine houses, and I think you'll like them a lot. We'll see those on another day, when we aren't tying up the Governor's time."

Pearl's hips swung with a little extra effort, sending the dots on her skirt into a sensual dance as she ushered the men and the children through vacant rooms and explained an endless string of possibilities. She beamed at her well-behaved children. Abby could not remember seeing her mother as radiant.

"You children are a Divine Gift from God," hollered Uncle Boyd. His voice echoed in the empty building. "A Divine Gift from God, indeed. I have Divine Gifts of my own. All boys— well, young men now. Divine Gifts, each and every one. You'll get to meet them all in due time. In due time."

The governor never said if he had Divine Gifts or not, but Abby figured he did not, since he didn't speak up to brag on them like Uncle Boyd had.

"Are we going to have a marina?" Matt asked.

"Brilliant idea," bellowed Uncle Boyd. "Just brilliant. The place could attract sports fisherman in droves. Why, from all over the world with the fine fishing right out there." Uncle Boyd pointed toward the bay and the Gulf. "Brilliant idea. In fact, I believe I'll put you in charge of the marina," he said looking straight at Matt. "Hell, your mamma will have to pay you."

Uncle Boyd looked at Abby, hiding behind her mother's skirt and said, "Young Lady, please forgive my French. I forget I'm in the presence of young ladies."

She was thrilled that he had spoken directly to her. Abby liked Uncle Boyd. Yes, she liked him indeed, she decided. She mimicked his speech patterns to herself so she could talk like him later. She wasn't too sure yet about the governor. But, maybe if he was a friend of Uncle Boyd's, he might be okay. She smiled at Uncle Boyd when he patted her on the top of her head. She brushed her hand over her hair to see if she could feel any spit from her mother's wiping. Abby was relieved to find her head dry.

"Well, little lady," Uncle Boyd said to Abby. "Help your mamma get this fine resort pulled together. I have to go back to the District, do the Lord's work in the name of my constituents. And the Governor's got to get back to governing … after a few days on that fine yacht of his. Just a few days."

A tall man in a uniform opened the back doors to the long car. Uncle Boyd gave Pearl a smack right on her mouth. There was some discussion of a motor boat parked just up the road that would take the governor back to his yacht. Then both men climbed into the long car and waved good bye. Matt could have sworn he saw his mother curtsy as they sped away.

Restoration, 1955

Pearl stood with her hands on her hips, looking at the old buildings and thinking about all that had to be done. She thought back to times she had started projects on so many things, never to have completed one, that she could think of at least. This was different. This she planned on doing with passion and perfection. She would make sure it would be finished. There was too much at stake for her to get side-tracked and not get this accomplished. She smiled, her new determination setting well with her. She glanced at the old watch on her wrist. The watch had been her mother's and reminded Pearl that good Christians always win, that a job well done is worth doing and most importantly, spare the rod and spoil the child. It was that time of day. Confessions were due. But, she had to tell the children what would be expected of them in the future, too. She decided she'd skip line up and confess for the day.

"Children!" All four showed up, ready for the leg switching. All were surprised when their mother seemed to be in a different state of mind. The children wiggled, confused, but tried to hold rank. "We are now running with the Big Dogs," Pearl proudly announced. "In fact, we *are* Big Dogs. That means each and every one of you must do your part. Whatever I ask you to do, or whatever Uncle Boyd wants, you are simply to be good dogs and follow orders. Am I clear?"

All four heads nodded. It was clear to all of the children that this was a new role for Pearl, no longer good mother or bad mother, but the Big Dog in Charge.

Pearl had many talents. She could paint a life like portrait or write a fairy tale fit for publishing. She could talk herself out of a corner without effort or lie so well even she believed it. And, most importantly, she could make anything or any-

34

where look beautiful. An ordinary cardboard box could become a puppet show house or a gift box from Tiffany's. Give her a couple of rooms to spiff up and she'd invite you into a makeover that was as pretty as a penthouse apartment in New York City.

They all moved into the central room on the second floor of the same building as Room 23. It was a suite, of sorts, with a small central room, two small bedrooms and a bath. At night, Abby tucked herself into a bed in the smallest bedroom. Late at night she heard her sisters creep up the old stairs, the steps creaking with each weary step. She heard Mags complain that she was so tired the backs of her knees hurt. Mary's normally curly hair would be in a wet wad by bedtime each night, but she, too, was so tired she didn't do anything with it.

"I'll be damned if I'll live with you girls," Matt announced one day soon after moving to the suite. "Y'all are the nastiest bunch of girls on Earth." That was the last they saw of him in their little suite. No one had a clue where Pearl slept and no one brought it up.

Matt made himself an apartment out in the wash house, the building behind the old motel. He set up a single bed behind the washers and cobbled together a make-shift closet. He found an old dresser for his clothes and things. Pearl seemed to have forgotten about the record player, and he put it on top of his dresser. He wasn't crazy about his mother's waltz records, but they sounded good after he had scrubbed floors with Red Devil Lye all day.

"Mamma," Abby whined, "I don't like that water from the shower rushing down in my nose and eyes. Is there a bath tub here, anywhere?"

"Stop fussing, Abby. You're a big girl and big girls shower. If you keep whining, I'm going to give you something to whine about."

Abby risked a switching but she didn't care. "I'm gonna drown, Mamma, and it's gonna be all your fault."

The older children snickered at Abby as she continued to complain about showering. They had bigger things to worry about, like chores that seemed endless, including laundry for the entire Inn.

Outside of the wash house, which Matt now called his apartment, were several, long clotheslines. Mags and Mary spent most of their time washing linens and towels, hanging them on the lines to be dried by salt filled air.

"The guests are just going to love this smell!" Pearl said. "Fresh air, sunshine and sea and salt. Wish I could bottle this delicious aroma!"

When Mags and Mary made the beds with fresh white linens, they would shake out the crisp sheets with a pop. Abby loved to watch them, and gave into the temptation with each snap to dive under the poufy cloud the sheet created as it came to rest on the bed. The sisters let her get away with the antic a few times, but soon got fed up and ran Abby out.

Abby spent most of her days wandering the beaches, the rock wall, and the old fort, all day, every day. There was more than enough entertainment for a curious little girl.

"This compound is 420 acres," Pearl told Abby. "You can go anywhere you want and do anything you want, as long as you don't cross the seawall and you stay inside the compound. The seawall crosses the road right where we come in."

"Is there a line around the compound, Mamma? How will I know where the edge is?"

"The seawalls are the borders on two sides. The bay and the Gulf are the boundaries on the other two sides. You figure it out. Hell, I don't care if you hitch a ride on a shrimp boat as long as you stay out of my hair."

While Abby was out exploring her new range, the flurry of cleaning and scrubbing and re-scrubbing was non-stop until it suited Pearl. New bedspreads, curtains, and rugs came on a truck and each room had its own theme. Several were, of course, a beach theme, the curtains and spreads adorned with fish and seaweed. Additional rooms flaunted the Victorian period, teapots and roses everywhere. Others were old English libraries. The possibilities were endless with Pearl's imagination and Boyd's money. The old, moldy tiles were shiny and clean. When the slick old carpets were pulled up, the hardwood floors underneath sent Pearl into a dance of happiness.

Between both floors there were sixty rooms and four suites. Pearl boasted that once all these rooms were filled with guests, they would be rich, rich, rich. Abby could hardly wait. They had never been rich before and Abby wondered if that meant she could get a horse.

"Not only are we going to be stinking rich," Pearl told her

children in a quiet voice, "We are going to be included in a circle of people that are rich, too. And rich people have impeccable manners, blue blood and, most importantly, they have culture. I will teach you how to have culture and good manners. But for now, back to work!" she sang as her skirts rustled back through what would become the restaurant.

Matt gripped the handle of the big brush broom and spread out more hot water and Red Devil Lye on the wide planked floors of the would-be kitchen. "Abby, don't get near this stuff," he said. "If it touches your skin it will eat it right off, right down to the bone. You'll look like a skeleton," He smiled at her and winked. "That's why I have on these giant boots."

While her sisters prepared the rooms and Matt scrubbed floors, Abby played out in the shelled parking lot. What once had been shiny oyster shells were now ground down shards of shell and sand. As Abby became more familiar with her surroundings, she found out that most of the vegetation on this wind-swept and sandy peninsular were vicious cacti and sand spurs.

Daring to walk back inside where work was underway, Abby went in to lodge her latest grumble. "Mamma, these flip flops hurt my toes," Abby complained. "And those cactus stickers just jump off the bush and stick in my legs. Sand spurs are everywhere. What good is it to live on the beach if I can't even go barefoot? I need a horse, that's what I need."

"We'll see," answered Pearl. Abby knew that meant no. She shrugged her shoulders, blew her bangs out of her face, and went on exploring. She noticed that most of the trees on the point were oleanders. There was an occasional thorny ash tree, which Abby learned the hard way were mean when she tried to climb the barbed branches. The oleanders had been undisturbed for years and were as tall as the old buildings, their sticky sweet aroma so thick it seemed to stick in the back of Abby's throat and in her nose. The aroma wafted around on the sea breeze, and Abby could find no place to hide from it.

"Those oleanders are practically historic," Pearl said. "They are also deadly poisonous, so don't burn them, and Abby, don't eat them!"

The worst thing about oleanders was their long leathery branches. Abby didn't like them because if she got too sassy or too whiny or otherwise in the way of work, Pearl would strip

37

the leaves off in one smooth motion, leaving the bare switch and the business that it meant. Her mother, thinking herself clever, called these switchings "Oleander Tea." Sometimes her mamma would make Abby pick her own switch. Abby soon learned that smaller is not better when it came to switches. Her legs were covered in mosquito bites and red welts from all-too frequent rounds of Oleander Tea.

During her exploration of her new domain, Abby saw cats everywhere in the rock walls. She spent hours trying to coax a small black one to come near but it and all the others were too wild and scared.

"They look just like Grandmaw's cats," Abby told her mother. "But even if I give them food they won't come to me. They just don't like people."

"You stay away from those cats," Pearl said. "They are feral and probably have a dozen diseases. God knows what they carry. They are as mean as baby coons, Abby, and if you get too close, they will bite your head off." Pearl turned to Matt. "We've got to get rid of those cats before our guests start arriving. We don't need a damned cat bite to start things off."

Abby gave up on the cats, and sunbathed on the rock seawall and tiptoed down to the small beach of the bay. The sand was a mid-morning yellowish, not snow white like it was just around the bend at the Gulf. The water was clear, green, shallow and warm. Abby could see the bottom which helped her avoid stepping on the blue crabs that inhabited the waters and the hermit crabs that scuttled around the bottom near the shore.

"Mags," Abby said one night after a long day's work, "I learnt to swim all by myself. And I can open my eyes under water, but it burns because the water is so salty. Then I get used to it and you wouldn't believe how many crabs and minnows are in the water."

"One day soon, I'll come see what all you've discovered, Abby. I will lie on that beach and get some sun. If I live that long. Mamma's about to work us to death," Mags replied.

"Are you gonna die, really?" Abby asked with worry.

"No, Abby, just some days are so long and so hard, I wish I would die, that's all. But we are almost finished. The big kitchen stove is put in, and Mamma had a spit put in the kitchen fireplace to roast chickens on. She's having somebody build the tables, and they won't be too much longer. Now go to sleep, Abby. I'm dog tired. We'll talk some more tomorrow."

As always, Mags was out of the door to go to work early the next morning and Abby knew she'd be tired again tonight. So, as usual, Abby went to the beach alone. Abby spent the morning talking to the little hermit crabs. She believed she made friends with them. A fisherman who came to fish off the small pier near the end of the point told Abby that hermit crabs shop for new shells, just like her mamma shopped for new dresses. "When it outgrows its shell, it looks around and finds another one," the man said.

"Hey," Abby said to another fisherman on the pier. "What you fishing for with that big string?"

"Hey, yourself. I've got chicken necks tied to these strings. I'm gonna catch me a slew of blue crabs," he said. "Anyhow, what you doing down here all by yourself, little un? You could fall right off this wharf and drown. Where's your mamma?"

"My mamma is fixing up the Inn right there." Abby pointed to the motel which remained unpainted. "We're gonna be rich, too."

"Well, that would be real nice," the fisherman said. "I heard somebody was trying to fix that old place up. That'll be good. Those old buildings are just eyesores."

"So, crabs like chicken necks?"

"Yes, ma'am. It's their favorite. Especially rotten."

"Did I tell you I just turned six? But we don't get birthday cake. Our mamma don't believe in birthdays, except for our Lord Jesus Christ," she said, her eyes bright. Abby said in her most grown-up voice, "And I know how to swim, so I ain't gonna drown. Besides, Mamma said if I did fall in the porpoises would push me back to shore. That's what they do, you know. Besides that, have you seen those needle fish that puff up when fishermen pull them in? I would never fall in close to one of those things!"

Abby really liked the fishermen she talked to, how they treated her. They drank their beer and talked to her, just like she was part of the group. The fisherman looked at her, guessed she was about eight, based on her height. He noticed how tan she was and the thin red stripes on her legs. "You want a swig of this beer? You allowed to drink beer?" he asked. "Those spiny fish you talking about? Them's blowfish and they will sting you, so be careful."

"Yes sir, I sure do want a sip. Mamma ain't never said I couldn't drink some beer."

The man handed her his long neck beer and Abby took a big slug, just like she had watched him do. She spewed most of it out, some spraying out through her nose. The fisherman laughed and gently tugged on one of the crab trap strings.

"That tastes like horse piss," Abby said.

"Now, how does a girl like you know how horse piss tastes?" The fisherman laughed. By this time a few more fishermen had circled around, watching the child spray the beer across the pier and laughing at her description of the taste. Foam from the beer was on her nose and around her mouth.

"Well, I ain't never tasted horse piss," Abby said. "But I bet it tastes like that beer."

"Here, have another pull," the fisherman said. "Only not so much this time. Just a little sip 'til you get used to it."

Abby did as she was told and before long, one of the other fishermen opened another bottle and handed it to her. "Here's your very own, little girl." Each looked at the other and snickered. They'd played similar tricks on their own children and knew the kid would be no worse for the wear.

The fisherman went back to the string, easing it up, crabs hanging on to the raw chicken neck at the end. Slowly he slid a long handled net in the water from the other side, eased the line almost to the top of the water and slipped his net under the catch.

"Well, I'll be damned," Abby said. It was her first bad word. The men stood around laughing, hands low on their hip bones, tan backs to the sunshine.

Abby drifted away from the fishermen, went down the dock and got sleepy watching the porpoises swim by, roll to the top and blow, roll to the top and blow. She lay down on the warm boards and peered through slits of the pier and saw a hammerhead shark circling around in the clear water below. A pilot fish was stuck to its side, traveling along with it. The fishermen tossed over the fish they didn't want and the shark snatched them from the water. Abby watched the shark gulp the bait fish and questioned the safety of her favorite swimming hole. Abby gave a shiver when it dawned on her how many times she'd swam right there in that very spot.

The sun sunk lower in the afternoon sky and Abby felt lazy, hypnotized by the porpoises. She didn't know the beer was working on her. She nodded off on the pier with the fishermen laughing and talking nearby, the gentle noise of talk and laughter lulling her to sleep.

"Hey, Little 'un," a hard-toed boot gently nudged her leg. "It's getting dark out here and we are packing up to leave. You better get your little self home."

Abby blinked her eyes and tried her best to wake up. The beer and warm sunshine won though as she dozed back off. She woke up with a start and then dozed back off, the sun feeling like a soft blanket on her back. When she finally awoke, the fishermen were all gone and the sky was inky black, millions of stars twinkling overhead. It was as dark as she could remember and Abby was scared. She heard a strange noise in the distance and wondered if it was the bob cat way up in the woods her mamma had warned her about. She heard the wild cats scuttling up and down the rock walls and the wild oats on the dunes rustle in the wind. The water had grown rough and the waves slapped against the shore line. Abby ran like a bat out of hell back up to the suite in the center hall where she knew she'd be safe. But before Abby fell exhausted into her bed, she glanced around the corner into her sister's bedroom across the hall from her own room. She was measuring how much trouble she was in for staying out too late. Mags and Mary were both sound asleep. Abby was a little afraid that nobody even knew she was missing. She lay in bed wondering about that when the lingering effects of her beer put her back to sleep.

The Inn

*O*ver the last few months, Pearl's renovation of the compound and grounds had gone at a hefty clip. The barracks had undergone a complete transformation, including fresh white wash on the exterior. Some men had to be hired, but the children had worked alongside them every day.

"I'm leaving these steps just the way they are," Pearl announced. "I know, they look like an old swayback mare that's dropped one too many foals, but they add history and interest to the place, don't you think?"

"When are we going to start on the marina?" Matt asked.

"We've got a lot to do before we even think about that marina," Pearl replied. "Boyd wants this place up, open, and swinging with happy customers by summer. Besides, the marina will mean big machines and more money! Nothing Boyd needs to hear right now!"

The old porches now had dozens of rocking chairs. Pearl had ordered Matt to dig up wild lantana plants that dotted the landscape and they now sat in big clay pots up and down the porches. An occasional giant fern hung from the rafters. Abby loved the new sign out front of the restaurant. It proudly boasted "The Light House Inn and Restaurant," and it hung over a huge red Coca-Cola circle surrounded by tall oleanders. You could see that big, red dot from a good distance. Abby noticed the parking lot had been re-shelled. The new shells hurt Abby's feet when she tried to go bare foot but she liked the shiny new, bleached oyster shells with the lavender spots in the middle. She remembered seeing the pretty purple dot in an oyster shell before when Matt told her that oysters can actually make a pearl out of a little piece of sand. She wondered, out of all of these shells, how many pearls had been made.

Inside, final touches were underway. "Matt, you, Mags, and

Mary go down to the point. I want a big piece of drift wood. I don't want a scrawny little branch. I want a tree. The whole tree, a big one, nice and long. Go see what you can find," Pearl ordered.

"What are you doing with a drift wood tree?" Mary asked. "And do we have to take Abby?"

"It's a surprise," she said. "It's going to be beautiful. No, Miss Priss Abby can stay here with me. I've got a few things I need to show her anyway."

Pearl treated the older children as if they were grown, working them like a construction crew. She gave them no time off to do kid things at all, only sent them to school. Mags had not yet even made it to the beach with Abby, though Abby whined and pleaded with her daily.

Things seemed to be changing for the better for the kids when Pearl surprised Matt and Mags and told them they could drive the Studebaker. "Hell, just stay local," Pearl said. "Nobody on this place but us chickens, the Coast Guard folks that live on the point, and that old man at the fort. Nobody knows or cares how old you are, Matt." With that statement, on that day, Pearl made her own law and, as far as Matt cared, had pronounced him a man. Officially.

"Let's take the car down to the beach road and see what we can find!" Matt threw open the car door and jumped in. No chance they'd make any huge discoveries of driftwood trees there, but this was as good an excuse as any to drive. Matt wondered what would they do if they found a tree-size piece of driftwood, but he'd worry about that later. For now, the drive might as well have been a road trip to the county fair. They were elated. The tired three found new energy as they climbed out of the car, finally able to put their toes in the sand and take a break, even if just a short one. Their feet made squeaking noises as they drug them through the snow white sand. "Let's jump in!" Matt said. Glancing up and down the beach they saw no one, and all three stripped off everything they had on but their underwear and dove headfirst into the chilly waters of the Gulf of Mexico. It was spring and the water was still quite cold. They all came up shocked and laughing, trying to get their breath. Matt only allowed them a few minutes of splashing and playing, and no one complained when he said, "That's enough of this. We'll get pneumonia!"

43

They got dressed and strolled the beaches, casually and slowly, so their clothes and hair would dry. They saw several pieces of driftwood in all sizes, but the biggest so far was the size of a man's leg. Finally, they happened upon a huge tree trunk, silvered from the sun. Matt tried to move it, but it did not budge. He pushed with his full weight behind him, his feet dug into the sand. He couldn't even roll it over. Both girls joined in the pushing and pulling of the half buried tree. Still, it did not move an inch.

"Well, I think this is probably what she wants," he said. "But the damned thing is too heavy for us. I need some help and a truck."

Their clothes and hair were dry enough to risk climbing in the car and heading back to the Inn without getting caught fooling around and swimming.

"My hair is a curly mess," Mary noted. "She'll know we've been swimming for sure."

"Nah. We'll swear we broke into a sweat trying to get that damned tree dislodged," Matt assured her.

They drove up and saw Abby just where they'd left her, in the parking lot. Matt carefully parked the car and glanced at Abby when a dilapidated old car suddenly sped into the parking lot, skidding to a stop just before it hit the brand new steps up to the front door of the restaurant. The car door was one color, the hood another, and the trunk yet another. There were plenty of dents. And rust everywhere. The windshield was cracked and a rear window was covered with cardboard held in place with duct tape. The doors sounded like barn gates as they opened. From the driver's side Abby saw a filthy man get out. His tee shirt was yellowed and stained. When he tilted his head to squint at the sun, as if to tell the time, he drew back his lips and Abby could see he had no teeth. Greasy tendrils of hair hung down from beneath a once white sea-captain's hat. Abby looked at the passenger, a fat man, and he looked a mess, too. He smiled at Abby. He had nice teeth. The men were holding beer cans. They both took a swallow.

"Where's Miss Pearl?" asked the one with no teeth.

"She's in the restaurant," Abby said, pointing to the big building in front of them. "But Mamma's busy right now and she don't want nobody getting under her feet. Are you a Clark or a Cantor?" Abby asked.

It was long standing rule in the family, all the way back to her old grandmother, that none of them could play with a Clark or a Cantor. Abby was pretty sure these men had to be one or the other.

"Naw. We ain't them. We's here to see Miss Pearl. She sent word for us to come see her."

"Well, go on in then," Abby said. "She's in there somewhere, most likely in the kitchen at the way, way back of the building." Abby went back to what she had been doing, watching the one cat, a lanky tabby, the only one with nerve enough to approach the Inn. A mockingbird was dive bombing the cat and Abby watched as the cat spun and twisted and snatched the bird out of flight. She waved at her brother and sisters as Matt took the steps two-by-two into the restaurant, following the dirty new arrivals.

Abby waited for the fun when her mother would chase these two hooligans out with a black skillet in her hand. It seemed like a hot forever had passed, and the two men were still inside. She decided to sneak in and see what was going on.

Abby heard her mother speaking and then the sloppy slurred voice of the toothless one out on the porch behind the kitchen. She tried to sneak closer in, and hide behind the door, but Pearl saw her. Matt was standing on the porch with the men, hands in his pockets, eyebrows drawn together, paying close attention to the plans being laid out.

"Abby," Pearl called. "Come out here. I want you to meet Uncle Homer."

What? One of these dirty men was her uncle?

Abby walked out on the porch, stood behind her mother, clinging to her skirt. She knew Pearl did not like for her to tug on her skirts, but it was a habit Abby couldn't seem to break.

"Abby, this is Uncle Homer," Pearl chirped. She gestured toward the toothless one. Abby did not think the Big Dogs would approve of this man.

"I think we already met," Uncle Homer slurred. He had taken off his white cap and his hair hung in wads and strings. He wiped tobacco juice from the corners of his lips with a nasty blue handkerchief.

"Uncle Homer and his brother, Uncle Bud," Pearl said, "are going to build us a walk-in cooler, right here on this porch.

45

Uncle Bud has to stay home and tend to his old mamma, but Uncle Homer is going to live with us right here in the Inn."

"Where's he gonna stay, Mamma?" Abby wanted to know. "All the guest rooms are clean and ready for guests. Matt lives in the wash house."

"You let *me* worry about that, Missy," Pearl said, her voice sharp. "For the time being, anyway, I think it would be very hospitable of you if we let him stay in your room. You don't take up much space." Pearl's eyes sparkled fire, *Don't you dare say a word!*

"There isn't any room in there for a grown man," Abby dared, "but I guess Mags would let me stay with her for a few nights. Until you figure this out." She stepped from behind her mother's skirts and put her hands on her hips. This was one battle she meant to win.

"Don't be silly, you skinny, brainless child. There is plenty of room and a double bed in your room. The matter is settled, until we can make better accommodations! You won't even have to bother Mags. We'll get Homer a mattress for the floor ... or something." Uncle Homer patted Abby on the head.

Better accommodations for her or for Uncle Homer, Abby wondered. She had heard the older sisters talking about Mamma setting up a large suite of their own at the end of the first floor.

Abby announced she had somewhere to go. She stuck her lips out, her chin up and took long strides leaving the room. 'Thwack, thwack, thwack' was the noise made by her flip flops as she left the room. Matt looked at his mother with a question mark in his eye. Pearl glared at Matt, silently daring him to open his mouth.

Abby escaped the restaurant as fast as she could. When she got to the edge of the yard, she started crying. Not just tears coming down her face, but big sobs that made her choke. Sharks swimming in the water and dark nights alone stirred together in her head. What mother was this, worse than bad, who had very, very important new friends and very, very scary and dirty friends? Abby did not want another uncle. Uncle Boyd and Uncle Jim seemed okay. At least they had a long shiny car and a big boat that she might get to ride in if she was good. But this old toothless man? Abby was so mad she could spit. The madder she got, the more she cried. After all, she had offered to sleep with Mags, but noooo, her important Mamma wanted that dirty old thing to sleep in her room. This was something that she would tell her aunts about for sure. That'd make Pearl mad! Abby mumbled and stomped and cried until she could find Mary and Mags to tell them all about the new 'uncles.'

"Don't you worry, baby sister. Of course you can bunk with me. I'm sure Mamma didn't mean the hired help would sleep with you." Mags stroked Abby's tangled hair and looked at Mary. The heaving sobs turned into snuffles and Abby eventually stopped crying.

"But he's taking my very own room," Abby wailed as the sobs started again. "It's the first room I've ever had of my own."

"Don't worry. I'm sure that's not what Mamma meant," assured Mary. Worn out from crying, Mags tucked Abby into her own bed with fresh sheets. "Just take a nap while we go find out what Mamma's real plans are. We saw that grimy pair when we pulled in. I am quite sure he will have his own room."

The last sounds Abby heard that afternoon was Mary opening the window for a breeze and the two of them walking down the center stairs. They must have run into Matt, because as Abby dozed off, she heard the three of them talking.

Though spring, it was already hot. "Hotter than Hades," Pearl said. Pearl told Abby that Hades meant hell. "Don't you ever let me catch you saying *hell*. You can say Hades. But not a dirty word, do you hear?"

Pearl drug in an old single mattress and dropped it at the foot of Abby's double bed and allowed the old man sleep in Abby's room even with the older children objecting. Abby was so mad she decided she'd pay closer attention to those fishermen and learn every cuss word she could. Some day she might just let one slip in front of the men in the black limousine. "That would serve her just right," Abby muttered to herself. With that decision made, she walked slowly, stepping around the stickers, to her beach, hermit crabs, and the fishermen.

Abby dove head first from the beach into the clear green waters and opened her eyes. They stung for a minute but she got used to it. She swam under water humming, "You Are My Sunshine." She stayed under as long as she could and kept an eye out for that hammerhead shark. She could not stay under long enough to hum the entire song. She'd get as far as "when skies are gray" and pop up for air. It was the only song she knew all of the words to. When she stood up in the water and looked at her hands, her skin was all wrinkled. Abby waded onto the beach, went up the rock wall and peered toward the restaurant. That ugly car was gone.

"Hell, I think I'll go meet that old man at the fort," she said to no one in particular. "I bet he knows a lot about this place. And he probably knows me by now. He's been looking in my direction for a long time."

With that, Abby wrapped her sun bleached beach towel around her. Her bathing suit was two sizes too small and rode up her crack. She slid into her flip flops and took a route she'd not taken before. She was surprised to come into a clearing and find a sidewalk leading to the building.

The little building had a small, hand-painted sign on front. Abby studied it, sounding out the letters and making the words. Point Mobile and Fort Morgan Historic Society. Abby knew how to read pretty well, thanks to her big brother. She saw another sign. It said, OPEN. So Abby knocked on the door and went in.

"Well, come in. Come in," the man inside said to her.

She stepped into the small office. The man went behind his desk and sat down. Each time she had seen this old man, he had watched her. He kept his eyes on her as she climbed through the fort, or as she wandered up the shell road to the Coast Guard station. She had never said anything to him. He hadn't said anything to her, so she stood there. She didn't know what to say.

"I was wondering when you were coming to meet me," the old gray-haired man said, while trying to puff his pipe. "I've seen you around my fort. I figured you'd get curious enough to come for a visit." He waited for Abby to speak, and when still she said nothing, watching him, he said, "Your mamma the one restoring the barracks?"

He struck a match to relight his pipe, and Abby remembered the governor's pipe. "Pipes just don't work very good," she said. The old man laughed. She decided the short old man was friendly.

"Yes, Sir," she said. "Mamma and Uncle Boyd are partners now. She's fixing to run the hotel and restaurant. She got a lease on it. We're gonna be rich." The old man nodded, keeping an eye on Abby, smiling. "Oh, I am Abigail Delaney Whitney. People call me Abby, but my aunts call me Frog."

"Uncle Boyd," the old man said as he squinted his eyes and relit the pipe in his hand. "Now how does your Mamma know Uncle Boyd? Is he really your uncle?" The old man was being slow and careful while he tried to glean information from the tall but slight built child in front of him.

"No, he isn't my real uncle. Mamma makes us call almost everybody uncle. She says it's polite. She met him because she used to be a land-man. Do you know what that is? She'd go find owners of land that nobody else could find. So, she worked for Uncle Boyd up in North Mobile as a land-man. She said it was a big oil play up in Citronelle." Abby took a step closer.

Abby looked around the little room and watched the old man strike another match and stick it to the pipe end. "So, what's your name? I watch you hang them flags up every morning."

"Oh, pardon me," he said, standing, and giving a slight bow. "I was so curious my manners got away from me. I am Axil Chapin Gunter. I am the official caretaker of this fine fort. I've been here for years. When I first came down here, you couldn't even walk on the property because of all the underbrush and overgrowth." He rocked back on his heels and took a smokeless puff from his pipe, his old eyes glittering with pride. "Do you want me to call you Abby or Frog?"

"I like Abby. Frog is such a baby name and I ain't no baby."

"You do realize, my dear, using the word 'ain't' makes you sound like you're from the swamps. I doubt that you are, given the company your mother keeps." He lit his pipe, puffing hard until smoke finally came out of the bowl. "How old are you, Abby?"

"I'm almost six-and-a-half, but I'm tall for my age. Most people think I'm eight or nine. I hate being tall."

"Would you like to come in and see the museum?" he asked. Abby nodded, her eyes widening. Mr. Gunter stood and led Abby past his desk to the first of the exhibits.

Abby saw cases with glass fronts and glass tops. Mr. Gunter told her she was looking at parts of old cannon balls, bullet shells, buttons and coins. There were maps on the wall, one a diagram of the fort. Axil saw her looking at the diagram. She saw a sign she liked "Damned the torpedoes. Full speed ahead." She'd try to remember that and use it in front of her mamma's friends. She could say she read it on a sign and still get to use a dirty word!

"This old fort has five stars, five corners, and was built around a fort designed by Michelangelo! Isn't that utterly amazing?" He was rocking on his feet again.

"Well, Mr. Axil Gunter. Thanks for showing me your history stuff. I better be getting back to the restaurant." She reached out to shake his hand as a big girl would do. Mr. Gunter nodded and smiled, taking her hand and giving it a good firm shake. "Can I come back sometime?"

"Anytime, young lady. I'll show you how to hang and take down the flags when you're ready. There's quite an art to it that I think you'll appreciate. Nice meeting you, Miss Abigail Delaney. You may call me Axil. And by the way, don't let those fishermen give you any more beer to drink."

"Yes, sir," Abby stuttered, and left red-faced wondering if he might tell her Mamma.

Mc Allister

"Hey, Mamma," Abby said the day after meeting Mr. Axil. "I met that old man at the fort. His name is Mr. Axil Gunter and he's pretty nice. He says he is the caretaker of the fort and he has been down here a long time."

"Don't 'Hey Mamma' me," Pearl said. "You use your manners and address me with respect. I don't want to hear 'Hey Mamma' again, like you're calling a dog or something. Now, stay away from that old man! I think he's a kook. Remember when we first moved into the Inn and we heard strange things at night? Well, I think it was him trying to scare us away. Boyd says he's a nut and the State only lets him stay because nobody else will take the job."

"But Mamma," Abby said. "He said he would teach me how to hang up those flags over the entrance of the fort. And he can teach me lots of history."

"Well, just keep your eyes open. I suppose if he teaches you history and about the flags, you can tell the tourist's children and keep them entertained."

"Kind of like a babysitter?" Abby was all ears.

"You're a little young for that, but I still bet those children will want to play with you. You play in that fort a lot. You should know your way around by now. Now, scoot on out of here. I have lots of work to do."

As she wandered down to the fort, keeping an eye open for any new wild kittens, Abby realized she had indeed explored just about every inch of the original fort and she had even been in the newer, World War II rifle batteries as well. Her head filled with good ideas for the tourist's children, and she thought it would really be fun to have someone to play with. When she had the fort all to herself, which was quite often, she straddled all of the cannons like the horse she dreamed of having one day and climbed around on the cannon balls that were piled up and concreted together. Bored with riding a stationary cannon horse, Abby decided to go see Mr. Axil.

"Good Afternoon, Mr. Axil," Abby said. She had barely opened the door and was peeking in, just to make sure she didn't disturb him.

"Well, good afternoon, Miss Abigail," Mr. Axil replied. "I've watched you out riding the cannons and counting the cannon balls. Why, when I first got here, you could barely get in that big old door from overgrowth of vines and weeds, bushes of all sorts. The cannon balls were tossed this way and that and had to be gathered and stacked and mortared in place. That's pretty back breaking work and the state wouldn't send me any help. But, this is my work, by God, and I got it done. Come, let me show you some interesting things. Stalagmites and stalactites."

Abby had already seen them, though she didn't know the name of them, and was happy to have company that was actually interested in her. Abby followed as Mr. Axil led her into one of the huge domed chambers in the fort. She loved the giant arched doorways that separated each space. It was there, in those rounded entrances, that Mr. Axil pointed.

"See," he said, pointing to mounds on the ground that looked like ice. "Those are formed from the minerals in the water that seep up through the brick plus the water that drips down from the ceiling. Stalagmites. The ones that look like icicles? They are the same thing, but they drip down. Those are the stalactites. That's the only difference. Look. Some are so large they look like marble statues."

"I'll have to bring Mamma to see these for sure," Abby said.

"Now, let me show you a secret place, one you could show your mother, but nobody else."

Mr. Axil led her back out of the front through the large opening into the main fort, the wide entry path made of the same brick as the fort.

"That opening into the fort is called a Sally Port," Mr. Axil said to Abby.

"It looks like a giant mouth to me," Abby said. "The brick road going in looks like it's a big ol' tongue."

Abby squinted her eyes as they made their way out of the

dim and damp fort. He was leading her over to a battery. Although she had explored it many times, she didn't say a word. She was bathing in the attention of Mr. Axil and never wanted it to end. But instead of taking her up into the battery, he turned and went into a very dark doorway. She had noticed it before but stayed away from it. It was too dark and she was sure there were snakes in there. Snakes were all over this place and Abby kept an eye out for them.

"Are we going in there?" she asked, her eyes round and wide.

"Yes, but don't worry. I know all the tricks for finding my way in and out. You're safe with me. It's called a dungeon. It's a dark place where they kept prisoners during the wars. The hall zigzags and at each turn there is a very deep hole. So when I ask for your hand, give it to me and I'll swing you over the hole. The holes were dug to keep the prisoners from escaping."

Finally, after several swings over what she assumed were very deep holes, they got to the main room where the prisoners had been kept. Light flooded in from narrow slits in the upper part of the wall. Mr. Axil picked her up so she could peer through the slits.

"Why, we're right next to the beach and the pier!" she exclaimed.

"Yes, we are, little madam. Now that I've given you *part* of the personal tour, I have to get back to work."

True to his word, Mr. Axil led them back out of the dungeon into the afternoon sun. Abby bid Mr. Axil goodbye for the day. She walked along, wondering how in the world she could show the tourist children the dungeon. She decided she'd come back and get used to it like Mr. Axil had but she'd ask Matt to come with her first and bring his flashlight. Maybe Matt would let her borrow his flashlight for showing the dungeon!

Walking slowly back to the Inn, engrossed in her thoughts about how to show that dungeon, she was startled when her mother asked "Abby, have you been down there with that kooky old man again?"

"Yes ma'am. He showed me lots of fun things in the fort that I can show the visiting children. I can be an official tour guide, Mr. Axil said."

"Most people are afraid of that old goat," Pearl said. "Are you not afraid of him?"

"No ma'am. He's real nice. He's written two history books on this fort. He knows a lot and he treats me just like a grown up."

"Well, don't so much as whisper to him what we are doing up here," Pearl warned. "Uncle Boyd does not like him and does not trust him. You keep that big mouth shut, but keep your big ears open. You tell me everything Axil Gunter says to you. Do you understand?"

"Yes ma'am. I bet Uncle Boyd don't like him because Mr. Axil says this place belongs to the State of Alabama and that they leased it to someone else, not Uncle Boyd." Abby saw her mother's eyebrows raise, ever so slightly.

"Really? What else did Mr. Axil have to say? And it's doesn't, not don't. You really need to watch your English. That's the kind of talk you pick up hanging around with those fishermen."

"He said that Uncle Boyd was a rascal and you should be very careful with him. That's not the word he used. It was a big word and I can't remember it. He said Uncle Boyd couldn't lease you this Inn because it wasn't his to lease. He said a woman like you ought not be running around with the likes of Uncle Boyd. He also said Uncle Boyd isn't a big dog at all, but just poor white trash without an education."

"Well, aren't you full of talk? I know what he's referring to and it's nothing for you to repeat."

With that, Pearl's skirts began their swing as she walked out of the room, leaving Abby standing alone in the big kitchen. A lot of work had been done. It now had stoves and ovens and giant refrigerators. The fireplace had been fitted with a slow turning spit, and the walk-in cooler on the porch was almost finished.

Some very old man came and went from the fort, someone Abby hadn't met before and someone her mother didn't bother introducing her to. He was trying to make the side by side sinks wash the dishes by themselves and had installed fans in the bottom of the sinks. He warned everyone, not just Abby, to keep their hands away from the fan blades. The dishes were put in large metal baskets and lowered into boiling water and the fans spun. The plan worked on some dishes but some

54

came out with food still stuck on them. This man smoked a pipe, too, and bent over the sinks sketching and puzzling as he puffed and lit and relit his pipe.

The huge driftwood tree had been hosed off and dragged into the building by Uncle Homer, Matt, and a few other hired hands. It now sat right in the middle of the dining room with different colors of orchids artfully plopped into every nook and cranny. Pearl said the barnacles left on the tree added to the authenticity.

"Well the tables look great," Pearl said as Abby entered the dining room. Abby stopped to study the driftwood tree. Her mother called her over. "These tables are called Lazy Susan, Abby. See, the large centers go around so we can serve family-ly-styled meals to our customers. They can have as much as they want! We want people to get their money's worth. Plus, our linen costs will be lower." A few regular square tables were inserted here and there with a group of them in a private corner that led to the screened porch.

"These are for the upper-ups," Pearl said, pointing to the private tables. "They can order off the special menu. I've hired a wonderful cook," she told her daughter. "He's from up North and is quite well known. He should be here somewhere. Come, let me introduce you."

Abby followed her mother into the kitchen glancing back over her shoulder to look at the fish nets hung on the wall. They had shells and starfish and little pieces of driftwood stuck in them. She bumped into her mother and looked up. There stood the tallest, skinniest Negro Abby had ever seen. They were not allowed to use the word nigger like most of the people around here. Her mamma told her it was rude and unnecessary. Once, when they still lived in the cottage by the gully, Pearl and Abby were driving downtown and there, in front of the Methodist Church at Broad Street, was an old Negro man on a broken down bicycle. The kids on the corner had been throwing rocks at him and calling him names.

"See that man?" Pearl asked Abby.

"Yes ma'am."

"I better never catch you treating another human being like those children are doing. I will pinch your head off and roll it down the hill. People are people. We are all human beings. Nobody wants to be mistreated. The color of a person's skin does not change that one degree."

Abby blushed as her mamma ran off the kids and asked the old man if there was anything she could do to help. The look on the man's face was one Abby would never forget.

"Naw," he had answered. "But I sho appreciate you trying to teach them young'uns something. Not likely to take, though. They mamma and daddy prob'ly just as rude."

Abby had heard her aunts say Pearl was too liberal. They said she was going to ruin the children. Pearl laughed and told them right to their faces they were just a bunch of country bumpkins who didn't know the difference between ruin and right. Abby wanted to be nice to all people, a liberal, just like her mother. She did not want to be a country bumpkin.

"Hello, Abby," said the tall mahogany colored man. "My name is McAllister. It is a pleasure to make your acquaintance. You come around when I am not too busy when the restaurant opens, and I'll cook whatever your little heart desires. I'm a mighty fine cook."

His teeth were huge and white and his smile went from ear to ear. He offered Abby his hand to shake. His fingers were long and skinny and, based on his big ol' shoes, his feet were long and skinny, too. Just like she saw Matt do when he met Uncle Boyd, Abby clasped his hand firmly. She looked him square in the eyes.

"Hello, Mr. McAllister," Abby answered. Right away, she liked McAllister. The thought of having someone cook for her, anything she wanted, made her smile a smile almost as big as McAllister's. "What mighty fine things do you cook?" Abby wanted to know.

"Well, I make the best gumbo you ever gonna taste. You like gumbo?" Abby nodded her head yes. "I make chicken and dumplings that will melt in your mouth! And biscuits? Ooooh ... eeee ... my biscuits are like hot buttered clouds. A little honey and you could float on up to heaven." By this time, Mr. McAllister was becoming more animated, walking through the kitchen, pointing at giant pots and pans as he talked. "And fresh fish? Whoo-eeee, what McAllister can do with a fresh fish. You just wait and see! I bakes a whole hog. I mean all of the pig and stuff an apple in his mouth, for special parties. The best pork you'll ever eat."

"You got any children, Mr. McAllister? And where do you

live?" Abby had lots of questions for this man she liked better all the time.

"Now, Abby," Pearl interrupted. "Don't pester McAllister to death. He's getting the kitchen set up to his liking."

"Well, yes I do have children. I moved them and my wife, Bessie, right down here to the fort with me. I have nine children. Mostly boys, but they's some little girls 'bout your size to play with. We live in that little cottage you mamma set up for us at the end of the airstrip."

"We have an airstrip?" Abby asked, looking up at Pearl.

"Well, it's sort of an airstrip," Pearl said. "Right now it's just 2,000 feet of grass. Uncle Boyd is going to ask the governor to pave it so we can have fly-in conventions." Her chest was swelled beneath her white blouse as she wiggled the belt buckle on her small waist, making sure it was aligned properly. "Now, leave McAllister alone and go play."

Abby decided to wander around the inside for a while. As long as she stayed out of her mamma's way, she thought it'd be okay to look around a bit. Abby was seeing the transformation of the inside of the restaurant for the first time. The right side had the big dining room with the round tables and the kitchen was behind two swinging doors at the back. Abby wandered to the left on her tiptoes, into the foyer where the stairs went up. Her mother had said people would have little stores up there.

Abby's eyes widened as she walked into the room to the left of the entrance. Upon entering the big room on the left, Abby saw stools in front of a long, curving bar that was varnished and shiny. Fishnet hung on the back wall with starfish caught in the mesh. A wooden sign, that looked old, said, Tiki Bar. Orchids sat on the bar in giant shells. Glasses were carefully cleaned and lined up on shelves. She crept quietly past the bar into the main room.

"Good God from Vicksburg!" Abby said louder than she intended. She had heard Pearl say that on many an occasion. The room was huge with tall ceilings. Floor to ceiling poles, covered in decorated tin, stood throughout the enormous room. At the very back was a small hut covered in palmetto leaves, from top to bottom. It even had a palmetto thatched roof. A sign hung over the propped open window that said Sugar Shack. The hut was more than Abby could resist. The small door creaked just a bit as she opened it and she snuck into the leafy hut.

Abby lost track of time and place in the hut and sauntered back out into the big room. She was engrossed with her surroundings, not even aware of the sound of her own voice. The poles beckoned her to climb them, a temptation she could not resist. She wrapped her skinny legs around the poles, ankles crossed and locked. She inched her way up all the way to the top, touched the ceiling, and slid down, her sweaty skin squeaking against the fancy tin.

"Abigail Delaney!" Pearl yelled. It was never a good sign when Pearl used both of her names. "Get your monkey fanny off those columns and out of this room right this instant, young lady!"

"Mamma, is that my playhouse?" Abby asked, sliding down the pole and pointing at the frond covered house at the back of the room.

"No ma'am, it is NOT! This is the ball room and the Tiki Bar. That," she said pointing to the palmetto hut, "is the Sugar Shack, where your sisters will give kisses for money. Now you get your behind out of here and stay out or you can bank on a good switching!"

"We have a bar?" Abby asked.

"Thanks to Uncle Boyd," Pearl responded. "Our first fly-in convention is on their way in, grass landing strip and all. It's going to be busy around here and I expect to see very little of you. Now scoot!"

Abby walked down the sidewalk that led from the convention center all the way down to the grass landing strip. Abby had never thought about all that grass as she had explored cisterns and the old battery on the other side of the grass. She made her way down to McAllister's cottage. There, busy as bees fixing up the porch, were McAllister's grown boys. They were men really. They glanced at her with suspicion, brows furrowed.

"Hey. I'm Abby. I'm Miss Pearl's daughter," she said as she stuck out her hand like McAllister had done.

The boys just kept working. One nodded his head toward the door on the tiny house and said, "The girls are inside. I guess that's who you came to see."

Abby climbed the rickety steps up to the front porch,

which was in bad need of a paint job. She looked at the fig tree at the end of the porch. A snake hung lazily on the branches, its body slinking down like an old hose.

"You seen that snake?" she asked. She pointed to it.

The boys stopped what they were doing and grabbed pieces of brick that was everywhere on the ground and all over the fort compound. They started chunking the brick ammunition at the snake. "No ma'am," said one of the boys. "We don't like snakes." He hurled another brick at the snake that lay undisturbed and still on the branch.

"It's just a little ol' corn snake," Abby informed them, tickled that a little snake had them so scared. Abby knocked on the front door. A lady with her hair tied up in a scarf and a little baby hanging over her arm answered the door, her eyes sleepy and disinterested.

"Are you Miss Bessie?" Abby asked and again stuck out her hand. It was ignored again.

"Yes'm," replied the lady. "Who you and what you want?"

"I'm Abby, Miss Pearl's daughter. Mr. McAllister said you had some little girls I could play with."

"Mister McAllister," the lady laughed. She wiped snuff juice from the side of her mouth. "Mister McAllister," she said again, like it was the funniest thing she had heard. "Come on in. The girls, they in the bedroom." She pointed toward one of the few doors.

The main room was a living room, a small kitchen and dining area. There was a bedroom on each end of the house. Abby did not see a bathroom. She was sure they had one somewhere. She heard giggles come out of one of the rooms and headed in. The giggling stopped as two brown girls, one about the size and age of Abby, stopped playing and just stared.

"Hey, I'm Abby. Mr. McAllister said you might want to play."

"Hey," they said in unison.

"Our mamma crazy," said the tallest one.

"Mine is, too," said Abby and they all burst into giggles. Within the hour, Abby had shed her own clothes and put on one of the girl's sun suits, so they would all match. They all went out to play. Abby loved the combination of yellow and orange they all had on, stripes and dots going this way and that in unison as they walked.

59

"Wanna go over the air strip and see that gray fort over there?" Abby asked as she pointed to the battery at the end of the grassy strip.

"We have to ask our brothers," said Cindy, the tallest one. Becky was the little one and she was six. Cindy, the same size as Abby, was ten years old.

The brothers ignored the little girls, questions and all. The snake was no longer in the tree, but instead was lying on the sidewalk with the head bludgeoned, a bloody brick-bat nearby being the weapon of death of that snake. Bessie still looked blank. She had the baby over her knees, bouncing them up and down, as she hummed a song. The three little girls went stomping over the grass strip in matching sun suits, complaining about sand spurs and swatting at mosquitoes on their legs.

"A fly-in convention is coming soon," said Abby.

"Who coming and what is a fly-in convention?" asked Cindy.

"I'm not sure. Mamma said they're coming, though."

Cindy had a question in her mind, one she wasn't sure she would ask, one she'd heard her Daddy talk about. She considered it and glanced at Abby a few times. After all, this was the first time they had met and she wanted the girl to come back and play. But, she got up her nerve and spat it out. "Dat old white man sleep wid you?" Cindy finally asked.

Abby felt her face turn red, knowing her embarrassment was visible to both girls and wondered how they knew so much so soon. "Well, my mamma makes him sleep on a mattress on the floor in my room," answered Abby. "He dudn't really sleep *with* me. How did you know about him?"

"I heard Daddy tell da boys to keep that ol' coot away from here. Dat it was bad enough he got to sleep with you. Dat old devil better not come round here. He be like that snake on da sidewalk if my brothers get holt of him."

Abby couldn't speak, not quite sure how to answer the lingering question about Uncle Homer coming around McAllister's girls. Maybe McAllister would talk to Pearl, too, and she wouldn't have to worry about him anymore. As if the subject had never been broached, the girls went stomping through the old fort battery, the high grass on the airstrip and finally back to the sanctuary of Cindy's bedroom where they played with paper dolls.

Mr. BB & Mrs. Chi-Chi

Pearl had a passion for dogs. She wasn't loyal to any particular breed of dog but she was loyal to the *thought* of breeding dogs. This time she brought home two black, standard poodles. The female was named Mrs. Chi-Chi and Pearl told Abby that Chi-Chi was a milk thief. She said you could tell she was a milk thief because of the white beard Mrs. Chi-Chi wore on her otherwise black face. The male was called Mr. BB. Pearl told Abby that BB was short for Beelzebub and that Mr. BB was a devil of a dog, still very much a puppy and needing lots of training. She told Abby that poodles were very smart, especially standards, and she was waiting for them to get old enough to have babies. Abby was excited about the idea of having puppies. She liked the way their breath smelled when they were little. For now, though, both dogs were good companions, even though Becky and Cindy were scared of them. Cindy said they were too big. Becky thought they were too black.

BB was Abby's favorite and he stayed right on her heels, even in the dungeon, if Pearl hadn't locked him away in his kennel. Pearl had failed to consider that poodles are water dogs. They splashed in the bay anytime they were near it, climbing out tired, matted and sandy. Abby was careful to take BB to her secret swimming spot at Navy Cove, far away from the hammerhead sharks at the pier. She hummed underwater while BB splashed around her and occasionally held her under water, trying to hold on to her. Abby came up sputtering and laughing. The sand spurs stuck in the dog's coats which caused Pearl hours of combing and clipping and grooming. So she locked them up in their crates quite often. Abby would sneak and let BB out so that he could go on her adventures with her. She ran her fingers through his thick curly hair and he would look up at her, brown black eyes that stared at her with total love. Today, she and BB had been to the beach and had run through the dungeon. She had to drag him by his collar to get him back in his kennel before Pearl caught her or saw the dog out.

Playing and then wrestling with BB to get him back in his kennel left Abby hot and sweaty. She had been all over the fort, her companion at her heels, in and out of that dungeon at least a dozen times. Matt let her borrow the flashlight and she used it at first. But now, like Mr. Axil, she knew her way. She showered off the sweat and sand, but it was early for bed, at least for Abby. McAllister had stuffed her with a fine piece of steak and his secret recipe mashed potatoes. She was full, clean and ready to lie down and read her book.

She drifted into a light sleep and awoke when she heard the back stairs squeak, then Uncle Homer's old boots tromp and slide down the hall. He fell into the walls and groaned as he stumbled toward the bedroom, ricocheting from side to side. Though she had become used to his drunken entrances and his sleeping on the single mattress that was still not elevated off the floor, she dreaded his arrival each night. Tonight Abby pretended to be asleep. She had learned not to squeeze her eyes shut when acting like she was sleeping. That was a dead giveaway, and she didn't want this toothless old drunk to know she was now wide awake. She peeped at the wall she was facing. The porch light, shining through the window blinds, made shadows and patterns on the wall. She moved closer to the wall but turned over so she could keep an eye on the man. The old door complained on its hinges as he entered the room. Abby focused on her breathing, trying to remember how her sisters sounded when they were asleep.

Abby tried to quiet her thoughts while also trying to keep her breaths deep and even. *I wish he would take a bath. He said he would be nice.* Abby's thoughts crawled through her brain as her ears took in every sound the man made. She heard him tiptoe, or try to tiptoe, into the bedroom. She remained frozen. Her bed moved a little as he sat down on the edge and she heard him kick off his boots. She could feel his glare when he turned around and looked at her. He lit a non-filtered cigarette and sat on the side of her bed smoking it, Abby trying her best not to cough or move her nose as the smoke filled the corner. She peeped out of one eye and saw him rub the hot cherry of the burning cigarette with his little finger, ashes falling into the palm of his hand. He smoked until the cigarette burned his lips, then he mashed it out on the window sill. She watched through barely open eyelids while the man slid out of his filthy work pants and stained tee shirt. She could smell him. In one quick move, his hand was on her arm. Abby jumped and drew back. His unexpected touch shocked her.

"It's okay, little one," he said. "I ain't goin' to hurt you. But I know you is pretending to be sleeping." He chuckled. "Since I got that cooler finished up for your mamma, I figured I could use a good night's sleep in a real bed instead of down there on the floor on that mattress. I know you don't mind."

Abby opened her eyes. No sense in pretending anymore, she thought. "I'm not allowed to sleep with anybody but my sisters or brother," Abby answered as she crinkled her nose. His smell reminded her of an old mop her grandmother had once left in the mop bucket until it soured. She saw the cigarette butt on the window sill and thought this old goat was going to be in big trouble with her mamma. He stood with his back to her. There was a rip up the back seam of his underwear and she could see his bony rear hanging out right there in front of her. His sailor hat was off and his slick hair looked like fake hair on a plastic doll.

She heard the bark of a dog, first in the distance, but coming closer. Then sharp dog claws racing up the shiny, slick steps. She wondered if she had forgotten to put Mr. BB up but was glad he was on his way. She had been trying to send him a silent SOS when she heard the scratch at her bedroom door. *Attaboy,* she thought.

"Uncle Homer," Abby said. "That's my dog, Mr. BB, scratching at the door. I'm gonna let him in so he doesn't scrape up the door, but you better be real still because he's my guard dog Mamma bought." She thought guard dog sounded really good. The scratching became more intense and the dog was growling just outside the door. "Really, if he keeps pawing at the door and messes up the new paint, I'll be in trouble." Abby slid out of her bed and walked toward the door. "Now, I'm gonna hold him by the collar until he gets used to you. But he's pretty big and sometimes I just can't hold on to him."

"Don't you let that damned dog in here," Uncle Homer

said. "I'm scared of him and he don't like me anyhow. Ever time I get near him, he bares his front teeth at me. That ain't a good sign."

"I'm going out into the hall then. You can sleep in my bed tonight, this one time, since you're so tired, but it's the *only* time. If you try to sleep in my bed again, I'll let my dog eat you in one big ol' bite. I'll go sleep with Mags tonight, but you need to tell Mamma you need your own room." Abby inched the door open, pushing Mr. BB's nose back while she slid through the narrowest crack in the door she could make. She'd never heard him growl, much less snarl, but he was doing both tonight. "Good boy, BB," she whispered. She grabbed his collar and tugged him back down the stairs, him trying to claw his way back up to her bedroom. She finally got him back down to his kennel. The chubby and lazy Mrs. Chi-Chi was sound asleep in her crate. She kissed BB square in the mouth and nudged him into his own crate, walked back across the darkened yard and slipped as quietly as she could up the back stairs and into Mags and Mary's room.

"Mags," Abby whispered. "Mags, move over. I have to sleep with you because Uncle Homer wants to sleep in my bed tonight. I am not sleeping with him!" Her whisper had become an indignant full voice.

Mags stirred and Mary sat straight up in her bed. "Okay," Mags said sleepily, barely awake. "Climb in and I'll talk to Mamma about it tomorrow."

"You damned straight we'll talk to Mamma about this," added a fully awake Mary. "He is crazy. This is crazy. He shouldn't even be sleeping on your floor! He better be careful or Matt'll take him off in the swamps and lose him."

"Mags?" Abby asked in a hushed tone, "Will you change my sheets tomorrow?"

"Emm-hmmm," responded a sleeping Mags.

The Lighthouse Inn and Restaurant

"Now children," Pearl said to the row of clean and shiny children standing in front of her, "since the Inn is officially *open for business*, it's important that you all stay clean, dressed and always prepared to meet almost anyone you could imagine!" Her normally flashy green eyes were blue, matching the dress she had on. "Based on the success we had with the last convention and thanks to Uncle Boyd, both the Bachelors and the Débutantes will have their conventions here, too!"

Mary, having heard this speech before, was bored. She smiled to herself and decided it was time to tease her baby sister. "Abby, your epidermis is showing!"

"It is not!" Abby retorted, puffing out her lips into the biggest pout she could muster. She didn't know what epidermis was, but she was sure she had nothing showing.

"Yes it is!" added Matt. "*And* you slumbered in your bed last night!" The three older children laughed so hard that Matt bent over and held his stomach. Tears ran down Mary's cheeks. She covered her mouth with her fist as she tried to control laughter that she couldn't stop. Mags chuckled but felt a bit sorry for Abby.

Abby's face went from sun-tanned to bleached-white to hot-red. She wasn't sure what slumbered meant, but whatever it was, she was sure she had not done it in her bed!

Mary said, in a soft, cooing, teasing voice, "Oh, look, Abby is blushing!" She and Matt broke into another round of giggles.

"Leave the child alone! Stop teasing her so much," Pearl said. "We are open for business and don't have time for this foolishness. Since it's summer and you are out of school, your duties will be consistent. Margaret and Mary, you will help serve food in the dining room and keep your tips, which should be substantial. Matt, you will work the air strip. You will have to learn to anchor the small planes that risk landing on grass. Don't ask me! I sure as hell don't know! I'm sure the pilots will teach you."

Pearl told Matt the pilots would tip him and maybe pay him to wash their planes. Matt showed his excitement for the prospect of getting rich from the rich people who'd be coming here. He patted his pocket as though it was already bulging with cash.

"And Abby," Pearl continued, sighing. "Well, Abby, you can show the guests to their rooms, a very important job. The main thing, and I mean the very main thing you all must do is *practice discretion*. Abby, that means keep your mouth shut. A lot of our guests will be important politicians who want to be incommunicado while on vacation. Abby, incommunicado means they do not want to speak to anyone. Now, does everyone understand?"

All nodded their heads. Pearl was bent on going on with her instructions when the front screened door swung open and shut with a loud slam. Uncle Boyd strode in. He was puffed up and proud as always in his polished black shoes that clicked on newly polished wood floors.

"Well, my little hard working crew," Uncle Boyd's voice reverberated. "Hard working, indeed. Your lovely mother said she would meet my deadline and by God, with the Lord's help, she did. Met my deadline. You little sailors all did your jobs, too, from what I understand. Yes, indeed, a great group of sailors! We make a fine team, a fine team indeed."

"Hello, Boyd," Pearl said, tilting her head, batting her eyelashes, pushing her hip to the side. "I wasn't expecting you today. We are just going over a few running rules here. Like, how to be discrete!"

She smiled and he roared with laughter. "Yes, little soldiers. Listen to your mamma. Discretion is important!"

Pearl was relieved she had insisted the children bathe and dress. "See," she whispered to Mary, "you never know who will come through that door."

"Well, my lovely Miss Pearl," Uncle Boyd said. "I understand your entertaining cannot be topped. Nosirree. Cannot be topped. The conventioneers said the hospitality was the best. The best they've ever had. They had lots to say about McAllister's fine food, too. Fine Food. Seems you've got yourself a booming business just at the blossom here, Miss Pearl. Just ready to bloom. I'm mighty proud of you. Mighty proud. I knew it just took the right person. My money and your taste and flair, well, we have ourselves a winning combination. Winning combination."

The mention of Boyd's money answered a lot of questions on Matt's mind. He wondered where his mother was getting all the money to pay for the work done on the buildings. He had asked her once, but in typical fashion she told him it came from her bank account. Matt had known better and also not to argue with her.

"Now y'all run on," Pearl said to the children. "Uncle Boyd and I have business to talk."

"I have some excellent news," Uncle Boyd said. "Brad Caldwell, *the* famous baseball pitcher, *and* a *famous* rocket scientist, who will go by another name for *discretion,* are going to be our guests! A rocket scientist! Comp their rooms, food, booze ... anything they want. Make sure it is top class, would you please Miss Pearl? I'm just proud to have such important guests. So proud. Important guests. I will see that the newspapers get wind of this."

"But if we comp every room for every famous person you send down here, we will not make any money," she said playfully, not wanting Boyd to think she was complaining. But Pearl wanted her share of the rewards from this place.

Boyd clasped his meaty hands behind his back, stood on his tiptoes and beamed. He thought she'd complimented his influential circle.

She knew her charisma and hospitality would be a dollar-for-dollar match for Boyd's leverage with rich and famous people. Still, they needed each other and she didn't mind stroking his huge ego one little bit as long as she got her share of the money.

As Boyd had told her, the following week the baseball player and the rocket scientist sat in the rockers on the front porch of the restaurant, enjoying each other's company, the drinks, beach breezes, and the beautiful scenery. Matt was on cloud nine just to meet the scientist, who also took a liking for Matt and gave him an airplane ride in his mustard yellow Piper Cub with pontoons. Matt loved every minute around the brilliant man and got in trouble for "dereliction of duty," as Pearl called it.

Abby had no idea who either of the Inn's important guests were, but they didn't go by Uncle and they seemed very nice. She had been very proud of herself when she picked up the keys to the first suite and said, "Come with me, Dr. Brown. I'll show you to your room. It's real nice. My mamma fixed it up herself." She had not understood his name through his heavy accent, so the scientist became Dr. Brown from that day forward.

Brad Caldwell had flown in a few days ahead of Dr. Brown in his little Beech-craft. He took Mags, Mary and Abby for a ride in his plane. Abby was amazed to see schools of fish so clearly from the sky. She also saw schools of sharks swimming just off the beach. She liked flying and hoped that more of their guests would bring planes with them. Matt learned to block and tether the planes correctly, and had a growing interest in all aspects of flying.

Pearl was wheeling through the restaurant, up and down the porches, shaking hands and making sure her customers were happy. She breezed into the kitchen and said, "Well, McAllister. The restaurant is booked for weeks. Your reputation has spread far and wide. We have people coming from Florida and Mississippi to taste your fine cuisine! The Inn is all but full. It's going to be a great summer. That phone is ringing off the hook. Thank God we only have one."

When Pearl left the kitchen, McAllister got back to his cooking. And while he worked he sang. He sang all the time, it seemed, mostly old hymns he'd heard in church since the time he was a child, he'd told Abby. Good ol' songs, he'd said to her. Abby stayed in the kitchen and out of her mother's hair as much as possible. "Why do you sing so much, Mr. McAllister?" Abby asked.

"I like to praise the Lord all day long!" McAllister was the happiest person Abby had ever known. She could not think of a single person she liked better.

"See here, sugar pie," he said to her one day while she sat on a stool. "I make two pots of gumbo. One with oysters. One without. Not everybody loves oysters. See dose?" he asked pointing to pieces of white shells in the gumbo pot. "That's the bodies of da crabs. I break em in half and put the whole things in there so the people can dig out that sweet white meat. You like crabs?" Abby nodded yes. "I don't like making that home cooking for those merry go round tables your mamma put out there. But that goes with da job. You'll learn that as you grow up. You just have to take the good with the bad. That new woman? That Miss Donna? You stay away from her, chile. She a prostitute!" McAllister had stopped what he was doing and looked right at Abby with that instruction. Abby wasn't sure what a prostitute was, but she could tell by the way McAllister said it, it couldn't be good. She'd ask Matt later, she decided.

The kitchen was full of gray smoke that made Abby's eyes tear up. "You got to cook this roux as slow as possible," he said, as he turned back to his cooking. McAllister slowly stirred the flour, and the smoke billowed out from the cast iron pot. "This flour gots to be cooked to just the right shade of brown so da gumbo be good. Sometime it takes hours. Some folks cheat and use lard to speed up da process. But, little girl, when you start cooking, McAllister wants you to do it da right way, okay?" Abby nodded her head, proud that McAllister was teaching her how to cook.

Sometimes, at the end of a busy Saturday night, Pearl put money in the juke box in the ballroom. McAllister let Abby stand on top of his long feet and she wrapped her arms around his skinny waist and held on as tight as she could. They danced and danced. "I wish you were my daddy," Abby told him. He just shook his head and smiled.

"Law, chile. That would bring this world to a stop. But, I got to tell you my little girls pretty jealous about you. So you's kinda like my child."

A few days later, McAllister asked Abby to help in the kitchen. He needed the fresh squid cleaned and showed her how it was done. When the backbone slid out, her mouth dropped open. She looked at McAllister and back at the squid and its spine.

"Really?" she said to McAllister. "They are invisible and look like little tiny feathers!" Abby's blue-green eyes sparkled.

"I thought you'd like that," McAllister beamed. "Praise da Lawd!"

"Can I have that big old pickle jar, the empty one?" she asked.

"You certainly can. What you gonna do with it?" McAllister asked.

Abby washed the jar nice and clean until it hadn't a hint of pickle smell. In her neatest handwriting, she had made a sign for the jar "Fairy Fountain Pens~1 Penny." McAllister laughed.

"Ain't you something, chile?" McAllister stated rather than asked. Abby was happy. She now had a steady job of back-boning the squid and had a built in clientele of children to buy them. Within a few weeks, she lost track of how many pennies she had saved. It was a big pile. She was saving for a horse. Mary and Mags waited tables and changed sheets and towels, keeping guest rooms clean. Matt did the laundry and scrubbed pots in the boiling hot kitchen water. Much harder work, in Abby's opinion, then selling Fairy Fountain Pens.

Mags spied a kite in Abby's hand as she announced she was going to play with Cindy and Becky. "Make sure you fly that on the beach or somewhere away from the airstrip. Abby, are you listening?" asked Mags.

"Mr. McAllister bought us kites!" an excited Abby explained, not hearing a word of the warning her sister had issued. On the airstrip, she, Cindy, and Becky slowly let the strings out, racing down the airstrip until their kites caught the wind. They stood in childhood glee as they watched the colorful kites skittle in the blue sky above. A small plane was circling when Mags came storming out of the building with a blue hair brush in her hand, the first weapon she saw in her fury. She stomped out to the airfield and beat Abby's butt until the brush broke into two pieces.

"Do you ever listen? If your kite gets caught up in a propeller, Abby, you could cause a plane to crash. Mamma would get sued and it'd be all over but the crying for you, young lady. Fly your kites on the damned beach."

Cindy and Becky stood by, waiting for Mags to spank them, too. Instead, Mags stormed back into the kitchen. The kites, with Mags assistance, now laid on the ground, flat as flitters and utterly lifeless. Abby twisted around trying to get a look at her butt. "Is it black and blue?" she asked Cindy.

Instead of flying kites and risking another spanking, the three girls hid behind the fig trees next to the restaurant, spying as guests arrived in station wagons full of eager children, beach balls and hula-hoops springing out as soon as car doors opened. At first, local people came down from neighboring towns, most simply curious about who had refurbished the old buildings and what the place looked like. The locals usually ordered the cheapest thing on the menu, hamburgers, which sent McAllister into a tail spin each time.

"I am a gourmet cook," he told Pearl. "Gourmet cooks don't cook no damned hamburgers!"

"You'll cook what our customers order," Pearl said. "They are our bread and butter." Pearl spun, irritated by McAllister's attitude, and went into the dining room to greet more guests, including Mobileans who had summer cottages on the beach. Abby had lots of new kids to play with, but she felt lanky and awkward in their presence so she mostly played with Cindy and Becky.

Small town gossip rode the wind off the peninsula and soon word was out that something wasn't quite right down at that Inn. Word was passed among local wives who would not let their husbands come to the Tiki Bar. Families rarely came to dine. Wives whispered to other wives about the constant flow of beautiful young women in and out of the Inn. Mention was also made of the two pretty girls who lived there and of a woman named Donna. One newspaper piece wondered if the Governor spent more time at the Inn than at the State Capital. But all the talk hardly made a dent in the business. When Matt asked about the gossip, Pearl took a devil-may-care attitude.

"Matt, I don't care what the locals think," she said. "And neither should you! Just do your work. Our good customers can afford to pay for peace, privacy, and a good meal. The gossipy old women in town are not our problem." Pearl was busy replacing and rearranging orchids in the drift wood tree and shells in the fish nets on the walls. "You need to mind your own business, young man."

Matt wanted to tell Pearl that his girlfriend's parents heard the rumors and threatened to not let her see him anymore. That *was* his business. But he kept his mouth shut and walked out to the airstrip to check the blocks under the plane's wheels. The wind had kicked up and he needed to make sure they were secure.

Stonewall Jackson

Uncle Boyd spread the word among politicians, both in state and around the South, who became regulars at the Inn. Since they typically came without their families and wanted to remain out of touch, they were pleased when strolling into a room in which a phone did not sit on the night stand. In case of emergency a phone perched, somewhat glaringly out of place, on the old desk in the kitchen, just past the swinging doors. The downside to having only this phone was it was in earshot of McAllister and guests were never too sure if their conversations were private. Few calls were made, but when they were, Abby was the eardrum wrapped around every word of their conversations, not the tall black cook who was absorbed in praising the Lord at the back of the kitchen.

Abby hung around doors into the kitchen, just on the other side of where the desk and the phone sat gathering dust. She'd follow some "important" person when she saw them head that way, and after she heard a congressman or a senator pipe sweet nothings into the ears of whomever was on the other end of the line, she would race down to Mr. Axil to report the goings on. She did not fully understand what she heard, but she could tell by the low voice, even whispers, that it was likely something Mr. Axil, and maybe even her mother, would want to hear.

She found Mr. Axil bent over his typewriter as usual and slipped in the door, without so much as a knock. "Mr. Axil," Abby said just barely above a whisper. "You know that senator from some state up north?"

"There are a lot of states up north, my dear," Axil answered. "Anyone in particular?"

"It starts with an O. Maybe Oya or something like that," Abby answered, trying her best to remember which state her

72

mother said he was from. "Mamma's excited because she said word is getting out that this is *the* Inn to come to. She said she's happy folks from up north are discovering us!"

"Could it be Ohio? Senator Furling?" asked Mr. Axil.

"Yes sir. That's it. Ohio. Well, he was telling somebody how much he loved them and that he wanted them to get down here as quick as possible!"

"Maybe it was his wife?" asked Axil, puffing his pipe and raising his eyebrows just a bit.

"Why would he whisper to his wife, is what I was wondering," said Abby. "Mamma says we have to keep our mouths shut because a lot of these men don't want their wives to know where they are, anyway,"

"To tell you the truth, little one," Axil paused and puffed a little harder, "you shouldn't be listening in on other folks when they are on the phone. But that one has a reputation as being a lady's man, so I have to tell you, I am not surprised."

"Boy, Mr. Axil, I bet my mother doesn't know that he is a lady's man," Abby replied, wondering exactly what a lady's man was. Having Mr. Axil share gossip made her feel very important and she did not want him to know what all she didn't know.

"My dear," he said kindly. "I think you should tell your mother everything you hear and see and everything I tell you. The more knowledge one has, the better. You never know when one can use all that stored information." He bent back down and began typing, her signal that for now, their time was up. She waved a silent goodbye and walked out of the history building, not quite sure how more knowledge would help, but trusting if Mr. Axil said so, it must be true.

Abby wandered back up to the Inn, deciding on what she should tell her mother, or even *if* she would tell her mother. Information was one thing. Listening in on a private conversation of an important guest was another. She was weighing whether or not she would get in trouble when she saw her mother whip her car into the parking lot, either angry or excited, based on the amount of dust kicked up by the car tires caused by the rapid entry.

Pearl climbed out of the car, smiling from ear to ear, clutching a very wiggly bundle of brown, black, and white puppy. He was so squirmy Pearl was having a difficult time not dropping him.

"Who, or what, is this?" asked an excited Abby, running over to the car. A new puppy was almost as good as a horse!

"Meet Stonewall Jackson," Pearl proudly announced to Abby. "He is a purebred beagle pup! Uncle Boyd thinks if I am going to raise dogs, and of course I am, I should raise really good beagles. He has all kinds of customers looking for good ones. So I bought him out of Boyd's newest litter. Isn't he wonderful? He's from an award-winning bloodline and I am going to start breeding beagles!"

"What about Mr. BB and Mrs. Chi-Chi?" whined a concerned Abby.

"Oh, of course, we'll keep them, too. I just won't plan on breeding Chi-Chi. Besides, she's so fat, she'd probably roll over on her pups and smother them," Pearl chirped, struggling to keep the puppy in her arms. She reached into the car and brought out a new leather leash, still stiff from the package, and promptly hooked it to his collar. Stonewall Jackson pulled against the restraint and wrapped the tether around Pearl's legs, almost toppling her. As she unwound herself she added, "Of course, he is only twelve weeks old and hasn't started training yet. It looks like the leash will be first on the agenda. Abby, a perfect job for you! Teaching Ole Stoney here how to be polite on a leash. I'll show you the basics." Pearl was in a great mood, very pleased with her new plan. "I've got to go find Uncle Homer. Make him build a decent kennel." With that, she dragged the reluctant Stonewall Jackson with her, him backing up and practically sitting down like a stubborn old mule not ready to plow.

Abby watched, amused at her mother's lack of control over a little bitty puppy, as Pearl pulled Stonewall through the sandy, sand-spurred yard. Abby decided to go see if any fishermen were about and would then go tell Mr. Axil about the new pup. As she walked down to the pier she noticed hundreds, maybe thousands, of butterflies and black love bugs in the air. Abby knew this meant summer was dwindling away. The love bugs were so thick, their blackness against that blue sky looked like a giant black spider web slowly moving in the wind. If she dared to open her mouth, she'd have a mouth full. Earlier, when Abby inhaled one, hacking and coughing, Pearl told her bugs are pure protein. "Just swallow it!" Pearl had said.

"No way!" Abby replied, when she found her voice. "Mr. Axil told me they breed while they fly. That is nasty!"

"Well good for Mr. Axil," Pearl said sarcastically. "Mr. Axil does seem to know a little of everything, now doesn't he?"

On the same day Mr. Axil informed Abby of the breeding habits of Love Bugs, he also told her the orange and black butterflies were Monarchs that simply passed over the little peninsula on their way to Mexico. He told her they laid their eggs on the milkweed and those eggs turn into long black and cream caterpillars. Then they spin a clear chrysalis before turning back into butterflies. "Wait until you see them. Quite fascinating. Our spit of land is just a resting spot for them."

Abby wandered around, scuffing the toes of her tennie shoes in the shelled and sandy parking lot at the Inn, dodging flying, breeding Love Bugs and bored as no fishermen were about and hermit crabs were nowhere to be found. Abby saw Pearl outside with her new puppy. She couldn't remember ever having seen her mother pay so much attention to a dog before. Matt, Mary, and Mags were all gathered around, holding the restless puppy in turn, him licking their faces before leaning downward to the ground. Each drew him around on the leash a bit, and already he was getting the knack of it, not pulling against it so hard.

"Damn, he's a smart one!" Pearl said. "Matt, school will be starting soon and you're going to have to drive the girls to the store to catch the school bus this year. Then, you have to take McAllister's boys to their school. I just do not have the time to run around dropping you off and picking you up every day."

"Mamma, I'm not old enough for a driver's license. And I don't have a car! I mean driving around here, where there are no policemen is one thing, but all the way to school?"

"Well, since McAllister's boys have to go to the colored school, the county, by law, has to provide transportation and that is quite expensive, especially for just a few children. So, Uncle Boyd talked to the sheriff and it's okay for you to drive the kids to school instead of the county having to send a bus. That will make it legal, more or less, because the county needs you to do it. We'll get you a jalopy of some sort before school starts."

"Mags, Mary, Abby ... come here," Matt called to the girls

who were over playing with the new puppy, yowling occasionally as its sharp baby teeth hit skin. "You won't believe this! Mamma's gonna get me a car so I can drive y'all to Snyder's to catch the bus. And I even get to take McAllister's boys to school! And it's okay with the county! I can drive!"

"She is not going to buy you a car," Mags snorted. "You're as big a liar as she is!"

"No. It's true. Something about the county and Uncle Boyd. They got it all worked out so I can drive."

"Well, why not drive us all the way to school then? Why do you have to stop at the store?" Mary asked.

"Number One, y'all are girls and I don't want you in my car more than absolutely necessary. Number Two, with McAllister's boys riding, too, we'll be packed to the gills," Matt said. Matt smiled at his sisters, excited at the prospect of his own car.

Snyder's store was about half way up the twenty-two-mile road from Fort Morgan to Gulf Shores. The schools were in Foley, another twelve or so miles away. The county school bus only came as far as the store. Kids from all along the peninsula met there to catch the big yellow bus number ten. Snyder's was a bait and fishing store with an assortment of rods and reels, fishing lures, and four different kinds of crab traps. It also sold cold drinks and some produce, including lemons. The girls always bought a coke and a lemon to share. Abby had to admit, as much as she hated getting up early, she was ready to get off this peninsula and go to school. She hoped, now that she was almost seven, her sisters might share the lemon and Coke with her, too.

Pearl did a good deal of shopping for some type of car for Matt. After asking friends and a bit of wheeling and dealing, she finally found a suitable one that would hold a lot of children and that Matt would like. Abby thought it was really ugly; an old black hump-back roach is what she thought it looked like. A Palmetto bug. Matt thought it was a beauty and didn't mind the slow start or the smoke that puffed out of the tailpipe when the engine turned over.

He waited as patiently as he could until the morning finally came when he packed all of the children into his car to head off to school. "Come on, girls! We're gonna be late. Mary, who cares if your damned hair is curly? Somebody, try to get the tangles out of Abby's hair. Never mind. Do it in the car. Just come on," Matt ordered.

McAllister's boys, Andrew, Robert, and Jessie, were waiting in the car, two in the front seat and Jessie, the smallest, in the back. Girls squished in around him, Abby having no choice but to sit in Jessie's lap. The early morning sun was changing from summer hot-yellow to an autumn pale-yellow. The short ride to Snyder's Store got rid of the girls. Matt would drop the boys off at their school and proudly drive onto campus in his own wheels. Abby was finally on bus number ten, sleepily peering at acres of gladiolas planted between Gulf Shores and Foley as the bus lumbered along. Later in the day, the girls were dropped off at Snyder's store. Mags bought a Coke and a lemon which she asked the clerk to cut in half. After taking a long sip of Coke, her lips slathered in her newest color of coral lipstick, Mags noticed the look on Abby's face.

"Thirsty?" Mags asked her. "Here, have a sip. You're too young to suck on this lemon, though. It's bad for your teeth since most of yours are new."

Abby gladly grabbed the small green bottle from her sister's hand, parched from the ride home. As she sipped, she noticed the drink had a peculiar taste. "Mags, this don't taste right," Abby said as she handed the bottle back to her sister. Mags took another sip to test it herself.

"Doesn't, Abigail, not don't." She took a sip. "No. It's fine." Mary wandered over, reaching out for the Coke bottle. She, too, took a swig.

"Mary, that Coke taste normal to you?" Abby asked.

"Yep. You're just tasting Mags' new lipstick. Makes it taste like a Pepsi," Mary answered.

Matt showed up, a full thirty minutes behind the bus since he'd picked up the boys, all kind of laughter going on in the black hump-backed car. The girls piled in, skin to skin, sticking to each other as the afternoon humidity increased. When Matt pulled into the parking lot, Abby noticed Uncle Homer idling on the steps of the porch to the Inn, casually drinking a beer as if he had not a thing in the world to do.

"Thanks for the ride, Matt." Andrew waved as the three boys sauntered down to the little house at the end of the airstrip. The girls were out of the car, tugging on blouses that were fine this morning, but too hot now in the afternoon. Mags and Mary went straight into the restaurant to drop books and begin the set up for supper for the guests while Matt went around back to check on the airplanes before joining McAllister in the kitchen.

The First Day of School

Abby climbed out of the sticky hot car and skipped over the oyster-shelled driveway, up past Uncle Homer lounging on the steps, to the center room to change from her school dress to a sun suit, ready to go play with Cindy and Becky.

The first day of school had been good and she was thinking that her very old teacher, Mrs. Jewell, smelled like baby powder. In her room, she stripped down to her panties, enjoying the breeze from the window on her hot skin, completely absorbed in what all she had to tell Cindy and Becky about school and wondering why they didn't go to school, too. When she turned around, there he stood, a half drunk, toothless smile on his face. Abby jumped, startled that she was not alone and mad because the old geezer was staring at her bare body, covered by nothing but a tiny pair of pink cotton under-panties.

"Well, ain't you the all growed-up school girl?" Uncle Homer slurred. "Look at them little titties. Looks like they startin to grow." Abby reached over to the bed and grabbed a pillow to put in front of her, the sun suit forgotten, still hanging in her hand.

"Git out of here, Uncle Homer!" Abby yelled. "This ain't your room. I ain't dressed!"

"I just come up to take a little nap," he said. "I am sure you ready to rest a little after your big day in what ... second grade? Third grade?"

"First grade. And I said get out. I'm gonna call my sisters if you don't leave."

"You sisters and brother, busy. You Mamma ain't here. Had some biness in Mobile. You all by yourself, except for me. Now come here and gimme some sugar." He took another long draw on his beer, a fresh new one, icy condensation dripping off the sides of the long necked glass bottle.

Abby dropped the pillow and the sun suit, aiming for the only door in the room when his bony but muscular arms stopped her dash and scooped her up. "Put me down!" Abby screamed. "Mags! Help!"

"Oh I gonna put you down alright," he said as he tossed her like a rag doll onto the double bed. "Today is the day you gonna learn about love, little 'un. Don't worry. I be real sweet."

Abby screamed as loud as she could for her sisters, her brother, and Mr. BB, but no one showed up. Homer moved over to the bed, took his dirty clothes off and reached for her. She kicked and scratched as he attempted to pin her small arms next to her body.

"You a little wild cat like you mamma," Uncle Homer said, a wide toothless grin on his face, purple gums visible from side to side. "They ain't no need for you to scream and holler. Ain't nobody gonna hear ya, anyway." He put his calloused hand over her mouth and she bit the palm of his hand as hard as she could. That just made him laugh and he snickered as he forced her arms over her head, holding both of them with one of his strong hands. With his free hand he ripped off her panties. "Shhhh," he said. "You be still and quiet and I ain't gonna hurt you. Grown-ups do this all the time and like it. You gonna like it, too, once you used to it." He spat in his hand and rubbed the spit on her private parts.

"Uncle Homer," she mumbled. "Mamma says that if a man touches my private parts, I'll have to be a mother. Please don't touch my girl parts. I won't tell anybody you already ripped my panties and spit on me."

He laughed again. "You ain't gone be no mamma. You too young."

Those were the last words Abby heard before a searing pain shot though her. She was crying and could hear her own wails, as if the sounds were from a faraway place. She soon found out if she kicked or wiggled, the pain just got worse.

"Now, hush crying and be still," he said as he continued with his mission. "It ain't gonna hurt next time, I promise."

When Homer was at last through with Abby, she laid on her favorite feather pillow on her side, facing the wall, crying, sobbing, wondering why even Mr. BB didn't hear her. She noticed blood all over her stomach and on her fresh new sheets.

Uncle Homer was sitting with his back to her, hunched over on the edge of the bed smoking, occasionally taking a drink of his beer.

"My mamma's gonna fire your ass," she finally said, furious and hurt and confused, as she turned back over to face his back. "You can't do things like that to me. You just wait and see." Abby was past crying, now ready to get up and kick the man, kick him until he was black and blue. But she was not about to get out from under her sheet and let him see her naked again. "And you're going to get in trouble for leaving cigarette butts in the window, too."

Homer reached down to the floor, grabbed his dirty white tee shirt and yellowed boxer shorts, putting them on right in front of her. He slowly turned around and looked right into her eyes. "You mamma's not gonna fire me because this is our little secret." He had a sober, hard, mean look on his lean face, dark whisker stubbles moving as he talked. The glare scared Abby but she was not giving up.

"Oh, yes she is," sassed Abby, "because I'm gonna tell her myself. I'm gonna show her how you got blood on my new sheets, too. Oh, yes sir, you are going to be in bad trouble."

"Well, little 'un. You's mine now. If you go blabbing our little secret, well something serious bad might happen to your brother ... or maybe that mean ol' black dog. I'd think about that if I was you." His tone was low but hard as steel. "I gotta go start a fire for the pig roast. I'm gonna wad these sheets up and throw em in the fire. I'm telling you, priss-pot, you know what's good for you, you keep your mouth shut." He smiled at her and deliberately stubbed his cigarette out on the sill of the window, pulled on his grimy green overalls and stepped in his boots. He slicked his greasy hair back out of his face with his hand and then he turned so quickly that Abby backed up into the corner her bed made where it hit the wall. He snatched the sheet off of the top of Abby, leaving her fully exposed, and ripped the bottom sheet off last. She again clutched her pillow as cover and he quietly laughed, putting his pointer finger up to his lips, "Shhhhh." He turned, sheets balled into a tight bundle under his arm and left the room. Abby stared at the closed door, then laid down with no sheets or cover, and cried herself to sleep. In her sleep, she thought she heard Mr. BB scratching at her door.

Pearl's New Car

The children were in school and business was at the predicted season's ebb, the restaurant and Inn quiet. The year, financially, had been a good one. She drove to Mobile to make the Monday morning delivery to Boyd's office, a small brown sack of cash in her hand. Pearl was surprised when she found Boyd in the office. As a rule, she or Matt handed off the cash to Hamilton, his son.

"What a pleasant surprise." Boyd smiled as the attractive woman seemed to glide into his office. "Is it pay day, already?"

"It is a nice surprise to see you, too, Boyd. I thought you'd be in D.C.," Pearl replied, smoothing the skirt tail of her dress, tucking it under her bottom as she sat in the leather chair in front of his enormous desk. She looked around at the office walls displaying photographs of Boyd with the President and this or that diplomat. Newspaper articles carefully clipped out, matted and framed, littered the walls. Ribbon cuttings, bottles being smashed across ship hulls, all of his accomplishments, framed and ready to be seen. "Well, the sack has grown a little smaller. Business peaked a few weeks ago. Now it's down to a few die-hards." She laughed and handed the bag over to him. He peered in the sack and set it on the edge of his desk.

"Well, it's been plenty stuffed up until now," Boyd responded. "And to thank you for a most excellent first year, I've a little surprise for you. To show you my appreciation. And our customer's appreciation, too. They finally have a safe, private and snug little hideaway." He reached in his desk and handed her a fat envelope, one that she waited until she was back in her car to open. She peeped in the envelope, and the amount stunned her. She knew exactly where her next stop would be.

Pearl pulled into the parking lot in front of the Inn and smiled at the children who had gathered on the front porch when they heard the sound of tires crunching on the shells. Their eyes and mouths were wide open in surprise. She was driving a brand new, well, slightly-used as a demo, 1955 sea-foam green Nomad Belaire Station Wagon. "Well, children, what do you think?" Pearl beamed as she stepped out of the shiny new car.

"Whose is it?" Matt asked.

"What do you mean? It's mine, silly. We've done quite well this year, and with a little help from Uncle Boyd, this baby is ours. We needed a station wagon to haul in supplies, anyway. Look on the floor board. See it? It's air conditioning, for the car!"

Both doors and the rear hatch were now open and all four children inspected every inch of the interior. There, mounted in the middle of the front floor and saddling the center hump, was a gray box.

"What is that?" asked Matt.

"It's the air-conditioner!" Pearl was about to burst with joy. "Can you imagine? It was an extra. Uncle Boyd surprised me by having the dealer add it on! Hell, even our rooms are not air-conditioned! That Uncle Boyd is just the kindest, most generous man!"

"Can we ride in it?" asked Abby.

"Of course we can. Let's take her for a shake-down cruise. Abby, make sure your hands are not sticky and dirty."

"Matt, when you drive to Mobile to take Uncle Boyd his share every week, I'll let you take the wagon. I'll bet that girlfriend of yours will be impressed!" Almost every Monday Matt, now that he was allowed to drive, took the cash stuffed brown bag to Boyd's office. Hamilton, Boyd's son, grabbed the cash and ushered Matt out as quickly as possible. During his weekly run, Matt picked up Jane, his girlfriend, so they could have a little ride together. He knew Jane would love the new car because it had soft fake leather and tweed fabric on the interior, not the scratchy wool his old car had.

Pearl watched as each child got into the car. "Make sure you brush the sand off your feet," she instructed as they crawled in. Abby rubbed her fingertips over the soft interior.

Matt sat in the front seat, Pearl showing him which buttons to push to make the air-conditioner work. Mags and Mary were in the back seat and Abby had the entire rear compartment to herself.

"Mamma, I can feel the wind from that air-conditioner all the way back here," Abby announced. She watched the fort and the Inn disappear behind her through the rear window and felt the thump-thump beneath the tires as they bumped over the seawall where it crossed the road. Other than to school, this was as far off the compound Abby had been since they arrived. They drove down the beach road where Pearl got out and walked around the front of the car. Matt got out, too, and passed her in front of the hood. She was actually going to let him drive it today! He slid the gear handle into place. He had only driven a column-shifted car once and prayed to himself he remembered where the gears were. He released the clutch and the car slid along, as smooth as silk. He looked at Pearl and smiled.

"I knew coming down here was a great move for us," crowed Pearl, proud the Inn was so successful and that she now had a new, almost new, car to show for her hard work.

Glancing at Matt and acknowledging how well he handled the new car, Pearl said, "Matt, now that fall is here, business will all but halt shortly. We have to get the Winter Inn ready." Pearl intended to turn one of the three houses on Officer's Row into a small inn, for the few guests who might want a getaway in the winter. Boyd had agreed it was a fine idea.

"Winter Inn?" a puzzled Matt asked. He did not dare glance away from the road, even though he knew it by heart.

"Yes. The three buildings up the road? That used to be officer housing during the War? We'll fix up one to live in and the other will be a Winter Inn. We won't have the same clientele as we do during the summer, but some sport fishermen will come. Uncle Boyd will, of course, send his companions. We'll fix the third house up later." She looked out the window. "Yes, it's only going to get better. Boyd said he thinks the State is going to fund paving of the air strip. Maybe even this winter, without the guests flying in it will be a perfect time to do it."

"What about the marina?" Matt asked.

"I think Boyd wants it opened by next summer," Pearl answered. "He and his engineers have it all figured out. He's found some useless old surplus barges. He says the bottoms are practically rotted out, but that will suit our purposes anyway. He intends to anchor them starting right at the beach, then lash each one together. The bottoms have some holes, he said, but that will allow the water in and make them more stable. I suspect the ones in the deepest water will have to be on piers." Matt nodded, listening intently with the plan.

Abby was all ears, even way back in the car. The air conditioning blew her mother's curly hair around and Abby wondered what it was like up there, how cool was it and how did an air conditioner even make cold air?

"In the meantime, girls," Pearl said, turning around in her seat to look at Mary and Mags. "I've finished Suite 31. It has two bedrooms, a bath *with* a tub and a small kitchenette. Until our house in Officer's Row is ready, we're going to live there."

"Mamma, am I going to sleep with you, like I did in our old house?" asked Abby from the far rear.

"Not yet," Pearl said. "You'll stay with Uncle Homer until the house is ready. No sense in moving everything twice. Besides, the bedrooms are quite small. You'll be fine, right?"

Abby sucked in air through her nose, dreading the idea that her sisters would be farther away than across the hall. So far, she had heeded Uncle Homer's warning and kept their little secret. He bothered her almost every night now, except for the nights she snuck off to sleep at Cindy's house or when he was gone to see his mother. Her eyes welled up with tears, which she wiped away with her fingertips. "Mamma, I want to live with you," she cried.

"Oh, don't be such a baby," Pearl said from the front seat. "The house will be finished soon and then there will be plenty of room for you and Uncle Homer can keep your current room. Now cooperate, please. I have too much to think about without you pitching a fit every time I turn around. Just to show you how much he likes you, Uncle Homer is bringing you a fine surprise. Wait until you see it! I bet you won't mind sharing a room a little while longer then."

Matt, having proven that he could indeed handle the new car and Pearl thinking the test drive was a success, the ride came to an end. Everyone oohed and ahhed one more time at the pretty new car as they got out.

Mags and Mary had Abby sandwiched between them as they climbed up the front steps to the restaurant. "I want to live with you," Abby said quietly. "Uncle Homer isn't nice and he stinks."

The older girls looked at each other, each knowing they were helpless to do a damned thing about the old drunk who slept in their baby sister's room. They had talked with their mother until they were blue in the face.

"Abby," Mary said very quietly. "Each of us has tried to talk to Mother about him being in there. But you know how Mamma is. When her mind is made up, there's nothing much that can change it. He doesn't hurt you, does he?" she asked.

"No," Abby quietly lied. She was not willing to risk her brother or her dog. "He stinks and I'm sick of him. I want to be close to you."

"But you said he isn't nice," Mags added.

"Just when he's drunk and he idn't exactly mean. I just don't like him," Abby replied. Again, her sisters exchanged looks, now more concerned than their mother seemed to be, helpless to do a thing about the situation.

"We'll talk to Mamma again," Mary added. "The house will be finished soon, too. If he does anything to you, you know, stuff he shouldn't do, you come straight to me or Mags and let us know!"

Once inside, the girls parted ways, Mags and Mary to attend their various duties and Abby upstairs to the gift shop. Abby had come to like the lady who opened the shop upstairs over the Tiki Bar. Her hair was red and frizzy, her skin almost as pale as Crazy Ruby's and she was short, round and soft. The skin under her arms hung long and jiggled when she talked. They reminded Abby of her old grandmother's 'wings' and she really wanted to feel them. But she didn't dare. Miss Tammy suggested that Abby collect shells for her to buy and then sell to the tourists. So far, the only shells she had were shellacked and shiny, not even off the Gulf beach. Miss Tammy said maybe they'd pay even more for local treasures. Abby was excited to have yet another way to make money for her savings for the horse.

Not only did she find some great shells for the shop, Abby also collected sand dollars on the beach. Miss Tammy was thrilled because Abby only brought her the whole ones and shells with no holes or chips. If the waves were not too high, Abby bounced out to a sand bar several yards offshore where sand dollar collection was always best. The Gulf was deep and choppy right outside of the mouth of the bay and she was not strong enough to swim out to the sandbar. She had learned that she could bounce along the bottom and pop her head above the waves with every spring. It was slow going, but in this way she could make it to the sand bar. For every five sand dollars Abby gave Miss Tammy, Miss Tammy would give Abby ten cents, or sometimes a quarter, and one paper ball about the size of the softballs that Matt swatted at occasionally in the parking lot. The ball was made of paper serpentine. Abby dug her fingers into the paper ball, unwrapping it strip by strip until there was a pile of paper at her feet and a trinket of some sort in her hands. She didn't care so much about the trinket but loved unwrapping the balls. She had hidden one under her bed in the center room upstairs and prayed that Uncle Homer wasn't around so she could take it out on the rocks to peel it open.

Since Miss Tammy had an actual real customer, Abby left to go see Cindy. Maybe Cindy could come up with a good idea that would make her mother let her move with the rest of the girls in the big suite. Abby saw Pearl and Matt walking up to Officer's Row. She guessed they were going to take a look at what would become the Winter Inn. She also saw Uncle Homer go into the center door of the Inn and decided she would hot foot it down to Cindy's and avoid him. Unwrapping her new paper ball would have to wait.

The Secret

Not much had to be done to two of the three houses at Officer's Row. Hurricanes had mostly spared the structures. On the other hand, there was much to do cosmetically and Pearl, as usual, had been at full throttle. The Winter Inn was ready. Adding a last touch, she tied a kitchen cord to a pencil. With one end of the string in her hand and the pencil tied to the other end, she drew a huge circle on the foyer wall. Then with a tiny artist's brush she painted the words to a poem she found to be almost perfect. The lines of the poem followed the circle, so you had to tilt your head side-to-side to read it. Pearl thought it very clever, especially the little scrolls she had added every so often.

> *Folks, you are welcome here, be at your ease.*
> *Get up when you're ready, go to bed when you please.*
> *We're happy to share with you such as we've got.*
> *Leaks in the roof and soup in the pot.*
> *You don't have to thank us, or laugh at our jokes.*
> *Just sit deep and come often, you're one of our folks.*
> –Author Unknown

She stepped back and admired her art work. "Damn, I'm just getting better at this," she said to a totally empty room.

The bay was just across the narrow paved lane from the houses at Officer's Row and the marina would be constructed right at that spot. The house she chose to be the Winter Inn had the most bedrooms and a larger kitchen, though it had no porch. It, too, had one phone installed in the kitchen, out of sight and out of mind. The house next door, that would become her home, had porches that wrapped all four sides and both floors. A little Red Devil Lye, hard scrubbing and paint would do the job, she reckoned.

There was another weather-beaten house across the street on the bay side, next to an old gas station. One of the county commissioners lived there. "Wonder who he pissed off?" Pearl asked aloud as she peered out her window. "Nothing like being stationed in Siberia." It had been Mag's job to make sure the drunken old commissioner made it home from the restaurant every night, hoisting him out of his chair or down from his barstool, placing his arm around her neck and putting her arm around his huge waist. Many nights she literally dragged him to the car with Matt's help. Mags dodged his sloppy, drunken kisses every night and often had to swat his hands away from her breasts.

"Don't use my car to take that old boozer home," Pearl instructed. "I don't want him to throw up in it. Matt, sorry bud, but you have to use your car."

Now that business was shifting to the Winter Inn, the commissioner could stumble across the street to his house. Still, sometimes he needed some support, but at least no one had to drive him. Pearl complained to Uncle Boyd that the commissioner had not yet paid for one meal or one drink. Uncle Boyd waved her off and assured her he would look into it.

The Winter Inn was near the end of the grassy airstrip and planes could be tied down right behind the building. Surveyors had been hammering sticks with orange flags that flapped in the breeze every few feet and bulldozers scraped up the grass. The promise of a paved airstrip was becoming reality.

McAllister's house stood at the end of the airfield, and he asked if they were going to pave right over him. His youngest kids sat on the porch, sucking on satsumas, watching the construction. Abby cuddled between the girls, grateful that it was the season for satsumas and kumquats. Bored with watching the airstrip construction, the three girls walked up to the Winter Inn and the house at Officer's Row. Abby was anxious to show them what would be her new bedroom. Pearl was directing men carrying furniture into the house when Abby, Cindy and Becky ambled in, Cindy surprised at the size of the house as compared to her own.

"Mamma, can me and Cindy and Becky walk the sea wall?" she asked as her mother was shooing her out of her way.

"I don't care what you do, as long as you stay out of my

way, Abby. It's eleven miles long, but if you think you can do it, go ahead and try. Of course, if you get stuck out in the middle, don't expect me to come rescue you."

Pearl didn't know that Abby had traveled the sea wall on many occasions, staying out of sight and mainly away from Uncle Homer, who was always around, doing some job or another for Pearl. It gave Abby the shivers because he seemed to know exactly where she was all of the time. Abby liked school days, which gave her some relief from being vigilant, and after school she usually went to Cindy's.

"I ain't sure I can walk that far," Cindy said. "But I am real sure Becky cain't. She's too little."

"I like watching them tractors, anyway," Becky chimed in. "Y'all just walk me home. I don't want to walk no eleven miles."

Abby and Cindy walked down the path east of the big building that had not been renovated, past the dozers to McAllister's little house. They handed Becky another orange and she sat back down on the porch, digging her little fingers into the skin of the fruit.

"Don't worry, Cindy," Abby said as they set off on their hike. "We don't have to walk the entire seawall. There's places in it that swerve in close to the big restaurant and we can take a short cut from there if you get tired. I'm glad Becky stayed home because I got a secret to tell you anyway. But you got to promise not to tell nobody." Abby was dead serious as she looked at the only real friend she had.

"Gosh, Abby. What is it? Daddy says secrets ain't good and that you shouldn't keep them."

"You won't tell your daddy, will you? Or anyone else?" Abby pleaded.

"Naw, I won't tell. I swear. What is it?"

"Uncle Homer? The one that you asked about sleeping in my room?"

"Yeah ..." Cindy picked up a small rock and threw it as hard as she could.

"A few weeks ago. The first day of school? He did really bad things to me. Things my Mamma says will make a girl a mother. Something she says proves God is not a woman. I didn't even hear him come into my room." Abby had tears rolling down her face.

"What happened, Abby?" Cindy had stopped walking and was squatting on the top of the concrete seawall. She stared up at her friend, watching Abby's tears cut a line through the dirt on her face.

"I was almost naked, getting ready to put on my sun suit to come play with you. All of a sudden, he was there. Standing in my room. Talking about my titties growing. I don't even have titties. Then, he ripped off my underwear and spitted on his hand and put his spit on my girl parts!" Abby was sobbing and sat down on the sun heated top of the seawall, as close to her friend as she could get. The breeze blew in from the Gulf. "Then, Cindy, he did something else. First with his fingers, then with his thing. It hurt so bad I wanted to die."

"Abby. I know I promised. But we got to tell my daddy and your mamma. Daddy warned me about men trying to do those things to girls. My daddy don't like him anyway. I'd bet he'd kill him for you if you wanted him to." Cindy was scratching another rock up and down the top of the concrete, the rock making white marks right on the concrete.

"No, please, no. You promised. He said he would hurt my brother and my dog if I told a living soul! We can't tell nobody. Please, Cindy?"

"Does he do it to you a lot?" Cindy wanted to know.

"Just about every day or night. Whenever he can find me and nobody's around. I been getting Mr. BB out of his cage everyday when I get home from school. I keep him with me until Mamma catches me with the dog out. She puts him back up in his cage. I don't know why. He don't bother nobody, but he sure hates Uncle Homer." Abby reached over the edge of the seawall and picked what was left of a wild lantana flower and started pulling the small petals off, one by one.

"Until we can figure something out, you jess need to come spend the night with me. With BB in the day and my brothers at night, you'll be safe. I bet one of my brothers would kill him. Want me to ask them?" Cindy was serious.

"No, we can't tell anyone, remember? I'll just start slipping down to your house when Mamma puts the dog up. You sure your mamma won't mind?" She tossed away the now empty lantana stem and reached to pick another. Her tears were dry but the streaks in her face remained.

"Mamma don't know what's going on half the time. Be-

91

sides, she don't care if you spend the night. I knew something was wrong with you, Abby. You ain't been acting very happy lately. I'm glad you told me. I won't tell no one, I promise."

"And stay away from that guy, too. Make sure you and Becky are safe."

Both girls stood up, Abby tossing the second stem away, Cindy casting her rock as far as she could fling it. They had come to the part of the seawall that jutted in toward the restaurant and hopped off the wall, walked past the old cisterns, dodged cacti, crossed the airstrip in a section that didn't have any heavy equipment on it, and made it safely back to McAllister's porch. Becky was still watching the bulldozers move the dirt around on the airstrip. "Hey, y'all" she said as the girls approached. "Did you already walk all eleven miles?"

"Naw," Cindy answered. "We just walked part way. It's too hot to walk the whole thing. Abby gone spend the night with us."

Abby and Cindy went into the house to find Bessie staring into space out of the kitchen window. "Mamma, Abby gone spend the night, okay?" Bessie continued gazing out of the window, not aware the girls were in the house, much less that Cindy had asked a question. "Your baby sure is growing, Miss Bessie," Abby added.

The girls went off to Cindy's room and Becky stayed out on the porch, mesmerized by how much dirt those big tractors could move at one time.

"One day, Cindy, if you want to, I'll take you to the secret dungeon Mr. Axil showed me. It's no big deal if you got a flashlight," Abby said.

"I'm scared of the dark," Cindy replied as she got down the shoe box full of paper dolls.

Timothy Seahorse

The next day after school Abby went to get Mr. BB out of his crate but was surprised to find the crate empty. She wondered if her mother had Mr. BB and if she did, why? Mrs. Chi-Chi was in her kennel, sleeping as always, and Stonewall Jackson was outside in his little pen. Abby went to Cindy's house but nobody answered the door. She hadn't seen Uncle Homer anywhere and hoped he was off visiting his mother. Abby decided she'd go see what Mr. Axil was doing. She knew he was probably still busy writing his history book. This would be his third, but he said it was the most important one. When she got to his office, he was hunched over his typewriter, hammering away, as he usually did until it was time to take down the flags.

She gently entered the office and sat down until he looked up and welcomed her. He had asked her a while back to come in and be quiet, lest she interrupt his train of thought. Once he had it down, he'd told her, then they could talk. At last, he looked up at Abby and started to light his pipe.

"Hey, Mr. Axil," Abby greeted the man.

"Hey yourself, young lady. And how are you this glorious afternoon?"

"I'm fine. But I can't find my dog. You seen him around? The big black one?" Abby asked.

"Can't say that I have," he replied, "but I had asked your mother to keep him up because he scares some of the people who come to tour the fort."

"Okay, thanks. I'm gonna keep looking for him. Bye, Mr. Axil." As Abby walked out of his office, she saw Uncle Homer's truck come slowly into the parking lot. Her mother was hanging off the porch of the restaurant and waving at her, motioning for her to come toward her. Maybe her mother found Mr. BB and was mad because he was out of his cage again. She slowly walked toward the flailing arms of her mother and the truck of Uncle Homer. Something big was in the back, but she couldn't be sure if she was seeing what she thought she was seeing. She sped up a little, then a lot. She was running by the time she got to the battered old truck.

"Hurry up, Abby," her mother yelled. Pearl was smiling, so Abby knew she wasn't in trouble. "I told you Uncle Homer had a surprise for you!"

"Lookie here, young 'un. Lookie what I brung you!" Uncle Homer yelled to the racing child. His speech was slurred and his bottom lip was puffed out, stuffed full of snuff, his tongue pushing against the snuff to keep it in place. He wiped the oozing corners of his lips with a dirty old rag that hung out of his back pocket. "I told you I loved you. See here. I meant it, too!"

In front of her, up in the truck bed, stood a small horse, blond in color with a creamy white mane and tail. There was a dab of black hair at the end of his tail and his muzzle was black, too. His tail switched back and forth, swatting flies.

"Oh, Mamma. Oh, Uncle Homer. That's just what I wanted. That's what I need. My very own horse!" squealed Abby.

"This isn't just *any* horse," Pearl said. "This is Timothy Seahorse, a special breed of Welsh Pony."

"Is that why he's so small? He's a pony and not a horse?" Abby was a little bit disappointed that this might be his full grown size.

"Naw, he just a baby," piped in Uncle Homer. "He'll grow so big you'll think he a farm horse."

"Does he have a saddle so I can ride him?" Abby asked.

"No, dear," Pearl interjected. "He isn't broken yet. He's green. Green means he hasn't been broken-in to ride," Pearl explained. "With his halter, that leather strap on his head, and a strong lead rope, you'll lead him around for a while until y'all become friends. Then in about a year, we'll saddle him up."

Uncle Homer laid two wide boards together on the tailgate, clipped the rope into the pony's halter, and backed him down to the ground. He handed the lead rope to Abby who stood there looking at the pony and smiled, glad he was bigger than she thought.

"Mamma, do ponies like snacks?"

"Yes ma'am. Let me see what I can find in the kitchen." Pearl turned around and walked back into the kitchen. She came out with a carrot and four apple slices.

"Now, Abby, when you feed him hold your hand open, almost flat. Not totally flat or he'll accidentally nip you. Just a nice shallow bowl and hold the apple in your palm."

Abby tentatively took the apple piece, folded her hand out like Pearl had done and made her first offering to Timothy Seahorse. The pony grabbed the apple so fast it startled her and she stepped back.

"Don't worry," said Pearl. "You'll get use to each other. Keep an apple slice in your pocket and he'll follow you anywhere," she said with a big smile on her face.

Abby approached the pony again, stepping over the lead line to get a little closer. The pony snorted and shook his head, scaring her again. She inched closer and fed him the carrot, holding it by the very end, taking not the slightest chance her fingers might get snapped by the pony's big teeth.

Uncle Homer pointed over toward the wash house. "See there," he said. "I built you a pony pen when I was building your mamma's dog kennel." Abby had noticed the roofed lean-to attached to the wash house but thought it was part of her mother's new dog project.

She gave Timothy Seahorse two more pieces of apple and stuck the last one in her pocket as her mother had told her. She led him around in small circles, then bigger circles, then back-and-forth in a straight line. "Mamma, look how smart he is! He's already learning to walk on the leash!"

"It's called a lead line, not a leash. If you're going to be a horse-woman, you need to learn the terminology. Matt is picking up a book for you from the library."

In reality, Timothy Seahorse was following the smell of apple and before Abby saw him coming at her, his head low and ears laid back, Timothy Seahorse ripped the pocket off of her favorite gingham dress. The apple fell onto the ground and the pony snatched it up, chewing it, his mouth moving from side to side creating an audible crunch. Abby started crying. "Mamma," she screamed, "this pony tore my best dress!"

Pearl smiled. "Lesson Number One of Horsemanship," she said. "Don't ever keep food in your pocket!" Pearl and Uncle Homer laughed. Abby did not find it funny and led the horse to the new paddock, unclipped the rope all by herself and shut the gate.

"Mamma, that was not a funny joke," Abby screamed.

"Oh, don't be such a baby. You've outgrown that dress anyway," Pearl said. "Ungrateful bratty child."

"Don't worry, Miz Pearl," Homer said. "I'll go look after her and make sure she alright. I'll help her with the pony, too. That pony was a real good idea," he said, smiling at Pearl.

"Mamma," Abby asked, not ready for another horse trick to be played, "I can't find Mr. BB. He's not in his cage and I can't find him anywhere. Do you have him?"

"If you took better care of him, I wouldn't have had to take him to the vet," Pearl snapped. "Seems someone left him out of his crate and he got bit by a snake."

"A snake? Is he gonna be okay?" Tears were trickling down Abby's face.

"He's going to be fine, but it's going to cost me an arm and a leg, Abby, just because you were careless. It's your fault. I'll pick him up tomorrow."

Homer looked over at her and smiled. "You gonna take better care of this pony?"

"Yes. Mamma." Abby asked glancing at Homer, "Can you pick BB up today?"

"No, the vet had to give him some medicine and wants to watch him a day or two," Pearl answered.

Abby, feeling friendless and trying to think of when she last let Mr. BB out of his cage, sullenly meandered to her room. She wasn't too sure about the pony, either. She fell on her bed and cried.

When Uncle Homer entered her bedroom, Abby yelled, "Don't you come near me! If you get near me, I'll tell Uncle Boyd. He will get the police! I'll call my real uncle and he will take care of you the old fashioned way." She had no idea what the old fashioned way was, but she had heard her mother say it enough times to believe it must be serious. Abby meant for him to know she was mad and would not be bought off with a mean pony. She worried about her brother and her dog but couldn't stop her outrage and screamed at the old drunk. "You better watch out, mister!"

Uncle Homer chuckled, amused at her temper tantrum and not the least bit worried about her threats. He leaned over, picked up a small bag and tossed it to her. Abby watched the paper bag fly through the air and clasped her hands together, determined to catch it. She was also keeping an eye on Uncle Homer and missed the catch. The bag landed at her feet, and when Uncle Homer made a move to come near and pick it up, Abby backed up. He stopped. He was grinning like an imbecile. Abby finally ventured a glance toward the floor. She saw a tuft of bright blue material peeking out of the bag. She kicked the bag, as if to shake out whatever was in it.

"Aw, shit, girl! Just pick it up. It's something good," Uncle Homer said.

Cautiously she bent forward, shot a look back at him to see if he was standing still, and then picked up the bag. She dropped the bag away and a pretty blue dress unfolded in her hands. It had a big square white collar with a red anchor sewed on it.

"Go on. It's yours to keep," Uncle Homer said. "It used to be my girl's sailor dress, but she done out-growed it. She said you can have it."

Abby looked back at him, wadded up the dress and threw it on the bed. Abby thought two presents in one day could only mean trouble later on. He and her mother couldn't be trusted, and this knowledge grew daily in her mind. She darted out of the bedroom and ran as hard and fast as she could. She did not see her mother in the yard, and didn't look over her shoulder all the way down to Mr. Axil's office.

"Hey, Mr. Axil," she panted, bursting through the door, mindlessly breaking the rule of quiet entry they had agreed upon. She bent over, hands on her knees, trying to catch her breath. She caught a whiff of something soured and realized that she was smelling her own body odor, the stale reek of sweat. She looked at Mr. Axil. There was no indication he could tell she was a bit stinky. She took a few steps closer to him, but kept a safe distance, just to be sure he didn't get a hint of her stench.

"Well, hello, Miss Abby. It's been a while since you've been to see me. I thought maybe you were very busy in school this year."

"I didn't want to take up your time while you are writing your book. You are still working on it, aren't you? Or is it finished?" Abby paused and looked at her hands to see if they were dirty. After she inspected them, Abby decided to be careful to touch nothing in the spotless office, especially the glass cabinets. Her hands were very dirty and sticky from the apple's juice and the pony's slobber.

"Mr. Axil, I been begging Mamma for a horse so I could ride everywhere," she said. "She and Uncle Homer bought me a Welsh Pony! It just got here a few hours ago. It's not a horse but it's close. Can you believe it? But he's too young to ride yet. Then Mamma and Uncle Homer played a dirty trick on me. Mamma told me to put an apple in my pocket. That stupid pony ripped the pocket right off my favorite dress trying to get to that stupid apple."

"Oh, my dear. I'm so sorry to hear that. That was a nasty trick. Your mother seems to be full of them, doesn't she? But, all in all, it's a pretty good day when a girl gets a pony!"

Mr. Axil noticed Abby was rather pallid, apparently not spending as much time outside as normal. Maybe because of school, he thought. He also noticed a twinge of disappointment on her face. He got up from his desk, straightened some papers there and asked, "Have you named your new pony yet?"

"Well, he came with a name. Or Mamma named him. But I like it. He's called Timothy Seahorse. I think that's a good name for a beach horse, don't you?"

"I do, yes I do like it. Very clever, that name. Now, if you feel like it, I'd like to tell you about what I consider to be the Cradle of American History. It's what I'm writing about. My book is nearly finished." Abby brightened up. She loved his personal history lessons. "By the way," Mr. Axil said, "just so you know to be careful, Welsh Ponies are known to be mean little things. Not all of them, and I am sure yours is not, but be aware until you get to know him. Now, come with me. I'm going to show you a genuine bloody hand print that one of the soldiers left when he was shot, before he fell way down into the fort."

Two Crows & a Shot

Abby hated her hair. It was long, thin and stringy and could not be plaited like Cindy and Becky's, whose thick hair stayed in place for days with pretty little beads woven within the plaits. Abby's stayed in knots and in her face. Rubber bands just slid out and headbands hurt her head. Her siblings gave their best shot at keeping it from becoming a giant nest of tangles, a chore they dreaded as much as Abby. Matt, Mary, and Mags would lie her down on Mary's bed and spread her hair out like a fan on the bedspread, grab a brush and wide-tooth comb and start the process of getting out the tangles. While the sisters worked on her hair, Matt played an old game with Abby he called "Two Crows in a Bar." Using his fingertips as make believe crow legs, he'd tiptoe up her chest and under her neck. When he got to the tickle spot, under her neck or under her arms, the familiar story would start. "Two crows went into a bar and begged the bartender for a SHOT!" Each time he yelled SHOT, he tickled Abby and she wriggled and giggled and for a moment was distracted from Mags' and Mary's work, combing like mad to get tangles out of her fine blonde hair. It was something they kept up for at least an hour, two or three times a week. When they were done, Abby would make a run for it and head for the fort or the beach.

Before escaping on this day, Abby tried one more time to get her sister to come to the beach with her. "Mags, you want to see what we can find on the beach? It's windy but not too cold. You wanna come with me?" Abby asked.

"I wish I could, doll, but Mamma has us working on the house at Officer's Row now. Best of all, *you* can live with us there and pretty soon, at the rate we're going! We'll get you close to us, don't you worry. It won't be long now." Mags wrapped her in a deep hug and said "You will just love how pretty it's going to be. My room is lavender and Mary's is yellow!"

"What color is my room?" asked Abby, clapping, waiting for details.

"I don't know. Mamma hasn't painted it yet. But it has very long, narrow French doors that lead out to a beautiful porch. Every room in the house has them and it is something to see! For my bed, she cut squares out of the hem of my lavender blanket, so it looks like the top of a castle! She is so creative," Mags said.

"What color is Mamma's room?" asked Abby. "Does it have a pretty bedspread, too?"

"It isn't painted or decorated yet either," answered Mags. "Lucky for us, Mamma's bedroom is downstairs so we have the whole second floor to ourselves! And a bath tub!"

"Matt, what color is your room?"

"I am NOT living with you girls. I prefer to stay down there in the wash house. It's kind of like my own apartment and I can keep it *clean!*" Matt headed for the door. "I've got work to do!" He missed catching the screened door before it slammed.

Abby left the suite, in which she was only allowed for the hair combing ordeal. Within minutes of hitting the windblown beach, on her way to the point at the Gulf to watch sting rays in the shallow water, her hair blew every which way and masses of knots had already started to form. She tucked it behind her ears and blew her mouth sideways trying to get it out of her eyes. As she walked along, noticing that the sting rays seemed to be following her in the shallow water as she made her way toward the point, she saw something lying on the beach, up near a sand dune. She trudged through the thick sand and realized what she had seen was a bleached out fish carcass, down to the skeletal head and the backbone, the remains of a fishermen's cleaned fish. She broke the head off and looked carefully at the bones that ran along the spine. As she has seen Mags do a hundred times, she took her messy hair and wrapped it into a French twist type knot at the back of her head and inserted the fish spine. Her new tool did a good job of holding her hair off her neck. The knot stayed firmly in place, only a few strands of hair still blowing in the wind. Abby was excited she'd solved her hair problem and couldn't wait to show her sisters.

"It's just like Mag's fancy hair combs!" she announced to a nearby palmetto. "Just wait till they see my new invention. If I can find enough, I'll sell them to the tourists!" She went in search of fish back bones.

Later in the day, at her mother's coffee time when she knew her mother and sisters would be in the suite, she decided she would surprise them with her invention. She snuck up to her bedroom. Uncle Homer wasn't there. In fact, she hadn't seen him all day. She pulled out the new blue sailor dress and slid it over her head, careful not to mess up her hair or let the fish bone slip out. The knot of hair had gotten lower on her head. The dress was wrinkled and it looked and smelled like it hadn't been washed lately. It was at least two sizes too large for Abby, but she loved the big collar with the bright red anchor. All in all, she believed she was presentable for calling on the suite. She jumped as high as she could to see herself in the mirror over the sink, but could only spy her head and the dirty white collar with its red anchor appliqué.

Abby gently, quietly, knocked on the screened door her mother had Uncle Homer install so she could enjoy the breeze without mosquitoes. Though late in the fall, the sticky sweet smell of oleanders still permeated the air. She politely knocked on the screened door again.

"Mamma? Are you in there? May I come in? I want to show you something." Abby said through the screen in the door.

"Oh, good God, Abby. Come on in. Now what've you done?" Pearl asked. Pearl looked at the scrawny child in the dress that was big enough to fit Mary and said "What in the hell are you wearing? Where in the hell did you get that rag?"

"Uncle Homer give it, gave it, to me. It was Paula's, his daughter." Abby answered.

"Well, its dirty and way too big. Take it off. Right now. Hand it to me." Pearl ordered.

Slipping out of the oversized garment took only a second and Abby stood there in her pale blue panties, chilled from the wind whistling in the open screened door. "Are you gonna wash it for me, Mamma?"

"Hell, no. I'm burning the damned thing. Is this what you came to show me?"

"I really like the collar. Can you save that?" Abby asked. "Look, Mamma. Go get Mary and Mags. I want to show you my new invention!"

Mary and Mags were already hanging at the edge of their bedroom door. They'd been alerted by their mother's raised tone of voice and were surprised to hear Abby at this unexpected time.

"There you are!" Abby beamed when she saw her sisters. "Mags, it's kind of like your fancy hair combs!" With that, she turned around, her little nipples protesting the cool air, and displayed her fish bone hair comb.

"Good God, Almighty!" Pearl screamed. "What in the hell do you have in your hair?"

"It's a fish backbone, Mamma. It holds my hair up off my neck! It won't get so tangled, maybe."

"Well, take it out!" Pearl screamed. "No wonder you stink. You little hellion. Why in the hell would you put a damned fish bone in your hair?"

Mary and Mags moved over to Abby's side. Mary slipped a sweater over Abby's pale skin and goose-bumps. Mags tried to jiggle the fish bone out of Abby's hair, knowing full well that Pearl would soon yank it out and any hair that was entangled along with it. The comb would not budge.

"Mamma, it's stuck. It won't come out," Mary said quietly.

"Oh, hell yes it will," Pearl snapped, getting up and storming into the kitchen. She returned from the kitchen carrying the large sewing scissors no one was allowed to touch for any reason. "Turn around, Abby," she said, taking the child by the shoulders and twisting her around roughly.

Snip, snip, snip. Abby heard the scissors while she watched her long hair fall to the floor. She held her breath, not daring to say a word. Mags and Mary leaned against the door frame, looking on. Clip, tug, clip and the bone hit the wood floor.

"Turn around again," ordered Pearl. Abby didn't have a chance to move before her mother spun her around. The scissors were placed against her forehead. Snip, snip, again. She didn't dare move to brush away the strands that fell on her chest and had begun to itch.

"There, by God. I told you I could get it out. Your hair looks better, anyway, and now, you don't have to worry about tangles. Mags, get her a mirror so she can see," Pearl said.

Mags held out her hand to Abby. She took it and they went into the bathroom where there was a small mirror over the sink. Mags lifted her up so she could see. "Just go ahead and sit in the sink. You've gotten too big for me to hold you up."

Abby could not believe her chopped off hair. It was shorter than a lot of boy's! She looked at the slanted bangs that covered her forehead and tried not to cry. She knew the kids at school would have a lot to say about the parts that were too short and just stuck up out of her head.

"It looks real nice, Mamma," Abby yelled from the bathroom. "Thank you."

Mags told Abby to sit still while she went to ask for the scissors to try to even up the bangs. Pearl offered no objection. Mags cut away to help improve the mess her mother had made. Little clippings of hair fell all over Abby's shoulders again. "Mags, it itches," she whispered.

"Mamma. The hair on her skin itches. May I give her a bath?" Mags called from the bathroom.

"For God's sake, yes. Plus, the child stinks. What if Uncle Boyd had been here to see this mess!"

Abby had not been in a bathtub since the family moved to the fort. The warm water all over her body felt like heaven. She slid her head down under the water, holding her breath and opening her eyes to look up at her sister. Mags beamed. When she slid up, Mags gently washed her hair and her body, and with a wash cloth, not just a bar of soap. Eventually, the water became cold and Mags took her out of the tub, hating to interrupt her enjoyment. After a gentle pat dry, Mags applied pink medicine on her mosquito bites. "At least now your hair's quick and easy to comb," Mags said. Mary stood by with a pair of very soft, well-worn pajamas and put them on Abby, rolling up the arms and sleeves so they almost fit.

"There you go, baby sister. All ready for bed. Have you eaten?" asked Mary.

"Yes. McAllister made me a broiled flounder stuffed with crab meat!" Abby answered. "It's a new recipe he's working on and it was delicious. I think I'll eat flounder every day!"

Standing out in the small hallway, listening and seething as she heard the older girls border on spoiling the youngest, Pearl said "Well, scoot back up to your room."

"Thanks for my haircut, Mamma. Thanks for the bath, Mags. Thanks for the pajamas, Mary." Abby finished her list of thanks and, inhaled and asked, "Mamma, will you save that collar before you burn that dress?"

"I'll think about it," said Pearl. Abby knew that meant no. She decided not to argue since her mother had calmed down. Abby went out, careful not to slam the screened door.

Abby climbed the steps to her room with as little noise possible. Her breathing increased and she felt her chest grow tight, wondering if Uncle Homer was in the room. Homer was sitting up in her bed, the wall serving as his back brace. He was smoking a cigarette and held a beer in the other hand.

"Now don't you look nice!" Uncle Homer said. Abby remained standing at the open bedroom door. "Your hair shore is short, though. I ain't even gonna ask what you done to have that hair of yor'n chopped off. Come here. Sit next to Uncle Homer." He patted the bed next to him. Abby obediently crawled in the bed and lay rigid underneath his waiting arm. The smell of his body and armpits was almost unbearable.

The Flaming Heart of Dixie

The next morning, Abby went out to walk the rock wall. Her hand went up to feel her neck when the wind hit her bare skin there, a few short wisps flying around. She shivered. She felt naked without her long hair hanging down on her neck. She went over to the fort office to show Mr. Axil her hair. It was early and the flags were not hung yet, so today might be the day she could help him. She walked up the sidewalk, peered through the window of the door and quietly slipped inside.

"Good Morning, Abigail," said Mr. Axil. "Looks like you've had a haircut." His hand was massaging his aching hip.

"I know. I hate it. I got a fish bone stuck in it and Mamma cut it out and off."

"It looks very becoming on you," Mr. Axil assured the child. "You look older."

Abby smiled. "Is today a good day to teach me to run the flags up the poles?"

"Actually, it's perfect," he smiled. "My arthritis is giving me fits and I needed a helper today. The first thing you need to know is never, ever let a flag, especially the American flag, touch the ground. Did you know," Mr. Axil asked, "that this old fort has been held under seven different flags? First we were under French control, so that flag goes up first. Then Great Britain, and then Spain. The American Flag always goes in the center. Then the Alabama Militia Flag, the Confederate States flag, and finally, the Alabama State Flag."

"How am I ever going to remember that, Mr. Axil?" Abby asked.

"Well, I'll be with you when we put them up. I'll also teach

105

you how to fold them when they come down. Once you've done it enough, you'll remember." Unconsciously, he rubbed his aching hip and took a seat in the closest chair. "They must be down by sunset and if the American flag is ever up after dark, a light must shine on it."

The flagpoles stood at attention over the sally port that led deep into the brick bowels of the old fort. The poles made a graceful arch as they ascended and descended the curvature of the ground over the mouth. Mr. Axil showed Abby how to loop the clamp into the top hole in the flag's rim, hoist a little, loop the bottom and then tug hard and quick. He made it look easy and the flags flapped into the wind without one of them touching the ground. He let Abby do the last two. "Well, my dear Abigail, you are quite the quick-study," he said.

"The Spanish arrived here more than two-hundred years before the English landed at Plymouth Rock," he told her proudly as he hobbled back to the office, Abby close at his side. The air was cool. "The Spanish name for the Mobile Bay was *Bahia del Espiritu Santo* which means 'Bay of the Holy Spirit.' Isn't that just lovely?" They entered the warmth of the building and Mr. Axil plopped down in the closest chair rather than the one behind his desk. "It was named that in the early 1500's, long before the Pilgrims came over! Most people don't know that." He patted his pockets for his pipe and some matches but had to get up and go over to his desk where the pipe lay dead in the oversized ashtray. "The first contact with the native citizens didn't go so well, the Spanish burning down their villages," he continued. Abby was hanging on to every word so she could impress her teacher and maybe remember it long enough to tell the tourist children next summer. "That is why Hernando De Soto, an explorer who came a few years later, met his fate with the Indians over on the Mississippi. It is rumored that his wife, Isabella De Soto, planted the origins of these beautiful oleanders, idling her time away here on this very peninsular, waiting for her husband who would never come." As he happily puffed, glad that at least one child was interested in the history of the place, he remembered something else he should tell her. "Also, the Creek Indians laid over here on their long, sad march to the Midwest. It was called the 'Trail of Tears' because the people were so sad to be forced off their very own land. Yes, this old fort has seen a lot of history."

106

Mr. Axil added, enjoying the dreamy look in Abby's eyes.

"The Governor has ordered the air strip paved and Uncle Boyd is going to build a marina, right across from Officer's Row." Abby blurted out with pride, interrupting his history lesson.

"Is that right?" Mr. Axil asked, pretending it was all news to him. He wondered what acts of evil Pearl and Boyd had committed to get those projects approved by the state.

"Yes! And my mamma tells the tourist women a funny history story," Abigail said. "You know those ol' cisterns back behind the airstrip?"

Mr. Axil nodded yes, his mouth clamped tightly on the stem of his pipe. One match after another died and he flicked them into the ashtray.

"Well, Mamma can spin a yarn. You might know that. Those women follow her down past those cisterns to this old iron pipe that sticks out of the ground. It's so rotted the top of it looks like lace. By the time they get there, they are already whipped into a frenzy. I've followed her a dozen times, I bet. The water spouts outta that rusted pipe and Mamma strikes a match and throws it in the water."

Mr. Axil's eyebrow was crooked up, listening intently to what the girl was telling him. He knew the outcome, but would let her finish her story, because her face was lit up and it was a joy for him to see.

"When the match hits the water, *Poof!* That water catches on fire! The ladies all ooh and ahh because who ever heard of water that can burn? Then Mamma stretches her arms out wide and smiles and tells the tourist, '*This* is **THE** Flaming Heart of Dixie!' The ladies all clap and Mamma brings them back up to the restaurant for lunch." When Abby first saw the pale blue and orange flames in the water, she wondered how water could burn. But it did. She had seen it herself. She looked at the ground as if studying something down there. "Mr. Axil, why does that water burn? I know it's not magic because my old grandmother says magic is the devil's work. My mamma is mean sometimes, but she would sure not be working for the devil!"

That's debatable, Mr. Axil thought and the way he pinched his lips together would have been a giveaway to an adult. "Well, Abby," he said, "we have a lot of natural gas in this area. It has to do with history that goes back so far, even I don't know it. Back to the dinosaur days. There's gas in that water. It doesn't have a smell like the gas in your house does, so nobody suspects it's there. That's a pretty good trick your mother plays on those tourists. I think she made that name up to entertain her guests. That's the kind of thing that keeps them coming back." He rocked back on his heels, envisioning the showmanship that Pearl demonstrated on a regular basis.

"Now, you keep your eyes on the sun today. Come before the sun hits the bay in the afternoon because these flags have to get down on time. Since it's your first time, why don't you come a little early?"

The Gray Lady

The next morning, Abby arrived early as Mr. Axil had asked, and was ready to begin with the job of hanging the flags. One after another went up, barely a word spoken between them during the process, Abby concentrating on the job at hand. They were almost at the end of the row when Mr. Axil said, "Oh, I've got a story to tell you. It's a true one and your mamma can tell our visitors. Does she know about the hurricane of 1906?"

"I don't know. I don't think so," Abby answered. "She never told me about it."

"Back in 1906 a stupendous hurricane roared over this peninsula." The last flag raised, he peered at the bay, thinking what the place might have looked like back then, perhaps a few houses scattered about, attempted gardens in the sand, maybe even fences. "The storm was so strong it washed Gulf sand all the way over to the bay, at least that's what they say. Now this is a fact, not fiction," he continued, his tone low and deadly serious. "When the tidal surge washed across here, the water was so strong and so deep it killed almost everyone." He stopped talking, deep in thought, thinking about tiny boats and tiny babes being washed out to sea. "The only ones to survive down here were camped in the fort. Except for one woman. They say that one poor woman was swept away in the rushing water and wound up in a pine tree down at Navy Cove, hanging on a branch by her hair! At the very top of a virgin pine, hanging by her hair! After the hurricane, a dense fog covered the entire area. The fog hid her from view for a few days so she became known as the Gray Lady. There's old sketches of her somewhere in one of my books. I'll try to find it for you. Just think, her hair saved her life, though she damn near starved to death before they found her. That oughta be interesting to the tourists." He nodded to Abigail, and continued trying to light his pipe.

"Gosh, Mr. Axil. That *is* a good story. My mamma sure will like to tell that one. She'll probably swear that woman up in the tree still haunts the place." Abby snickered at the thought of her mother scaring the ladies with some ghostly tale. "Well, I better get going. Thanks for telling me the stories."

Abby waved as she left and walked up the road past The Lighthouse Inn and Restaurant, past the old building that still sat un-renovated, its weather-worn wood the shade of the wild oats that grew on the dunes, and around a small curve in the road. She finally arrived at the three houses of Officers' Row. Curiosity was killing her and besides, Pearl had not told her she couldn't come up to see the progress of their house. She noticed a new sign hanging on the building at the end. It said *The Winter Inn at Lighthouse Point.* Abby decided she'd look at the Winter Inn first. She carefully opened the door to the building but it still squeaked an objection to being pushed open. She tiptoed into the front room. On the wall straight in front of her she saw a circle with her mother's swirly handwriting on a poem. She tipped her head from left to right and right to left, trying to read what was written there. She heard muffled conversation coming from the back of the building and snuck through the living room, then the dining room, until the voices were just ahead.

She peeped around the corner and saw the man her mamma was talking to. Abigail kept popping back her head, afraid she would be discovered.

"Here," her mother said. "Please keep this in your safe for me. And don't mention it to anyone, if you don't mind."

"I don't mind keeping it safe for you," the man replied. "But only if it's legal."

"Of course. I wouldn't ask you to hide something illegal. We've been friends a long time, Harris. You know me better than that! It's just some papers I need hidden from snooping eyes around this place." She gently laughed.

Abby decided she'd better scoot because it sounded like they were finishing with this business. She snuck back out the front door and hid in the oleander tree next to the building. A short man with a long red beard strode out of the building, Pearl right behind him. Pearl walked him out to the car and

110

bent down in the car window to say something else. The man started his car and drove away.

Once Pearl had gone back inside, Abby stood up, brushed off her knees and wondered who the man with beard was. As she stood there, she saw a pink and white car with wing-looking fenders and lots of shiny chrome pass Officer's Row. She followed the car, staying just off the road, jumping behind oleander trees like she was on a spy mission. It pulled into the restaurant parking lot, and the tall old gentleman got out, dressed in a white shirt with a striped tie. He strode inside like he owned the place. This was the same man she had seen numerous times before working on the sinks in the big kitchen. Pearl had told her that he was a friend, an engineer, but had never introduced him to Abby. He was trying to invent an automatic dish washing machine, Pearl told her. Abby wondered if he knew the big restaurant was closed for the winter.

Peter the Hungarian

"Well, the Winter Inn has worked out much better than even I anticipated," Pearl said as she arranged green branches with some red berries she had found. She plopped the arrangement in the middle of the dining room table which had been moved to the corner. With the juke box in the other corner, the dining room was now the dancing room.

Guests in from Vermont suggested she put up a Christmas tree. With her usual flair, Pearl led the visitors clomping into the swampy pine woods near Navy Cove to select a tree. The short needled pine tree they chose had to be cut several feet shorter once they got it home. It was too tall even for the sixteen-foot high ceilings at the Winter Inn.

"Oh just wait. We'll decorate it with sea shells and it will be beautiful," Pearl promised the new visitors.

With enthusiastic help from her guests, Pearl hung dainty dried seahorses and star fish along with some lights and a few ball ornaments. The aluminum tinsel she tossed on the branches moved each time the front door opened, reflecting light from nearby lamps. The lights on the tree were swathed with circles of fibrous angel hair that gave them an eerie glow. Abby was enthralled, unable to pry herself away from the lights at night.

The parlor was anchored by an old couch, long with tufted leather, given to Pearl by her beloved father many years ago. Politicians sat right alongside fishermen. Everybody got equal billing at this little inn. The mix was noisy in the parlor at night, smoking, talking politics and telling dirty stories. Abby was always nearby, but invisible.

Paving of the airstrip was finished and more guests flew in. Across the road, huge barges had been tugged into place making T-shaped marina docks ready for spring boaters and fishermen. A small store was under construction where Matt would run a marina business, and a dull aluminum ice house stood right next to the store. Uncle Boyd complained about money going down a dark hole, but Pearl just kept at the project.

"You know," Pearl said to Matt. "The airstrip needs some sort of lights. There are a bunch of those old black cauldrons under the old Inn. I think I'll have Homer haul them out. We can douse old rags with kerosene and light them at night when we are expecting fly-ins."

One such fly-in was already there, having flown in by a full moon the night after the folks from Vermont had arrived. He was a tall man with olive skin, dark hair and gold-green eyes. Every time he entered a room, his eyes swept from side to side, as if he were expecting to find something or someone and he spoke with a heavy accent. His name, he said, was Peter.

"Hey, ju," he said to Abby. "Little one, hiding behind ze door. I see you. Come out and talk wiz me."

Abby looked around for Pearl. She had made the mistake before of talking to people that she wasn't supposed to talk to. The coast seemed clear. She loved the funny way the man talked. She slipped out from her hiding spot and went into the parlor and stood in front him. She was aware of her dirty pants and remembered her face might even be smudged. She'd been playing hard outside today. This man with his musical voice was handsome, and Abby wanted to be clean and shiny. She missed her long hair.

"Das right," he cooed. "Come closer. I vill not hurt ju. My name is Peter. I come originally from Hungary. Ju remind me uf my own liddle girl."

"You have a little girl? Is she here?" asked Abby. She had not noticed any children.

"Sadly," he said, his eyes looking at the floor and tearing up, "I lost dem in the war. De big war. The Germans."

Abby stood silent. She squirmed, waiting for the man's eyes to reach hers again.

"I'll be seven in a few days," Abby said. "How old was your little girl?"

"She was eight," he said, "but was about jur size."

"I'm tall for my age," Abby said. "Everyone thinks I'm older because I'm so tall."

113

"Vell, Abby. Since you have a birdday, I tink we should celebrate, don't ju?"

"My mamma doesn't believe in celebrating birthdays, except for the birth of Jesus. She says too many presents spoil children." Abby glowed in this man's presence. His gentle manner wrapped around her with each soft word he spoke. She pulled at her short hair and glanced at her dirty hands. "Excuse me, Mr. Peter. I need to go wash my hands. I'll be right back!" Peter smiled as she left the room. As she walked away he said, "We go shopping. I'll ask jur mudder. I'll let ju buy anything ju want."

"We don't have any stores down here," Abby said as she turned around. She was disappointed at the thought of a lost shopping trip.

"Den, we go to where da stores are!" he said.

"Abigail Delaney!" Pearl scolded, but in a sweet voice in front of the gentleman. "Don't be pestering Mr. Peter. He's our guest and is here to rest, not to entertain you!"

"Miz Pearl," Peter said softly. "Abby remind me very much of my own liddle girl who I lost in da war. I would like to take her to town, to buy her someting to remember me by. Would dat be alright wid ju? Do you offer a car service?"

"Well, that's very nice of you. But, Abby, you shouldn't be fishing for presents, telling everyone it's your birthday!" Pearl said. "Peter, are you sure you want the company of an almost seven-year-old?" Pearl asked. Abby was surprised her mother knew how old she was.

"Ya. I'm very sure."

"Well, you can borrow my son's jalopy. He keeps it very clean and it runs well. Let me find the keys," Pearl said, as she left the room in search of Matt. A car service! Of course. Something she and Boyd had not thought about.

Abby could barely contain herself. "Mr. Peter. Let me wash my face and put on some clean clothes," she said. "I live just down the road in the big hotel. It won't take me long."

"Of course. Of course. Ladies always has to get ready before dey shop," he said, watching with pleasure as the child fled through the front door.

She ran down to her room in the big hotel, relieved that Uncle Homer was nowhere to be seen. A quick splash of cold water on her hands and face, a brush through her short hair, and some fresh pants and a shirt was all she needed. She hurried back to the Winter Inn, staying on the pavement so sand didn't get in her shoes and sand spurs didn't get stuck on her pants. She ran up the few steps, pushed open the door, looked at Mr. Peter and said, "See, that didn't take long! I'm all ready!"

Peter and Abby piled into Matt's old black Chevrolet with its woolly seats. They chatted all the way to Foley. Abigail had a million questions how someone is lost in the war. Peter resisted giving Abby full details, but enough for her to understand that his daughter and wife had been killed, not lost. He changed the subject. "So, Miss Abby. What ju tink we are shopping for? A doll? A dress?"

Abby knew he was avoiding the question, but did not want to upset him by continuing to ask. She could see the subject made him sad and decided to cheer him up by being an excellent tour guide. She pointed out of the car window on his side, her hand and finger right in front of his face, showing him where the gladioli farms were in the summer, told him all about Timothy Seahorse and how she had found part of a horseshoe crab shell on the beach. Peter smiled at her non-stop talk and asked a few questions about her life at the fort. She only told him the fun things and laughed when he laughed. When they reached town, he parked the old car in a parallel spot at the intersection of the two main streets. He came around to her door and opened it for her, just as she was reaching for the handle. It was mid-afternoon in the winter, getting dark early, and Abby wanted to hurry before the stores closed.

"No, my dahling," he gently said to her. "A lady always lets a gentleman open her door for her."

Abby tried to be graceful. She wanted to act like a lady and slid across the itchy woolen seats making sure her knees were together, like Mags had taught her. Her feet barely touched the sidewalk when Peter picked her up, twirled her around and laughed. As he carried her tall frame down the street, she felt like a small girl and loved the attention. She hugged the man's neck as tightly as she could without choking him and hoped he would stay for a long time.

"Mr. Peter? Will you please stay at Fort Morgan?" Abby asked.

"I vish I could," he said "but I have a busyness in Vermont.

Vis de udder people who came from Vermont. But today, my dear. Today, we celebrate each udder, togedder."

Though he insisted she buy everything she looked at for more than a second, Abby knew that being greedy was just unmannerly. She finally chose one doll named Leaner the Cleaner, a doll that came fully equipped with a mop, broom, apron and dust cloth.

"Oh, Mr. Peter," she said as they drove back toward the fort. "Thank you so much for my doll! She's a cleaning girl, so me and her can help my sisters clean the rooms at the Inn."

"Ju have brought me more joy dan ju can imagine," he answered with a smile.

By the time they reached the fort, the sun had set. Abby tried not to stare at the handsome man with his square jaw, lit by dashboard lights, but could not manage to take her eyes off of him. Without looking at her, he reached across the seat, his hand open, and she put her hand in his.

When they reached the fort, Uncle Homer and Pearl were out on the paved runway standing near a bunch of the smudge pots. Pearl was pointing to where the black pots were to be set.

"I'll fill them with oily rags," she told Peter and Abby as they walked up holding hands. "Then, I can light them at night so the pilots can see the strip." Pearl looked at Abigail then at Peter, her eyes narrowing as she looked at their hands clasped together. She cast a look at Uncle Homer who glanced over and gave Abby an ominous look. Abby dropped her hand to her side.

"What kind of pots are they, Mamma?" Abby asked nervously. Her mother was acting as if she had done something wrong, though she knew she had not.

"They're smudge pots and just what we need to light this little airstrip," Pearl answered, satisfied that Abby had picked up her silent signal and dropped Peter's hand. "Abby, I'm glad you had fun in town. What did you get?"

"Oh, Mamma! Mr. Peter bought me a wonderful doll named *Leaner the Cleaner*. She comes with all of her cleaning supplies so I can help Mary and Mags!" She looked up at Peter and smiled, then put her small hand back in his large one. He squeezed it. Homer watched.

Women's Army, Spring, 1956

Abby decided she'd go to the beach, even though it was pretty chilly, and planned afterwards to go talk to Mr. Axil about the man with the red beard and the man in the fancy car. She wondered if he knew either of them.

She walked down the seawall, outside of the fort compound, and headed down to the beach. She trudged up the enormous dunes, all topped in wild sea oats that her mother sometimes gathered in bundles as decorations for the restaurant. Her muscles were burning by the time she climbed up and down the dunes that were between herself and the Gulf. She thought there might be some good seashells on the beach this time of year. If she found some, maybe she could sell them to Miss Tammy in the upstairs shop. When she topped the last dune she couldn't believe what was happening on the beach right in front of her. She plopped down on her butt in the dune, partially hidden behind the wild oats, instinctively trying to hide. She sat and stared through the tall, grassy oats that swayed in the soft wind. Boy, this would be something to tell Mr. Axil. She stayed until the crew of women, all in army looking uniforms, got back into jeeps and trucks that were parked on the sand and drove away.

As a gentle winter faded into a blustery spring, coming down to hide in the dunes and watch the women on the beach had become almost a daily ritual. It meant Abby was missing a lot of school. She was glad her mother didn't seem to care if she went to school or not as long as she stayed out of the way. When not in school, Abby got up early to help Mr. Axil hang the flags then headed over to her camp she had set up on top of the dune. She was so busy watching the marching, she hadn't taken the time to ask Mr. Axil about the women or tell him what she was witnessing almost everyday. Abby had to pick her way through stickers and pointed palmettos, but she was not going to miss a minute of this show. She didn't even tell Cindy about her secret for fear she'd want to come along. Her black skin would stand out against the white sand and they would be caught. She certainly couldn't bring Mr. BB, and she missed the dog and the protection he provided.

Abby tucked herself behind the wild oats, lying on her stomach, her hands braced under her chin. She watched, making a mental note of every move that was made. The man with the red beard yelled orders and ladies dressed like men in soldier suits stomped up and down the beach, back and forth, turning on a dime when red beard commanded. Each woman had a long gun pushed firmly against her shoulder. A relay of orders resulted in guns swinging this way and that, winding up straight up and down against their bodies. Then, one female soldier blindfolded the woman next to her and each woman down the line followed in order. The man barked out more orders. On his order, each blindfolded woman took her gun apart and put it back together again. On command, each woman removed their blindfolds and inspected their work. They started marching again, coming closer to the dunes. Abby ducked down, closer to the sand, her chin separated from the sand only by her flat hand. Abigail decided she needed to go inform Mr. Axil about this right now, in case a war was coming and the state would take back the buildings. She slid backwards down the tall dune she was on trying to avoid anything that might stick her. When she finally reached the bottom, Abby ran down to Mr. Axil's office.

Though not yet full spring, the sun was bright and after climbing up and down dunes and trotting all the way down to Mr. Axil's office at the fort, Abby was sweating and hot. She hoped Mr. Axil had some cold water in his office. Sometimes the water fountain outside of his office worked and sometimes it didn't.

Panting, she approached the office and had a sip of water from the fountain. She frowned. She hated the water which always had the smell and taste of sulfur in it. She peeped in the glass windows and saw Mr. Axil hunched over the black typewriter, pipe going full steam, creating bushy looking clouds of smoke over his head.

Abby snuck in and sat in one of the padded chairs near his desk, waiting for him to stop typing and talk to her. She sat there picking at the cloth on the seat beneath her legs, trying to guess what print it might have been when it was new.

The clack, clack, clack of the typewriter keys came to a stop, Mr. Axil looked up and said, "Good afternoon, Miss Abby. You're all damp. Looks like you've been in a race. What brought you running to my office on this fine day?"

"Mr. Axil. I know my mamma's the biggest kind of liar and you might think I'm lying, too, when I tell you this, but I ain't. I mean I am *not* lying. I've been going down to the beach almost every day this week. Mr. Axil, there is a woman army down on the beach, stomping around with guns and everything. Oh, and those girls? They can take those rifles apart and put them back together, blindfolded! I'm not kidding and I'm not lying! And the man with the red beard that went to see Mamma a while back? Well, he seems to be in charge. Are we going to war?"

She had Mr. Axil's attention. "When did the man with the beard see your mother?" he asked.

"I don't know. Maybe two weeks ago? I couldn't hear what they were talking about. Just business stuff I guess."

"Well, it sounds like spring training has already begun. Nothing for you to be concerned about. Or that female army either. That's just old Harris Weeks. Been going on for years. He's quite sure U-boats are still in the Gulf. Thinks it's his responsibility to protect the coast line. The government wouldn't pay him any mind, so he started his own army. He chose women because in case of war, he figured all the men would be gone. He's eccentric but harmless. In fact, quite successful with his other businesses and hires only women for those, too. Were a war ever to come to pass, we would indeed be protected." Mr. Axil chuckled a little. "Quite an interesting gent, actually."

"Are we about to have another war, Mr. Axil? Is the state gonna take the barracks and the fort back over and make Mamma leave?"

"No, no, child. There's no threat of a war. This army is purely a product of Harris's imagination. I'm surprised the

119

federal government hasn't snuffed it out. I expect they will any day. And the old man up in Magnolia Springs that makes those machine guns for him, too."

Abby raised her eyebrows. "Those are machine guns?"

"Yes ma'am, they are. Homemade, right here in Baldwin County."

"Should I tell Mamma?"

"I imagine she knows all about it. You can tell her. It's no secret. Harris likes the ladies to practice on the beach, but only in the winter and early spring when there's less chance of being seen by a tourist or the law." Mr. Axil pushed back in his chair. "Anything else new in your world?" Axil asked.

"Well, Mamma told Matt that Uncle Boyd doesn't think he's getting his fair cut of money. But Mamma says he is. There is just less of it because of the time of year."

Abby paused to think what else was new. "That so called pony of mine?" she continued. "He's as mean as a snake. I couldn't ride him if I tried. He bit my oldest sister. He kicked my other sister right in the middle of her stomach when she was hanging out sheets. He jumps the fence of that little paddock and goes to see the fishermen because they give him beer. Mamma says he's a mean drunk. I didn't even know horses liked beer, but Timothy Seahorse sure does. The fishermen laugh when they give it to him."

"Yes, I've been meaning to talk to your mother about that pony. Come summer, that pony just can't wander around the fort like he does now. Especially if he bites and kicks. She's going to have to do something about him."

"Mr. Axil, I wanted a horse real bad. But I didn't want any mean pony."

"Well, I'll talk to her. See what we can do about Timothy Seahorse."

The next day, Abby watched Uncle Homer drag the pony into the back of his battered old truck. Timothy Seahorse bucked and kicked and raised horse hell all the way up the plank. Abby could see that even Uncle Homer was scared of him.

"Bye, Timothy Seahorse," Abby yelled as she waved to the pony. "You were NOT a good horse. I hope Uncle Homer can find you a good home." She watched the pony go out of sight in the truck then turned toward the airstrip. It was almost completely paved by now. She headed for Cindy's house. Cindy was scared to death of Timothy Seahorse, plus a million other things, and she would be glad to learn he was gone. Abby wanted Homer to be gone, but she was not so lucky.

The Miss Happiness & The Mis Hap

Spring was exceptionally warm that year, even the breezes blew hot off of the chilled water of the Gulf. With unusually warm weather people had already started coming down to the restaurant. The gift shop had reopened for the season and there was plenty to watch and do at the Inn. Matt was hard at work and happy as the marina had managed to open early. It was almost full of boats. Matt was busy between anchoring planes and getting boats in and out of the marina. The Winter Inn was closed for the summer. Pearl was busy finishing up the house in Officer's Row, but was often side-tracked from her decorating scheme with the flurry of unexpected spring business.

Uncle Boyd's grown children frequented the place often, and Abby was a little leery of them, for reasons she couldn't quite put her finger on. They all seemed nice enough. But there was something that stirred her intuition and she was careful to watch what she said around them, especially the one named Uncle Ham. The governor's yacht was once again parked off the pier, bright and white against an early summer sky. All was set for another busy summer, for a happy Uncle Boyd and maybe another big bonus for Pearl, like the new car she had gotten after last year's success.

Supplies were delivered to the restaurant by truck now and they could even afford to have a commercial laundry company do the linens. Occasionally, McAllister or Uncle Boyd or someone would need something special, something not on the normal order and Pearl would pile the older girls into the wagon to go pick up what they needed. Abby asked to go but Pearl kept assuring her she was too young and would get bored during the long car trips. Today was no exception. Mary, Mags, and Pearl were in the station wagon, off for what Abby thought was surely a shopping trip of some kind.

"Mamma, can I *please* go this time?" Abby pleaded. "I'm seven now. I'm old enough not to get bored. I promise, I won't whine."

"You can't go because there won't be enough room for you once we fill this car up with supplies. But, I suppose you could ride a short while with us," Pearl replied. "Uncle Ham has been asking if you could come see him. He misses his daughters. I'll take you there for the afternoon." Pearl got out of the station wagon, crossed the short expanse of yard, and walked through the back door of the kitchen. She went over to the phone on the desk, dialing a three-digit number.

"Ham? This is Pearl. Would you be a dear and watch Abby for me this afternoon? She is begging to go somewhere. Is to-day convenient? Good. Thank you so much. We'll be there in a bit." Pearl put the phone back on the receiver and marched back out of the kitchen.

"Okay," Pearl said to Abby as she walked back to the car. "It's all settled. Now, go get cleaned up and make it quick. We are already late. Wash your face and your hands and put on some clean clothes, please."

Abby didn't stop to think about what her mother had said. She only heard 'yes.' She jumped as high as she could and ran up the steps to her room, making sure she was fast, as her mother had asked. She squeezed her eyes tight as the she put the cold wash rag on her face. After putting on a fresh sun dress, she took a last glance into the mirror and thought she looked pretty good. She was tall enough now that she didn't have to jump to see herself.

Pearl and the girls were waiting in the running car, the air conditioner blowing full blast. Abby opened the car door and climbed in and over the back of the rear seat. After going over the seawall in the main road, Pearl suddenly turned right into a sandy drive, not far from the dunes where Abby had watched the female army's training exercises. In front of them was a small beach cottage up on stilts, with an unscreened porch wrapped all the way around it.

"Where we going, Mamma?" Abby asked.

"Well, you can't go all the way to Mobile," Pearl answered, "so I brought you to play with Uncle Ham, Uncle Boyd's youngest son."

"But he's a grown-up man, Mamma. I don't want to play with him. Does he have children? I wanted to go shopping with you," Abby protested.

"Well, he has some kids, but I don't think they came to the beach with him. He agreed to babysit while we are in Mobile," Pearl answered.

"Mamma, I'm too big! I never had a baby sitter before. Why do I need one now? I did turn seven, you know."

"Abby, stop whining," Pearl ordered. "You most certainly did have a babysitter. Who do you think Crazy Ruby was? Now just be quiet! Uncle Ham will take care of you while we run to town. You are to be a good girl and do exactly what he tells you. Stop complaining and maybe I'll bring you a surprise."

Uncle Ham stood on the front porch, leaning against the doorway, his hands in his pockets. Abby noticed how blue his eyes were. Unlike his short, round father, Uncle Ham was tall and lean with thin lips. Abby wondered how a son could be so different from his father. His brownish, thin hair hung wet down into his face.

"Abby, get out," Pearl said, then yelled out of the window. "Thanks, Ham. We'll be back in a few hours to pick her up."

Abby slowly clambered over the rear seat, accidentally stepping on Mary's hand, who howled. She got out of the door, which Pearl had walked around and opened for her. Glancing at her mother and then at Ham, she said quietly to Pearl, "Just take me back home, please. I just wanted to go shopping with you and the girls. I'm old enough now. I don't mind sitting on top of the supplies and I promise, I will not complain."

"Abby, you have wasted enough of my time this afternoon. Now Uncle Ham is being nice enough to let you visit and is waiting on you. You had better be a good girl!" Pearl pushed her toward Ham as she headed back around the front of the car, the hood hot from the running engine.

Abby drug her feet in the sand and stopped to swat at a mosquito before walking up to the deck where Ham was waiting. She kept her face down other than to turn to look at her mother and sisters. She watched her mother shift the car into gear as the wheels begin to turn.

"Please, Mamma?" she mouthed in her mother's direction. Pearl smiled and waved at her. Abby guessed her mother had not seen the final plea on her lips, because Pearl blew her a kiss as she drove away. After the car disappeared down the road, Abby walked up to the porch without looking at the man. She had met him a few times but he had never even spoken to her. She could feel his stare and knew his eyes had not moved from her since she got out of the car. She stole glances at him and then looked down at her feet. She hadn't liked him when she met him before and she didn't like him now.

"Hello, Abby," he said, keeping his voice low. "Let's see. What can we do today? I have a secret fort nearby. Maybe we could have some fun exploring it."

"The fort almost covered by sand?" Abby asked.

"I didn't think you were supposed to play around this far outside the fort," he said.

"I'm not. My brother told me about it," Abby lied. "Do you have any children?"

"I do. I have two girls just a little older than you. But they don't like to come down here for some reason. They like to stay at home with their mother."

Ham reached for her hand and said, "Well, come on. Let me show you this fort. The sand on the floor inside is so high the ceiling is real low. We'll have to stoop and maybe crawl!"

They walked over a short dune just past his house to the sand-buried battery. "It looks so dark in there," Abby said, still not taking his hand.

Ham just snickered as he reached and grabbed the girl's hand. He had to tug on her as she held back. He turned her hand loose and bent his head, stepping inside. He told Abby to come into the fort with him.

"It's cool in here," he said. "Even the sand is cool. You'll see. It feels good on your toes."

Abby was uneasy but stepped inside the partially buried room, squinting blindly into the darkness after having come in from bright sun. She stood still, waiting for her eyes to adjust. When she could see, her gaze went to the man. He had already sat down, his back against the concrete wall. She could see his face and a kind of lopsided grin. He unzipped his trousers. Her head twisted quickly in the direction of the light coming from the door. She might have run but she felt a

125

hand snatch her by the ankle. She tried to kick at Ham but he wouldn't let go of her foot.

"This is our little secret," he told her.

She was sitting on the top step of the deck, her eyes turned downward, when Pearl and the girls returned. Abby's sun dress was stained from a purple Popsicle Ham had given her, but that she had not eaten. When he went inside the house, she had thrown it on the sand, but not before it melted in her hand and dripped down the front of her dress. She stood and walked down the steps. At the bottom, she looked over her shoulder, but Ham Grantham had not come outside. At the car, there was no room in the very back for Abby, just as Pearl had predicted. She climbed into the back seat and sat between her sisters so each could sit next to a window. Abby didn't care. When Mags asked her how she messed up the front of her dress, Abby pretended not to hear. She just wanted to go home.

Instead of driving down to the Inn, Pearl wheeled the car into the makeshift parking lot at the marina, parking in the shade next to the ice house. The kids climbed out of the car and followed Pearl down the pier. Matt, who was stacking supplies on the new shelves of the new store, saw his mother pull into the parking lot. He stopped what he was doing and followed the family to see what was up.

"Watch out for holes in the top of the barges," Pearl turned around and called back to the following children. "They were used to load supplies into the barges when these old things were still in operation." She was walking backwards when she added, "Homer should have them all covered with wood and nailed closed by now. But keep your eyes open just in case. You don't want to fall into the bottom of this old thing. I have a big surprise! The first one that figures it out gets a dollar, a kiss, and a Coke," she said with a broad smile.

"Mamma! Don't walk backwards until we make sure all the hatches are closed!" Mary yelled.

Abby walked carefully out onto the old barges. Three of them had been latched together by steel straps. Just as Pearl had said, workmen cut big holes in the bottoms, allowing the sea water to come into the belly and help the structures stay stable. The ones in the deepest water were balanced on pilings that big machines had hammered into the sand. Abby kept her eyes open, looking for any hatches that were not covered. She only saw a few and they seemed to be safely battened down.

Abby was the first to see the new boat. "Mamma! Look! The stripe on that boat is the same color as your car!" It was a long, white and sleek Cabin Cruiser with a sea-foam green stripe painted all the way around it. The name *Miss Happiness* was painted in white over the green. "Do I get a dollar?"

"See? There she is!" exclaimed an excited Pearl. "Yes you do, Abby. Good eyes! Uncle Ham had a friend who needed to sell her and got me a great deal on it!"

"What? It's a new boat in the marina? So what?" asked Mary, holding her hand up to her brow against the glare of the setting sun.

"She's all mine. Ours," answered Pearl. "She's forty-two feet long!"

"Who's gonna drive it, Mamma?" asked Abby. "Can Matt drive a boat that big?"

"Well," answered Pearl. "Homer is a licensed captain. He can take our guests on fishing trips! One more way to make money, money, money. Come aboard!"

The boat was secured close to the dock. Rubber fenders were tied to the sides and hung between the vessel and the barge. Pearl jumped on as if she had made the move every day, while Mags and Mary offered each other a hand and cautiously climbed aboard. They each took one of Abby's hands and swung her aboard.

"You're almost too heavy to swing anymore!" Mags laughed at Abby. Matt took one long leap and joined them on the deck.

As they explored the boat, Abby commented to Matt that it looked a lot smaller on the inside than it did on the outside. "This is a stateroom," Pearl chimed in as they looked into the bedroom. The boat had a very small kitchen, called a galley according to Pearl. "What do you call this room, Mamma?" Abby asked, when they were in a bigger central room. Pearl informed them it was called the salon. Above the cabin, out on deck, were ample spaces to lie in the sun, or places where chairs could be set for fishermen, and latches in the floor that would hold them in place.

"When can we go for a ride?" Abby asked.

"Probably tomorrow," Pearl said. "Homer has to make sure she's seaworthy first. Then we'll take her way out in the Gulf and go deep-sea fishing! Doesn't that sound like fun?"

A few days later, Homer climbed aboard the *Miss Happiness*, plopped his dirty white sea captain's hat on his head and prepared for cast off. The passenger list included Pearl and her four offspring, plus one large black dog, Mr. BB, who sat on the rear deck, snarling a growl that was barely detectable.

"Miss Pearl," Homer asked. "You sure you want that dog on board for our very first cruise? We got a lot of safety things to go over. That dog makes me uneasy. I took the boat out yesterday. She handles like a dream. Now, so we don't get in trouble right off the bat, everybody got to put on one them life jackets," he said, pointing to a large orange pile. Mr. BB growled way down deep in his throat and Abby looked Homer right in the eye when the dog growled. She patted Mr. BB on the head. "Good boy," she said.

"Did you get any inspection stickers or licenses we might need?" asked Matt. "I didn't see anybody down here looking at her."

Homer pointed to the new sticker stuck on the windshield. "There's another one on the side of the boat, number painted on and all." Matt nodded at him and helped Abby get the clasps of her life jacket secured. The boat belched out dark diesel smoke, initially thick but thinning out as the motor came to life.

"I shore hope we get lots of fisherman, Miss Pearl," he said. Homer stopped talking and eased the boat out of the marina and into the placid waters of the bay. "I hope I make lots of tips. Beer money, ya know," he added.

Pearl was right about Uncle Homer and his captain skills. The water was extremely turbulent at the intersection of the bay and the Gulf, large waves leaping into the air as they clapped together, incoming against outgoing waters. Homer concentrated on what he was doing, leaving the safety of calm bay waters.

"First things first, Homer," Pearl said sternly. "First, go to town *today* and get yourself a clean cap, for God's sake. Second, if I hear a whisper of you drinking while captaining this fine boat, your ass will be fired. You may not drink before or during a fishing trip. Do you understand?"

"Oh, yes ma'am. I know not to drink while we have customers aboard. I'm just saying, we oughta have some happy customers. This Gulf is teeming with fish," he continued. "Lots of fish means good tips for the captain. That's all I meant." He stopped talking and focused on the channel in front of the boat, the changing of the waves and the changes in the water's color. Once the mouth had been cleared, he continued with his chat. This was his domain, one of the few things he could claim, for certain, to know about.

"What kind of fish are we talking about?" Matt asked Homer. "Are there any special lures or equipment I should get for the marine shop?"

"Depending on the season, we got Spanish and King Mackerel, Pompano and even Tarpon. I hear tell they's a giant Jew-fish out yonder near them wrecks. We got red fish, red snapper, flounder ... ain't no telling what all's out here." Homer enjoyed the attention and added, "McAllister gonna have fish to cook he never even heard of."

"What's a Jew-fish, Mamma?" Abby asked.

"It's properly called a Goliath Grouper. And you better use that name on this yacht from here forward, Homer," Pearl scolded. "Grouper, Homer. Did you hear me?" She turned to her daughter and told her that grouper could grow to eight feet long and weigh eight hundred pounds.

As Pearl's words hung in the salty air, Abby and the other three looked at each other wondering how their mother would know something like that. Matt raised his eyebrows as if to say he wasn't sure if their mother had one iota of an idea as to what she was spouting. Matt whispered to Mags, "I doubt there's a grouper that weighs any eight hundred pounds."

"Homer, you sure you got her? The water seems like it's getting rough again," Pearl asked, watching Mr. BB slide from side-to-side without picking up so much as a paw. Waves from cargo ships in the shipping lanes added to the confusion of the waters. The boat climbed up and down the waves, and Matt put a hand on Abby's shoulder. "I guess I'd better lay in a supply of sea sick pills for guests," Pearl said.

"Yes ma'am. Wouldn't be a bad idea," Homer agreed,

watching ahead and over the sides. "Y'all might oughta have on them life jackets, though. Even you growed up ones. The law wants you to wear them. Come here, baby girl," Homer said, looking at Abby. "We through the rough part now. Come drive this ship for me. Let me get me a cigarette."

Abby glanced at her mother and Matt. She was a mixture of happy and scared. "Really?"

"Get yore butt on over here," Homer playfully called Abby. She came close and he scooped her up and plopped her in the captain's chair. "You don't have to do nuttin. Just sit here and hold the wheel. Don't turn it like a car wheel. Just keep it straight. Steady-as-she-goes is what it's called."

Abby felt the wooden wheel under her hands. She could feel the water push against the boat and the vibration of the motor. She could tell that she could make it do what she wanted if she could drive good. She turned the wheel first this way, then the other, the boat shifting its course with each gentle touch. She finally got the boat straight again and held the wheel with one finger.

"Homer, I have an idea," Pearl said. "Not today, but maybe in the near future. Think if we tied lines and hooks on those life jackets and then spaced them, oh ten feet apart or so, like a trot line? Think we could hook a Tarpon?"

"If tarpons are running, we can hook them," he replied, looking over at her, then letting his gaze follow the length of her legs, not for the first time today.

"If we could snag one on a life jacket, all we'd have to do is follow it until the fish gives out," Pearl said. She noticed he was not looking at her face. "Homer," she scolded. She flashed him a warning with her narrow green eyes.

He blinked, took out his old white handkerchief and wiped his nose. "What'd be the point? The whole idea behind tarpon fishing is to fight with it for hours and entertain the hell out of serious fishermen."

"I'm just thinking it might be fun for some of our less experienced clientele. Make things easy like those hunting plantations do. They get bragging rights, you get a good tip."

"Yes ma'am, that oughta work. Hell, it might be damned fun, chasing them life jackets all over the Gulf. Course, getting a whole tarpon aboard is a whole other thing. A damn hammerhead will follow a line with a fish on it, and damned if they don't eat the thing before you can get the gaff hook in it. Either way, though, it'd make a helluva fish story for one them congressmen."

They arrived at a spot Homer said he knew for sure had good fishing. He shut off the engine and they drifted. "Once we get hooks in the water," Pearl told her children, "Homer will drive the boat at a slow speed, trolling for whatever is gonna bite today." All but Abby had their lines in the water. "I'll mess with her line," Pearl told Homer. "You get us moving."

When Homer tried to restart the *Miss Happiness*, nothing happened. Grinding. Groaning. Diesel smoke. But the engine did not start. He looked at Pearl. She looked at him, trying to decipher what was going on. Her face registered concern.

"Hang on," Homer said. "Just a minute." He retrieved his tool box from where it was stowed under the bench. He tinkered and tried to start it again. Nothing. More tinkering. More non-starting. "Damn," he said, mostly to himself. "Pearl, I think the crankshaft is broke."

"Can you fix it?" she asked?

"Probably. But not out here. We gonna need towed in." Homer got on the ship-to-shore radio and called the Coast Guard.

The Coast Guard base was within five miles and a towboat arrived within the hour. The captain of the rescue boat scolded Homer, telling him his passengers should be in life jackets in this situation. "You're lucky, folks, you've got water smooth as a mirror." Within a short while, the crew of the Coast Guard vessel had fixed a line to the bow of the *Miss Happiness*. In less than an hour they were back in their berth at the marina.

"You get your ass up in that engine compartment and get my boat fixed," Pearl told Homer. He wasted no time and soon had tools spread out and engine parts coming off. Pearl sat on the barge dock with an open can of sea-foam green paint next to her and a one-inch brush in her hand. She painted green over the white letters, first the "s" at the end of "miss," then "piness." And in less time than it took to unbolt a valve cover and lay it aside, Pearl had renamed her boat the *Mis Hap*.

"Renaming a boat is bad luck," Homer told her.

"No, what's going to be bad luck is what happens to you if you don't get my boat going," she said. "And bring that paint, and brush off the dock when you come." Pearl turned and went toward the Inn.

Homer had the engine running within a week, and over the summer the *Mis Hap* became a popular fishing charter boat. Homer earned a reputation for knowing where the fish ran, what was in season, and how to catch them. Pearl's guests and fishing charter parties were happy with her captain. He told Pearl his tips were more money than he'd had in his pants before. "When they offer me a beer, I tell them no," Homer revealed to Pearl. He did not tell her that if they offered again, he did not refuse, reckoning such to be bad manners and maybe even bad luck.

Big Chiefs

$\mathcal{L}$ate one afternoon, after a long day of fishing, soused and badly sunburned, Homer came to the Inn looking for Abby. He couldn't find her in the usual places, so he stumbled down to the beach. She was playing with the hermit crabs when he walked up behind her.

"Hey, baby doll. You been missin' me while I been a captain at sea?" Homer found himself funny and laughed. Abby, for her part, had hoped he might drown out on the *Mis Hap*. On most nights, she would go to McAllister's house, have greens and cornbread for dinner and climb into bed with McAllister's children. The shortage of beds meant some of the boys had to sleep with the girls. In order to make room, they lined up side-by-side rather than the normal up and down. Skin-to-skin, sweating in the summer night, Abby was happy. This night, she had not left the beach early enough to avoid Captain Homer's homecoming.

"Come on, baby doll," he said to her. "My tips is real good today and I'm gonna take you on an adventure! We'll take some of McAllister young'uns, too. I see if Matt wants to come." Abby ignored him, moving one hermit crab over here, made a pile of sand over there, playing a game in her mind. "Get your ass up, girl. We goin' on a fun trip. You don't want to make me mad, do you?"

Abby got up and climbed up the rocks. Homer walked up the pavement to the marine shop and found Matt. "Hey, son," Homer yelled to Matt who was busy fiddling with one of the diesel tanks that filled the boats. "We going on a little trip. You wanna go? We could take your car."

"Not tonight," Matt answered, finishing the job at hand and wiping his hand on a grease cloth. "It's date night for me!"

About that time, Jessie and Robert, two of McAllister's

133

sons, came out of the restaurant, their work day finished and a little pay day cash in their pockets. Homer was walking down to the parking lot to get his old truck when he saw them emerge from the building. "Hey boys, you wanna go to a real live juke-joint?" he yelled, his lips puckered out from lack of teeth.

"Naw, sir," answered Robert, the older of the two. "Them rednecks would kill us for sure." All three laughed as the boys kicked at the sand.

"Not so long as you with me," Homer responded. "You be all right."

The boys looked at each other and grinned. "Okay, give us a few minutes to clean up. We riding in the back of your truck?"

"We can all cram into the front, I think," Homer answered. "Abby, go get a dress on. Something cute so I can show you off."

"Jessie," Abby called as Jessie was walking toward his house. "See if Cindy can come."

Within minutes, Homer, Robert, Jessie, Cindy, and Abby were crammed into the front seat of Homer's battered old truck.

"Homer, this seat is jabbing me," Jessie complained as he shifted around, trying to find a spot where the plastic covering of the seat was not torn and jagged. Homer ignored the complaint. "It's too crowded in here, too. Maybe me and Robert ought to ride in the back?"

"Nah. It's not that far. Plus, I'm teaching Abby to drive," Homer said, glancing at the other children. "She can sit in my lap, give you a little more room. Don't worry, I be holding the wheel. I'm just letting her get a feel for it. Come on over here, baby. Sit in Uncle Homer's lap for your driving lesson." Abby moved over, out of Robert's lap, across Jessie and Cindy and into Homer's lap, her small hands taking hold of the steering wheel.

They drove for a long time, off the peninsular, but not as far as Foley. Homer turned left and then right. They were on a bumpy dirt road, the muddy potholes full of water from a recent shower. Jessie and Robert were laughing, exaggerating the bouncing, banging into each other side to side. Cindy was squealing as her brothers bumped into her. The truck slowed down and the hooting and hollering and playful mayhem came to a stop as the kids looked around them. They were all paying attention as the battered old truck swung into the grassy parking lot of a low slung, army green building. A huge bonfire was burning in the back of the building, men standing around it as if it were winter and they needed warmth.

There were two doors into the building, one marked WHITES, the other said COLORED. The boys held Cindy's hand and headed for the door that said COLORED. Once inside the separate doors, no matter which door you came in, there was one big room, with pool tables and bar stools lined up in front of a long polished bar and odds and ends of chairs along the outer walls, allowing room for a make-shift dance floor in the middle. A jukebox blared country music from the corner.

"Welcome to Big Chief's," Homer announced, once everyone was inside. "Here's where we have some beer, play a little pool. Have some fun." He lifted Abby up onto a leather-topped barstool, swung Cindy up on a stool on one side of Abby and took a seat on the other side of Abby. Lining the bar were tattooed white men in dirty tee shirts and women with heavy painted eyebrows and thick lipstick that smeared with each cigarette. Big Chief's fell quiet when the crew first walked in, but only for a moment. The raucous laughter and endless chatter resumed. The top of Abby's seat was cracked with age and use. It was brittle, scratching her behind. "Y'all relax. Ain't no rules in here. Ain't no law in here," Homer announced.

Homer told the bartender that everything the kids wanted was on his tab. "This here is my girlfriend," he told the bartender, pointing to Abby, but not calling her by name. "And she and her little friend needs a beer. So do them boys," he said, pointing at Jessie and Robert who were standing next to one of the pool tables, looking around the place.

Cindy looked at Abby. "I ain't never had a beer," she whispered. "Daddy might whup me first and then Mr. Homer."

"I'm surprised your daddy let you come," Abby answered. "But, I sure am glad."

"Daddy wadn't home," Cindy replied. "Mamma said it was okay, though." The girls chuckled, knowing Bessie would say yes to anything.

135

Homer grabbed his beer bottle and crawled off the bar-stool. "You girls sit right here while I go outside and see what's going on with everybody. Don't worry. You safe in here. Get whatever you want. They make hamburgers if you hungry." He walked out of the door. Abby and Cindy ordered a Coke and split a hamburger, their beer sitting on the counter getting warm. Homer spent the whole night drinking beer and stand-ing around the bonfire while Robert and Jessie drank beer and shot endless games of pool. Some people were dancing, and the noise in the joint grew louder as it got later. Stumbling, Homer came in and herded his group back outside and into the truck. Robert and Jessie elected to sit in the back bed of the truck.

"We gots to get home, else Miss Pearl gonna have my hide," Uncle Homer said, slurring, his eyes sleepy-looking. "But, now Baby, you done been to yore first honky-tonk," he said to Abby. "I guess it's your first juke-joint, too, eh, little one?" he asked Cindy. She nodded her head.

A few miles from the fort, the old truck just died. Homer muttered something as his passengers were ordered to get out and push. The moon was high and a pale yellow, casting bright light on the road ahead. Abby jumped to one side, al-most stepping on an injured crow on the road. She fell away from pushing for a moment and scooped up the bird to bring it home. The crow put up a bit of a struggle, but quickly set-tled heavily into Abby's hands. She caught up to the truck and put the bird into the truck-bed, hoping her mother could help it live. She thought of the longer wing feathers of the crow as she touched the skinny feather dangling near her ear. The bartender had taken it from a vase at Big Chief's and one of the waitresses had carefully bobby-pinned it into her short hair. She was barefoot and found the blacktop still warm from the day's sun. They finally pushed the truck into the marina parking lot, right up to the recently installed gas pump. Uncle Homer filled the truck, and it started right off. The crow was dead and Abby put it on the damp sand at the edge of the parking lot.

"I'm gonna teach you to drive this truck," Uncle Homer announced to Abby. "We gotta get these kids home and you gonna drive." Abby didn't answer, knowing driving meant she had to sit in his lap. She felt queasy.

Robert and Jessie had sobered up from pushing the truck down the road. "Hey, she might kill us just a few feet from our house," laughed Jessie. He and Robert climbed back into the truck bed while Cindy and Abby got in the front seat. "We can walk home," yelled Robert from the back.

"Naw. Sit tight while Abby gets a real lesson. I won't let her wreck," Homer said, his head hanging out of the driver's side window while he talked to the boys.

Abby reluctantly climbed into Uncle Homer's lap, ready for her new driving lesson. Holding it straight ahead should be easy, she thought. But when they came to the curve just past Officer's Row, Homer's hand popped up and swerved the truck back on the road. "You was headed straight for them rocks," Homer said. Abby was embarrassed. She could hear the boys hooting in the back. Cindy had fallen asleep in the seat next to her. Abby felt the swelling underneath her bottom and dreaded dropping off the children.

When they got to McAllister's house, Abby slid out of Homer's lap and gently shook Cindy awake. She heard the boys laughing in the back, teasing her about the near miss at the curve. They climbed out of the truck and came up to the window on the driver's side.

"Thanks, Mr. Homer," Robert said leaning in the window, Jessie standing to the side and back of him, shaking his head yes. "That was good fun. Don't tell our daddy we drank beer, though." Robert picked up Cindy and all three went into the little unlit house. It was late.

With Abby's driving lesson over for the night, Homer turned the truck around and headed towards the Inn. Abby tucked herself into the corner of the truck at the passenger door and dropped her head. She saw Uncle Boyd's big black car in the shelled lot of the Inn as she and Uncle Homer walked to her room in the center of the hotel.

Second Summer of Business

Pearl was thrilled that summer was here and that business had not only resumed but seemed to be better than last year. The marina was finished and almost full of boats, some planning on docking for the year. The air strip was paved, and rooms at the Inn were booked. The cauldrons full of oil-soaked rags lit up the air strip at night, and Pearl herself was alight with pleasure and pride in her Inn. Orchids bloomed in the driftwood tree in the dining room and more and more fishnet showed up on the walls of the ballroom. Abby's penny fairy fountain pens sold at a fast pace keeping her busy removing the backbones of squid. McAllister was glad that he had someone to do that tedious job.

Uncle Boyd's sons came to the Inn on a regular basis. Abby was relieved that Ham's family joined him most of the time. He had found only one other occasion to take Abby aside, and a beachcomber had almost caught them. Uncle Boyd's chubby grandson ordered hamburgers and French fries every lunch and dinner, then drowned them in a blanket of thick red catsup. McAllister reminded Pearl he was not a fry cook.

"McAllister, hush," Pearl ordered. "Boyd's grandchildren certainly get whatever they want. You're just getting uppity," She turned on her heel and stomped out of the kitchen. The heels of her pumps made a clicking noise on the hardwood floors giving McAllister, and anyone else around, notice that she was approaching.

"I sho' don't like that word or tone," McAllister said to Abby, who sat on a stool next to the black phone, all set to be the receptionist for the day.

"What does uppity mean?" Abby asked McAllister. This was one of the few times that McAllister was not smiling, so Abby knew the word must be bad.

"It means too big for my britches," McAllister answered. "But to me, it means something a lot worse. Now what you wanna eat, chile of my heart?"

"Did Mamma hurt your feelings?" Abby asked.

"No, honey. She just made me remember where I am." McAllister tried but could not put on his happy face for Abby.

"What do you mean?" Abby wanted to know.

"Aw, nothing for you to worry about at your age. Just times and place. Das all. Just grown-up stuff. Now, I ain't got all day. What you wanna eat?"

Abby was full of broiled flounder and boiled red potatoes that McAllister had seasoned with butter and parsley. After her lunch, she was feeling lazy and wandered out to her spot on the rock seawall and watched her sisters jump off the top of the Governor's yacht, squealing as they hit the water. Abby wondered if they, too, had to keep secrets. She was afraid to ask. Abby was thinking back on what her mother had told them about the Governor.

"The Governor is a private, but lonesome, man," Pearl had explained to her children. "He's so busy running the State that when he comes down here, he just wants to relax. Soaking in the salt water out in the bay is good for his arthritis, too. He likes to stay on his boat. If he comes inside, he has to meet and greet everybody, everyone wants a picture with him. He gets enough of that in Montgomery."

The governor almost always arrived by boat. Sometimes Uncle Boyd came in his big black car, but occasionally Matt had to pick him up in a little speed boat that Pearl acquired just for that purpose. When the call came, Matt climbed into the boat and made the run to pick up Uncle Boyd over at Dauphin Island, just across the bay.

"I like driving that speed boat," Matt told Abby. "It's like flying, bouncing over the waves in the bay. I'll ask Mamma if I can take you for a ride. You won't believe what it feels like racing across the wake from the cargo ships!" Abby learned how to time Matt's return and often waited on the dock for him. She never noticed a Mrs. Uncle Boyd and wondered if he was married. Sometimes she wondered if her mother was his girlfriend.

Uncle Boyd stepped onto the dock this morning, his thin hair standing up and blown every which way from the boat ride over. "Why, hello there, little Abby. You must be the secret ingredient here!" Abby looked at the smiling Uncle Boyd as he looked around the marina. "Just as I predicted. A full marina and an airstrip full of planes. Full!" he shouted. "This marina packing them in. Important, I mean important people, fishing for the first time ever. First time. Damned clever idea, those life jackets dragging tarpons around. Damned clever."

Abby left the dock while Matt showed Uncle Boyd the marine store. She walked back to the Inn and into the kitchen to say good morning to McAllister. She went through the swinging door and bumped right into Homer with a hard thud. She thought he had a fishing excursion, but here he was, standing right in front of her.

"I took me a little break, little one," he said, cutting his eyes toward McAllister. He fidgeted, as though he didn't want to be seen making his move on Abby. He put a hand on her shoulder and nudged her around and back out the door. Homer guided her straight to the center room.

McAllister shook his head as Homer and Abby exited the kitchen. "That's enough. I can't stand this anymore," McAllister said, throwing the potato peeler he had in his hand into the metal sink. The peeler bounced, clanging each time it hit the metal sink. He walked over to the desk and picked up the phone book. After flipping through a few pages, he picked up the receiver and dialed. "This gonna cost me my job," he said to himself while listening to the phone ring on the other end. "Hello?" he asked when someone finally picked up the phone.

Buddy

In her bedroom, Abby hypnotized herself by staring at the shapes and colors on the bedroom wall made by the light through the blinds. She saw tobacco juice stains and peeling wall paint. Her mind transformed them into images with all sorts of exotic places, castles with moats full of alligators and armed guards.

After Homer left, Abby lay in the dirty bed. She had always loved clean, soft sheets. None of it mattered to her anymore. She sat up cross-legged on the bed, peeling off sun-baked skin on her arms, when she heard footsteps at the bottom of the stairs. She heard the footsteps come up the steps, then down the hall. She held her breath as the door to her bedroom quietly opened.

"Hello," said a strange man, entering her bedroom. He stood in front of her, the door still ajar. "My name is Buddy. I took a ride down here on my motorcycle to see you."

"You better git out, mister," Abby yelled.

"I won't hurt you." His voice was gentle and convincing.

Abby's shoulders dropped as she relaxed a little, still curious, still cautious. He smelled of fresh soap, his black hair was shiny and windblown. He wore a tee shirt with a pack of cigarettes rolled up in the left sleeve and had tattoos on both arms. He took out his wallet and put his index finger over his lips, motioning her to be quiet. He flipped the black wallet open and showed her a shiny, star-shaped badge. Abby's eyes grew big and she could not have given him her name had he asked. He reached behind him, closing the door, slowly and quiet.

"It's okay," he said softly. "You are safe with me."

"Are you the police?" Abby barely whispered.

"Of a sort. May I sit by you?"

Abby nodded and the man sat on the side of the bed. He looked around at the scene in the room, beer cans and cigarette butts on the floor and the window sills, on the dresser tops. The walls were dingy and stained, the bed sheets filthy.

"The man who just left? Who is that?" Buddy asked.

"He's my mamma's hired man. I'm supposed to do whatever he tells me and if I don't he might kill my brother. He even said he'd hurt my dog."

"Does he do bad things to you?" Buddy asked gently.

Abby nodded slowly. She could feel a strange release, as if the secret had seeped out of her skin like sweat on a July day. Tears poured from her eyes. She hid her eyes behind her dirty hands and the tears made streaks on her smudged face.

"It's okay. You can cry. You want a hug?" He slowly slipped his hand around her shoulders.

She edged over next to him and leaned against his shoulder. Abby felt like a child in the comfort of this man, almost like she'd become a baby again. He gently swayed from side to side, the way the breeze moved the sea oats. Abby felt like she was being rocked in a cradle.

"Shhh. It's okay. The man who hurts you is not going to do that again," he assured her as he continued to rock and soothe her. "Does your mother know that he does bad things to you?"

"He says she does. I don't really know," Abby said weakly. She wanted to be strong and tough, but it was not working. She cleared her froggy voice and said, "I don't know if Uncle Boyd knows about Uncle Ham, either. He makes me keep a secret, too."

"Boyd Grantham, the congressman? Did I see him when I pulled in?" Buddy asked.

"Yes sir."

"Hmph. Well, I am going to make sure the good congressman sees me," he said, looking toward the window, as if he wasn't talking to Abby. He turned to face her. "Would you like to see my motorcycle?"

"Yes Sir. But you won't tell anybody what I told you?"

"No, but honey, I promise you. This isn't right, and it comes to a stop now."

"How can you make it stop if you don't tell anybody?" Abby asked, standing up. She remembered she only had on her underwear, and pulled the sheet from the bed to cover herself.

Buddy, smiled. "You're a quick one, young lady. But you can leave the police work to me. Don't you worry one bit."

Abby ran into the bathroom, put on the sun suit she wore yesterday and washed her hands and face. She wished for a shower, but this would have to do, and she came out of the dingy bathroom. "Okay, Mr. Buddy. Let's go see your motorcycle. I never been on a motorcycle. Can you take me for a ride?"

"Not this time, but I'll be back. When I come back, I will take you for a ride."

As they walked out to the parking lot where the bike was parked, Abby asked if she could touch the freshly polished, shiny black motorcycle. It had lots of shiny metal and strings hanging out of the handle bars. Mr. Buddy was looking in the direction of Uncle Boyd, who was looking at the two of them. Abby became nervous. "Am I going to get in trouble?" she asked. She tried not to move her lips.

"Not at all," Buddy said. "I will be back, and you are not to worry. If somebody asks who I am, you say you don't know, but that I showed you a badge." He straddled his motorcycle. "You especially tell that hired man." She nodded, and he patted her on the shoulder. Abby watched as he cranked his motorcycle and drove away. She saw Uncle Boyd, who was standing on the front porch, turn to watch him go.

Pearl also watched the man on the motorcycle ride away. She stood next to the walk-in cooler on the back porch. She looked at Uncle Homer and said, "You're going to have to tell your biker friends to be more discreet coming down here."

"I ain't never seen that man in my life," Homer said.

Pearl crooked her right eyebrow, opened the screened door and peered out into the road, trying to get a second look at the man and the motorcycle. But Buddy was long gone. She hoped for good.

Abby kept her eye on Uncle Boyd, and as she watched him head for the Inn, she suddenly saw her mother there on the porch with Homer. She snuck toward a clump of oleander bushes. She stopped behind the bush and squatted down to watch through the branches and leaves.

Her mother met Uncle Boyd at the top of the stairs, and

seemed about to greet him with a hug, when he pointed off in the direction of the retreating motorcycle. He also motioned in the direction of Homer. They all then turned and looked to where Abby had stood. Abby could tell there was something going on that looked like fussing. Uncle Boyd did most of the talking. Her mother took over and stood right in front of Homer to say something. Abby could only see part of Homer's face, but it was squeezed into a frown, and he shrugged and shook his head.

Pearl left the two men and came quickly across the yard in the direction of where Abby hid. She slid farther back in the bush, but her mother must have spied her.

"Young lady! You stop right there," Pearl yelled. "I see you spying, as usual."

Abby's heart raced and her mind tumbled. The man said she should say he had a badge. But that was it. Abby could not think how she supposed to answer questions. She almost teared up, but shook her head and squeezed them away. She had to be big now. Her mother was closing in fast.

"Abby, who was that man?" Pearl demanded.

"He said his name was Buddy," she said, trying to hold her voice steady.

"What did he want?" Pearl was now within arm's reach. Abby decided to lie.

"He didn't say. I was just going up to my room when he caught up with me on the porch. He asked me if I was Abigail. And I told him yes and asked him who he was. He said Buddy. Then," Abby cleared her throat, "he got in a hurry it seemed like. He said he was out riding his motorcycle and I asked him if I could have a ride on it. He said I can some other time."

"So, why the hell were you out in the yard with this stranger, then?" Pearl bent closer in her direction.

"I asked the man if I could look at his motorcycle up close, and he said I could. I thought, since he knew my name and all, he was a friend of yours. Or Uncle Homer." Abby made her muscles hard for the next part. "He said I could come look at his motorcycle if I would tell you and Uncle Homer that he showed me a star in his wallet. I think he's pretty proud of it."

"What the hell are you talking about? I don't understand what you're telling me, Abby."

"The man took out his wallet when I asked him to see his

motorcycle." Abby spoke very slowly. "He opened it up and showed me a gold star pinned inside it. Then I asked him if he was the police and he said, 'You just tell the hired man and your mother that you saw this star. That's all you gotta say, and I will let you look at my motorcycle'."

"Did he say he was coming back?"

"Yes, ma'am."

"When?"

"He didn't tell me that. But he said I could ride his motorcycle next time. Can I ride it, Mamma?"

"Damn it!" Pearl said, and started walking back and forth. Abby could not tell what she was saying to herself. She stopped right in front of Abby. "If that man ever so much as rides by this place, you let me know. You hear me, young lady? And you better not ever say another word to him or I will give you a whipping like you have never seen. And don't you dare go running down to tell Mr. Axil!"

As her mamma stomped away, almost losing her balance in the sand, Abby wondered what would happen now. Something was coming. But what? She watched her mother walk over to Uncle Boyd and watched as Uncle Boyd threw his hands in the air. They were talking back and forth but Abby couldn't hear a word. Uncle Homer was standing behind them, his head hung down, his sailor cap in his hand.

Chumming

The summer was busy with customers driving, flying and boating in. Uncle Boyd's grandchildren were regulars. His grandson, the fat one that ate all the hamburgers with the piles of catsup, seemed to get meaner each time he came. He tried to catch what was left of the cats in the rock wall and told Abby that as soon as he caught one, he was gonna chop its tail off.

"You got my ass rolling in the bunk on that boat, you did," Homer told Abby on the dock. She stepped backwards from him while he yelled. "Go on, just git! I ain't finished with you, little one. I ain't scared of no cop." Homer turned his back to her and Abby watched him storm off. Who'd have thought a little star could cause all this trouble, she wondered to herself. She also wondered if she could get one when she got big. She'd try to remember to ask Mr. Buddy about that when he came back. Abby didn't care what Uncle Homer said. It's what he didn't do that mattered to her, and since Mr. Buddy had been here, things had changed.

She walked from the marina down to the Inn. Her sisters were whizzing through the restaurant with trays on their arms, smiling and greeting customers, taking orders, delivering food. McAllister was in the kitchen, food sizzling and slung onto trays. Abby finally found her mother out on the back porch off the kitchen.

"Mamma, the fat boy, you know, Uncle Boyd's grandson? The mean one? Well, he says there's gonna be a fishing rodeo and they have a junior's division. Can I be in the rodeo?"

"Abby, I do not have time for this right now," Pearl said, rushing past on her way to the convention ball room. "Did you see that the Sugar Shack has new palmetto leaves? So pretty. I am just about ready for my first big political get-together."

146

Abby did not try to hide her pouty face. "But, Mamma," she sang back.

"Mamma nothing. Just go do something. You know full well how to do that. Now go. And call him Gregory, not the fat boy!" Pearl said over her shoulder, trotting away.

Bored, Abby wandered back down to the marina. She had seen Mr. Axil with a row of tourists in a line behind him and knew he was busy, too. Uncle Homer and Matt were down at marina, Homer washing the *Mis Hap*. Matt helped customers get all the supplies they would need for the fishing trip. Beer and ice seemed to be the best sellers, Abby thought, as Matt rung the register every few minutes. Abby went out on the dock, looking to make sure the boards over the big holes were still secured. They were. Matt had given her that job at the dock.

"Uncle Homer," Abby called as she climbed aboard the *Mis Hap*. "Gregory says there's gonna be a fishing rodeo. I sure want to be in it. Can you help me? Do you know how it works?"

"Whichun's Gregory?" Uncle Homer asked. "And why would I want to help you? You done got me in big trouble."

"He's the fat boy. Do you know about fishing rodeos?" Abby asked. Then, feeling sassy these days, she added, "And you'll help me because it's your job." She held her breath for just a minute when he glared up at her, his eyes saying what his mouth couldn't.

"Well, yes *ma'am*, I happen to know a little about fishing rodeos, your highness. First, we gotta get you a fishing hole chummed." Uncle Homer said while bent over at the engine compartment.

"What's chummed?"

"Well, you about to find out. We go out near the shipping channel where the big channel cats live. Then, we throw in chum ... rotten fish, meat that went bad, just about anything McAllister can give us out of the kitchen. Fish guts and innards and heads and all the parts McAllister ain't using. Dump it in the water ever day." He lifted his head out of the engine compartment and looked at Abby.

"Matt's gonna go with us," Abby said defiantly. "Just as soon as he's finished with his customers."

"He can come. I's gonna ask to borry his little boat anyway. You know, catfish eat anything. Go tell McAllister what we're doing and that we gonna need his garbage for a few weeks or so. Maybe he still has some from today and we can get started."

"Idn't that cheating? Feeding the fish and fattening them up?" Abby asked.

"Naw, it is fair. I suspect everybody does it."

Abby ran up and glanced in Matt's store. He looked over the register at her and raised his eyebrows, a silent question. Abby raised one finger and mouthed "I'll be right back." She ran down to the Inn and raided McAllister's basket of scraps that he kept next to one of the big stoves. She snuck into the walk-in freezer and grabbed a whole chicken and some bones, hoping McAllister might not miss them. She had a sack full of garbage by the time she was back at the marina. Matt's store was empty and he was outside with the water hose, washing down his car mats. "Matt, Uncle Homer said he'll take me out to chum the fish so I can be in the fishing rodeo. But I want you to come. Besides, he needs to use your little boat, anyway."

"Okay," Matt said. "Let me lock up and put up a sign. We won't be gone that long." Matt wasn't sure why, but his mother had told him to make sure that Homer was not around Abby alone, and this seemed like one of those times to him. After closing the small store, Matt started the little motor boat and they sped out to the channel. It was as close as Abby had been to the cargo ships.

"Is it safe being this close to them?" Abby held on to the side of the boat. "They make big waves and we are in a little boat."

"The closer we are to them," Homer said, sighing like she had asked a stupid question, "the smaller the waves are gonna be. Now you *know* your big brother wouldn't take you up this close if it wadn't safe." Homer glanced at Matt, wondering what he might know. "Blue marks the spot," Homer said, as he splashed a bright blue buoy into the water with an anchor attached. The boat rocked back and forth as the ship waves hit it. "This is the fishing hole. Where we do the chumming. Dump everything in that sack right over the edge, right here."

Chumming the hole became a daily exercise. Most of the time, Matt took her out to the blue marker which was okay with Abby. Every morning she hurried down to help Mr. Axil hang the flags. Then she ran up to the dock while it was still too early for hung-over congressmen to fish. Homer had little to say. If he had to take her, he kept his distance. He slowed the boat and circled up near the buoy. Abby emptied the garbage sack.

McAllister had started leaving extra things in the walk-in for her morning collection. "That rodeo is less than a month away, girl," McAllister told her, "and I wants the fattest channel cat ever caught brung right here to my kitchen. You just think you had something good to eat so far. You catch me that fish and I show you what good eatin' is."

Two Catches, One Day

Rodeo day was here. Abby and Pearl were at the judge's stands under the big tents, filling in the paperwork when Pearl ran into an old friend. A man of course, thought Abby. Abby watched as Pearl smiled and flirted, twirling her hair around her ringless ring finger. Abby was relieved that at least Homer was down at the boat, getting the rod, reel and bait ready.

"We ain't chumming the fish for the last two days," Homer had told her. "That way, they be good and hungry by the time you drop your bait."

Abby jumped and twirled around, counting the minutes until cast off. She was trying to contain herself, but the excitement overrode her behavior. Finally, Homer motioned for her to come get on the boat and Pearl bid her friend good-by. After the judge went through the list of what to do and what not to do over the bull horn, they were ready to go. Abby saw Gregory, the fat boy, get on a small but fancy boat with more fishing equipment than Abby knew existed. He shot her a bratty smile and a thumbs up. Homer gathered some last few supplies. He was sullen, as he had not been around Abby alone since the man with the star had been to the Inn. Buddy still had not come back, but the trick about telling Homer about his star sure worked. Homer had not been near Abby.

"This gonna cost you, little one," Homer said in a low voice as Abby climbed on the boat. She looked to see if her mother had heard him, disappointed to see Pearl still dallying around on the dock with the gentleman friend.

"Hurry, Mamma," Abby yelled. "It's time to go!"

It took what felt like a life time to Abby to reach the chummed hole. Homer had pulled up the buoy on the last trip out to chum just in case someone might see their hole. Abby was not sure he even knew where the fishing hole was without the marker. Finally, Homer circled the boat and dropped anchor. "It's all up to you, now," Homer said to her, reaching into the cooler for a beer. Pearl sat on the top deck, her shoestring strapped dress blowing in the wind. Pearl, showing off the *Mis Hap*, made her the fishing vessel today. As other boats went by, headed out to deeper waters, Pearl waved and the other boaters waved back, sometimes blowing a horn.

Abby's first cast was a disaster, going only a few feet out, the sinker tangling up in the fishing line and wrapping around the end of the rod. The faster she tried to get it untangled, the slower the project went. The judges had distinctly instructed that adults were not to help the contestants and she saw Uncle Homer swig his beer and sneer at her. Finally, her line straightened out, she cast again. Perfect. Plunk, right into the spot into which she aimed. The large sinker took the line down to the bottom where the cat fish were. Instantly, she had a nibble, then a bite. She could feel the weight on her pole and excitedly brought up her first catch, a middle sized cat, but not big enough to win a thing.

"Now unhook him like I showed you," Homer yelled above the wind. "Put them gloves on and don't let him stick you or you done for the day."

Abby carefully unhooked the fish, covering the needle fin from his top side with the thick leather glove Homer had given her. She kept an eye on the side fins, too, just as sharp and painful as the one on top. She threw the fish into an icy bath in the cooler, saving all catches for McAllister. She cast a few more times and each one caught a hungry cat fish, none quite as large as she wanted. With them all in the cooler, even if she didn't catch anything bigger, she had some pretty good choices and McAllister had enough cat fish to cook for a large lunch crowd.

"Uncle Homer," Abby yelled. "What else we got for bait? They biting the shrimp, but I'm not catching the big ones. We have anything larger and stinkier?"

Homer came over, dug through the ice chest, careful not to get stuck by one of a dozen catfish that lay half frozen in the chest. He pulled out some chicken parts McAllister had given him this morning but threw them back in the cooler. Then he grabbed the smallest catfish of the bunch, knocked it on the head with his knife, cut off the head, and then chopped it up into large pieces, pulling away the leather-like silver skin. "Here," he said. "Maybe they like catfish!" He laughed at his own joke as Abby reached for the biggest piece and threaded it on her hook. She decided to thread on some of the entrails Homer had left in a bloody pile on the floor of the boat. She spat on it for good measure, like she had seen the fishermen at the pier do. She made sure the parts were as secure as they could be so the fish wouldn't steal the bait. "That oughta do it," she said to Homer. She glanced up at her mother. Pearl's eyes were closed, her face turned up to the sun.

They had hours left before judging would begin, but Abby was in a hurry. By this time, the water in the fishing hole was churning and moving, the catfish awake and aware it was feeding time. Abby cast her special concoction of bait and watched as the line sunk right in the center of the swirling, hungry fish at the surface. She reeled a little, pulling the rod back with each reel to keep the slack out of her line. Then it struck. The tip of her rod bent way over and she started reeling and pulling, making sure the fish didn't get off because of too much slack. "Uncle Homer," she screamed. "I think I got a big one! Look at my pole!"

"Just keep the slack out of your line." Homer was smiling, the first time he had felt cheerful since that SOB Buddy had shown up. "Just keep pulling and reeling in you line." He moved over close to where she was standing, the rod propped on her belly, her arm going back and forth, reeling and pulling, reeling and pulling.

"Uncle Homer, get the net!" she screamed. "It's big and I don't want to lose him!"

Pearl had come to life, hearing all of the excitement and came down the ladder from the upper deck. "Good Girl," she yelled.

It took Abby at least fifteen minutes, maybe more, moving from side to side of the rear deck, making sure the tip of her rod stayed up, before she had her catch aboard. The fish fought hard, first stealing line that made a whir sound as the line went out, Abby reeling him back in. Her arms were beginning to tremble. Finally, the fish broke the water's surface and she reeled as fast as she could, Uncle Homer standing by to slip the net under him.

"Abby, I do believe that's the biggest catfish I've ever

seen," Pearl said, laughing and clapping. "Homer, don't you lose him, now."

"I got him," Homer said, bringing the net up to the deck, the fish flopping around, Homer, Pearl and Abby all hopping around to avoid the big needle fin sticking out of his head.

"Mamma! Look!" Abby was beside herself. The fish, long since out of the net, continued its dance across the deck of the boat when Abby stepped up and put her foot on his tail. "It makes the rest of them look like babies," she said with a huge smile on her sunburned face. She already had her hands in Homer's big gloves and covered the fins while she worked the hook out. "This fish swallowed this hook," she announced as she jiggled and pulled at it. When the hook came out, the bait, except for the guts, was still intact. "It was the guts that did it!" she happily announced.

Satisfied that she had caught the biggest catfish in the entire bay, she plopped down on a deck chair. Pearl handed her an ice cold Coke and they smiled at each other. Homer was raising the anchor and yelled "Land, Ho!"

Abby could hardly wait to get to the judges table where the big scales sat in wait. On the trip back to the docks, she kept getting up and going over to the ice chest to look at her prize. It was more than three times the size of the other fish. "Thanks, Uncle Homer, for helping me chum."

Homer pointed the boat in the direction of Dauphin Island and they motored back to the docks. He was drinking another beer, but Pearl hadn't said a word about it. He docked the *Mis Hap,* and Abby plunged her hands into the icy water to retrieve her fish. As she lugged her heavy haul toward the judging station, she looked at the board behind the judge's desk and noticed quite a few people had turned in their catches, each category of fish having its own column. Alligator Gar, Amberjack, Black Drum, Catfish-Channel, Catfish-white. The list went on and on, many of the fish she'd never even heard of. But there was a category for each one.

"Mister, here's my fish," Abby said, still several feet from the judge's table. It was so heavy she was dragging it through the sand. She was having a hard time getting it from the boat to the judges' table. Her hand and part of her arm were stuffed in the fish's mouth. The judge was laughing as she grunted, trying to swing, and then pushing, the huge catfish up on the table. "I'm registered and everything. My name is Abigail Delaney Whitney, but people call me Abby. And here's my catch!" Abby was panting from hauling her fish up to the table.

"Miss Abby, you got yourself a beauty there. Now, we gotta go over to the table and slice him open. You musta been fishing in the bay. Ain't no catfish this big in the Gulf. Follow me, so you can make sure there's no hanky-panky when I weigh your fish," said the tall judge. He still had a big smile on his face as he approached the next table.

"This little girl has caught herself a channel cat," he announced to the man at the other table. "Before we weigh it, let's cut him open."

"Why are you cutting him open?" Abby was worried. "What about all the blood he'll lose. Won't that make him lighter?"

Both men threw their heads back and laughed. Abby could see a gold tooth right in the top of one man's mouth. The one with the knife took a swig of beer. "Honey, he won't lose much. Not enough to affect the outcome. We have to make sure you ain't stuffed no weights in his gullet. Believe it or not, some people try to cheat!"

Abby, Pearl, and Homer stood by to watch the procedure. Abby frowned, wondering again if chumming was cheating and if she would get caught. But she had not stuffed any sinkers down the fish, though she was a little surprised her mother or Uncle Homer hadn't thought of it. The man with the curved knife sliced right into her fish's belly, pulled it opened and stuck his fingers up to the fish's throat.

"Abby, this is normal," Pearl said. "They do it to almost every fish that's brought in."

"Why don't they do it to all of them?" Abby asked. "It doesn't seem fair to pick and choose."

"Usually," answered one of the judges, "we can tell by the size of the fish if it's a contender or not. If not, if it's smaller than what we have in, we don't bother to cut it."

"Well, young lady," the judge proudly announced. "So far you are in first place with a whopping thirty-eight pounds, seven ounces. That's damned near the state record! Nice fish. Now you have to wait for all the others to bring in their fish. That'll be hard to beat, though," he said, smiling at the anxious child with chopped-off hair. He turned to the board behind him and entered 38lb 7oz next to the channel cat column.

154

People standing around clapped and Abby smiled. Someone took her picture.

Abby looked back at her mother to see if she had heard that so far, she was in first place. Pearl was smiling at her and was among the group clapping. Abby looked at her mother, pretty, dressed in a green sun dress that made her eyes seem even greener and her dark hair seem darker. By now, Pearl had a fishing hat on with a handful of lures hanging on the edge, sitting lopsided on her head, and was carrying on an animated conversation with a man in a blue judge's shirt, her hands flying up to her mouth, tucking her hair behind her ears.

Abby walked over and tugged on her mother's dress. "Abigail Delaney, I am so proud of you. I'd like you to meet Mister Caldwell. He's planning on coming over for a deep sea fishing excursion AND he's one of the judges!" Pearl winked at Abby. Silly, Abby thought. Her mother's flirtation wouldn't make her fish any bigger. Mister Caldwell said, "Well, it's near a state record, young lady. Somebody's gonna have a hard time beating that!"

"Now, here's money for a Coke. Go sit on the bench next to the weighing station so you can keep up!" She turned back to Mr. Caldwell, putting her hand lightly on his forearm.

Abby sat on the bench until the very last fish was weighed, her bottle of Coke long gone and the smell of fish clinging to her hair. She wondered how many showers she'd have to take to get rid of the stench. She showered every day these days, waiting for Mr. Buddy to come back. She wished he was here today, to see her big fish.

Just before the station was shuttered closed, fat Gregory ambled up, holding a catfish about the size of Abby's. Abby had her eyes on the judges. One judge winked at her and hauled the catfish over to the other table. The man with the knife sliced him open and crammed his fingers up the fish, just like he had done with hers. She looked at the clock on the wall and at the bucket where the fish were put for weighing. In plopped Gregory's fish. The needle on the scale swung back and forth as it settled into the final answer.

"Ladies and Gentlemen," called out judge number one. "We have a winner of the Young Angler's Rodeo." At least a dozen or more kids waited for the results. "At thirty-eight pounds, nine ounces, Mr. Gregory Grantham is our first place winner and Miss Abigail Whitney brings in a proud second place at thirty-eight pounds, seven ounces. That one was close! Good looking fish, young anglers! We hope to see you again next year." A grumble went around among the boys. Abby was the only girl. She shot a look over at Homer, the full understanding hitting her that he had chummed a hole for Gregory, too. Homer sent her an evil smile and took another swig of his beer.

Abby was not about to pout. She was proud to have won second place. After all, it was her first rodeo. She tugged on her mother's dress, again. Pearl was now cutting up a storm with another man. "Mamma, Uncle Homer chummed a hole for Gregory. I just know that he did!"

"Now, Abby, don't be a sore loser. You did really good coming in second," Pearl scolded. She accepted a glass of water from the man she'd been hanging on. The man ignored Abby's big news. She heard the man tell her mother that she was utterly fascinating.

Abby drug her fish down to the *Mis Hap*, tied and bobbing in the small harbor.

"I can't believe you did that, *Uncle* Homer," Abby sassed.

"I bet that little bastard stuffed lead down him," said Homer. "Them Grantham's gotta win at ever'thing. Bastards, all of 'em. I didn't do nothing to help him, I swear." He took another swig of another beer, smiled a puckered, toothless smile at Abby, and wandered over to crank the boat.

"Well, I promised McAllister I'd bring him the catfish for him to cook," Abby said, turning to go inside the lower salon to cool off. "And I don't believe you! The judge said it was almost a state record! How could there be two cat fish that big at the same place and same time? Got an answer for that, *Homer*?" It was the first time she had not called him Uncle.

"To hell with you. To hell with McAllister," Homer slurred. He took three steps and snatched the fish from Abby. "I'm a white man and I eat catfish. I earned this meat. Not that nigger." He tossed the gutted cat in the ice trough. Abby opened her mouth to say her mamma didn't like that word, but when she looked at Homer, his squinty eyes scared her and she backed up. She wished her mother would hurry up and get to the boat. Finally, she saw the green dress floating toward the boat, the fishing hat in her hand. The man in the blue shirt bent and kissed Pearl's hand. He looked at Abby and said, "Better luck next year! You can be proud, though. You caught a mighty fine fish." He squeezed Pearl's hand and walked away. The trip across the bay was not that far but Abby couldn't wait to get off the boat and away from Homer. Everyone was quiet.

The sun melted into the bay, shades of purple and orange filling the sky. Some stars were barely visible, already appearing when they reached the marina. Pearl was first to get off, rushing off toward the restaurant as if she had some important business to attend. Abby picked up her pace, looking over her shoulder. She did not want to be left alone with Homer who had been drinking all afternoon. He was still on the boat, and when she turned he was smiling that drunken smile she had seen before. The look in his eyes made her skin crawl and she made a bee-line to the edge of the boat and the safety of the dock. Before she had a chance to put her foot on the edge of the boat, Home grabbed her. "Come here, you little sassy-mouthed brat," he said, swinging her up into his arms like a baby doll. His hand immediately went to her private parts. She heard a motorcycle. Abby watched her mother run toward the *Mis Hap*. She was thrilled to see Mr. Buddy running right behind her mother.

"Homer," screamed Pearl. "Get your hands off of her this instant! Put Abby down." Pearl turned to make sure the man on the motorcycle had heard her. "You are fired. Get your sorry ass off my boat and off my property, now!"

Homer didn't put Abby down, he dropped her. He stood there staring at Pearl as if she had lost her mind. Then he saw the man right behind her. Buddy was on the boat before it registered with Homer as to who he was, though Homer briefly remembered seeing him before. Buddy first reached down and took Abby by the hands, pulled her up, picked her up and handed her over the edge of the boat to Pearl. Homer, drunk and wobbly, was lighting a cigarette when his face hit the deck of the boat with a hard thud. Buddy jammed his knee into Homer's back, right between his shoulder blades, making sure his captive was winded. With his free hand, he shoved Homer's face harder into the floor of the boat. Buddy sat on Homer, twisting both of Homer's arms around to his back. He slapped shiny handcuffs around Homer's wrists and squeezed them shut, as tight as they would go. Buddy wanted to beat the man to a bloody pulp, but was playing this by the book to make sure the bastard didn't get off on any technicality.

"Homer Williams," Buddy said in a stern voice, so low and guttural it sounded like an alligator growling. He was still sitting on Homer's back, making sure his full weight was being felt. "You are under arrest for Lewd and Lascivious Conduct with a Child, which I just personally witnessed, and Felony Sexual Assault of a Child." Buddy climbed off Homer's back, reached down and yanked on the handcuffs, dragging Homer to his feet. The handcuffs dug into the thin skin around Homer's wrists and he yelped. He squinted his eyes at Pearl and then at Abby. "You bitch!" Homer snarled, then spat on the boat deck.

Buddy pushed him up the dock toward a waiting car and wondered to himself if Homer was calling Abby or Pearl a bitch. "You're not gonna see God's blue sky for a long damned time," Buddy said to his prisoner. "I'll make sure you get the maximum sentence possible, you drunk pervert."

Matt was looking out of the marina store window when the motorcycle pulled in followed by an unmarked police car, a red light on the dashboard flashing. He stared as the man he had heard about, Buddy, shoved Homer into the back of the car, not making the effort to push Homer's head aside, instead letting it hit the door frame full force. Buddy said something to the uniformed officer and turned to walk back down the dock.

Abby was running up the dock, toward the unmarked car and Buddy, when he opened his arms and she flew into them. "Oh, Mr. Buddy," she said. "I knew you would come back. You said you would and you did!" She hugged him tightly around his neck and he watched as Pearl came loping up. Abby knew she stank but didn't care.

"How do, ma'am," he said with one hand outreached, Abby sitting in the crook of his elbow in the other arm. "I'm Agent Jeffrey Salaway, Alabama Bureau of Investigation, Exploited Children Division. Everybody just calls me Buddy." Pearl reached out and shook his hand.

"Mr. Buddy, show her your star," beamed Abby.

"Now, Abby," Pearl said. "Don't pester the man. Buddy, I can't tell you how grateful I am for your services, not to mention your timing." She laughed nervously. "I had no idea that man was such a polecat. Come inside, let me get you some-thing cold to drink."

"Ma'am, I appreciate it," he said, swapping Abby to his other arm. "But I promised this little girl a motorcycle ride and then I've got to get to the station to book that man. He is, by the way, more than a polecat. Is it alright with you if I take Abby for a short spin?"

"Well, of course it is," smiled Pearl. "But before you leave, I insist on quenching your thirst. Maybe I could even feed you before you go back?"

"No, ma'am, but thank you. Abby and I'll be right back." Buddy turned to Abby and said "Sweetie, I wish I had more time to take you on a longer ride, but for today, we'll do a quick tour of the fort, okay?"

Abby eagerly shook her head as he lowered her gently to the ground. Matt came out and shook hands with Buddy who was helping Abby get on the motorcycle, sitting right behind where he would sit. "Nice to meet you, Matt," Buddy said, shaking Matt's hand. Then he climbed on the motorcycle and instructed Abby to wrap both arms around his stomach and to hold on as tight as she could. He cranked the motorcycle and headed for the fort, up the gravel drive that wound up behind the fort to the lighthouse station, back down the main road all the way to the seawall and back to the shelled parking lot at the inn.

After he cut the engine and lifted Abby off, he pointed to the hot pipes that ran along each side of the bike, warning her to keep her distance from them. She took him by the hand and tugged until he laughed and gave way to her pull, following her up the steps into the restaurant.

"Mr. Buddy, I really like motorcycles," she exclaimed. "And I did what you told me last time. I told the hired man and my Mamma all about your star in your pocket. Guess what? Homer hadn't gotten near me since! At least, not until today. And I came in second in the Junior Fishing Rodeo! I even got a ribbon!"

Buddy was smiling while Abby rattled away and they walked into the restaurant, hand in hand. Pearl was waiting for them and had both of her older daughters ready to meet the famous Buddy. He politely shook hands, had a sip or two of iced-tea, and said his farewells. Abby hugged him, tall enough now to hug him around the waist.

"Are you coming back?" Abby asked while she escorted him back out to the shiny motorcycle.

"I might be back," he answered. "Sometimes my work takes me away for a long time, but I'll make sure we stay in touch. I'll send you a postcard from my next assignment." He leaned over and Abby put her arms around his neck and whispered into his ear, "Thank you, Mr. Buddy." He smiled, gave her a squeeze and got on his motorcycle. Abby stood in the parking lot watching him leave. Pearl was looking out of one of the front windows in the dining room.

Missing

Tired from the days' adventures, Abby still went to the big kitchen to tell McAllister all about her day. She had a lot to tell him. It was dinner time and the restaurant was full of happy people, chomping on fresh seafood. Abby busted through the swinging door to see Mags and Mary cooking up a storm right alongside McAllister. Abby was promptly shooed away from the deep fat fryers and out of the kitchen.

"I'm sure you had an exciting day," Mags said "and we want to hear all about it, but not now!"

McAllister looked over at Abby and grinned. "I sho'nough want to hear all about it," his sheepish smile a clue that he already knew the best part. "I heard you got yoself a big ol' fish and that Mr. Buddy caught him something, too!" McAllister laughed, pulling open the drawer to the broiler, sliding out a freshly cooked fish.

Abby laughed with him and said, "Okay, I'll come back in a while, after the rush is over and tell you all about it!"

"I want every juicy detail," McAllister said as he slid the fish on an oval platter, sprinkled some paprika on top and put some bright green, perfectly cooked broccoli on the side. He slid the plate under the heat lamp and rang the little bell. Mary stopped what she was doing and came to get that plate and the one next to it. "Every little thang," he said to Abby, smiling big.

Abby wandered over to her room, knowing for the first time that she was absolutely safe. She stripped off her fishy smelling clothes and climbed in the shower. She wanted to go see Cindy and tell her all about her day, too. She wondered what time it was as she climbed into her bed to lie down for a little while. She planned on getting up in just a few minutes but fell into an exhausted but peaceful sleep, the sound of a motorcycle engine still fresh in her ears.

The last customer had long since been gone and Mary and Mags, exhausted, had crept over to the suite for some well needed sleep. Pearl locked the restaurant doors, turned out most of the lights, dimmed a few others and went into the kitchen. McAllister was singing and scrubbing pots, this day turning out better than he had expected. He was singing and mumbling, saying something to himself that made him smile.

Pearl, nearby and with the ears of a bat, said, "What did you just say?"

McAllister jumped, startled that he was not alone. He was so engrossed in his singing and his imagining of the hand cuffs put on Homer, he had not seen nor heard her come in. "Well, hey, Miss Pearl. You just about scared me to death!" He smiled at her and continued scrubbing the pot.

"I asked you," she repeated in an even, low voice, "what you mumbled to yourself just now? Something about calling the state police, I believe?"

He beamed, pretty proud of himself. "Yes ma'am. It took me a while to be sho, and you don't wanna be going around of accusing somebody until you sho, but once I figured out what that Homer was doing to baby Abby, yes ma'am, I called the police, straight away."

"You idiot! You've single-handedly brought the attention of the damned law on every little thing that goes on around here. Boyd is not going to stand for this, McAllister, you can believe me when I tell you that. Your sorry, Yankee, nigger ass is fired, here and now. I want you and that family of yours off this fort and I mean tonight!" She whirled and pushed the swinging doors so hard they hit the walls behind them.

McAllister stopped moving, except for closing his jaw which hung open. He stopped scrubbing, he stopping cleaning, he didn't wipe another surface. He took off his tall, white chef's hat and pulled the dirty white apron over his head. He laid them both down on the counter and walked out of the kitchen. Stepping out into the darkest of nights, he thought, *Lawd, take care of that chile.*

Abby awoke and stretched, realizing she had slept late when she saw how much sunlight was pouring through her blinds. She dressed in a hurry, bursting at the seams to tell first McAllister, then Cindy, all about the day she'd had yesterday.

She came in through the back door of the kitchen to find McAllister, but didn't see him. Mags was bent over the stove again, hot and sweaty, stirring something. Matt had something on the spit in the fireplace. They both looked up as she came in.

"Where's McAllister?" Abby asked her frazzled brother and sister.

"I don't know, Abby, but I don't have time to talk right now. We have hungry people out front. Mary is seating them faster than we can cook," Mags answered while stirring first one, then a second pot full of gumbo. She ladled out a steamy hot bowl, and rang the small bell. Mary came darting into the kitchen and grabbed the gumbo. The swinging doors did not have a chance to close before she pushed them open again, using her hip to push them while balancing the gumbo and iced tea on a tray.

Abby scurried down to McAllister's house. She gently rapped on the door. No answer. Slowly she slid the door open. She'd never gone inside his house without knocking first. Nothing, and no one, was there. No sign of Bessie, McAllister, no Cindy, no Becky, no boys. McAllister and his family were gone. Some random pieces of furniture sat here and there. A calendar was nailed to a wall. The back door was open.

Abby closed the back door, then the front door, and went flying back up to restaurant to find her mother. She slowed down as she entered the dining room, knowing she'd get her butt blistered if she made a scene. She didn't see her mother. She swung open the double doors only to see the same sight she'd seen earlier. She left the restaurant and went down to the marina. She saw Pearl out on the dock near the *Mis Hap*.

"Mamma," Abby screamed long before her bare feet hit the docks. "McAllister is gone! He is really gone! His house is empty," She reached Pearl and gasped for air.

"Pipe down, Abby!" Pearl scolded. "I know he's gone. Took a job up North somewhere. Just proves, you cannot help some people even if you try. My son is right. I am going to drown in the milk of human kindness."

"Why didn't you tell me, so I could say good-bye?" Abby

sobbed, still catching her breath.

"Don't be so dramatic, Abby. For God's sake, he's just a cook. I'm going up to Jackson to pick up Maddie Man. She can cook just as good and won't go running off in the middle of the season. I'm going to wring that man's neck if I ever see him again!" Pearl played her lie well, convincing even herself she'd moved mountains for an ungrateful man who'd abandoned her.

Abby sat down on the dock, put her head on her knees and cried. She was sure that McAllister wouldn't leave without telling her good-bye and letting her tell Cindy and Becky good-bye. She knew her mother had something to do with his sudden departure, but didn't dare ask. She wouldn't even ask Matt.

Pearl meandered up to the small marine shop complaining to herself about all of the ungrateful people she had tried to help. "Abigail," Pearl shouted down to her. "Come up here and make yourself useful. You can put price tags on the new inventory Matt got in. Good God," she said to Matt, "that child is dramatic!"

Abby stood up, dragging her feet all the way to the marina store and mindlessly did as her mother told her. She wanted to go down to talk to Mr. Axil, but she knew it was getting late and most likely he had left his office. When she finished her chores at the marina store, she walked back over to McAllister's house and sat down in the middle of the room, in the place where Bessie's chair had been. She balanced her head between her two forearms that were on her knees and looked around. "Don't worry, Mr. McAllister," her voice echoed through the empty rooms. "I'll throw those cat fish away before anybody else gets to cook them."

The New House

"Oh, Mamma. It's beautiful," Abby said as she studied her new room. "I don't even care if it's not painted yet. Look, I have my own doors onto the porch! Can I have a rocker out there?"

"Well, my room is still beige, too" Pearl answered. "I just haven't had the time to do up my room or yours."

Abby was ear-to-ear smiles. "Look, there's a copy of *Alice in Wonderland* on my very own table! I've never had my very own table, either! Oh, thank you, Mamma!"

Pearl walked over to the marina to talk to Matt. Things seemed to be developing that made her uneasy. "Hey, son," she said as she walked in the small store. "Good thing school is starting... looks like you're almost sold out!"

"Well, I do need to keep a few supplies on hand," he said, looking around at the partially empty shelves. "But, Mom, I don't think I've sold all of this. I think someone is stealing stuff."

"Really?" Pearl said as she mulled over a thought. "I've been meaning to tell you. I walked to the store the other night, long after lights should have been out. I noticed a dim light in here and went to turn it off. There sat *Homer*, of all people, and a few other men around a table. I could tell they were whispering but I don't know about what. When I came in, they scattered like black birds."

"I thought that bastard was in jail?"

"I guess someone bailed him out until the trial." Pearl's eyes looked at the ceiling as the scene became clearer in her mind. "That crew is up to something. So you listen up and tell me everything you hear or see!"

"Yes ma'am," Matt replied. "I *have* seen some different people around, come to think of it. I just assumed they were guests."

"I'm going up to Jackson to get Maddie Man, too," Pearl continued, barely aware of what Matt was saying. "To cook at the Winter Inn and help you out over here while you're in school."

"You might want to tell Miss Busy Body, Abby, to keep her eyes open, too," Matt added. "She seems to know more about who's coming and going around here than anybody."

Maddie Man was very tall, at least six-foot-two, Pearl said, and wore a size twelve men's tennis shoe and still had to cut the toe section out in order for her huge feet to fit. Maddie Man had come to work for Pearl on occasion when they lived in the house next to the gully. But Pearl had to go get her out of jail on many weekends. Maddie Man went out on Saturday nights, got drunk, would throw a chair at someone and wind up in jail. Abby supposed, since there was only the Tiki Bar and no jails to be thrown into down on the peninsula, her Mamma must have decided it was okay for Maddie to work here. Maddie liked to cook and iron clothes, and she loved tucking Abby under her big, flabby arms to give her a hug. All that flesh, those huge breasts and strong arms, Abby wondered if she could be smothered by love.

"All my chilluns done growed up," Maddie told Abby one day. "I like me some sugar from Abby, das for sho."

"I am glad Uncle Homer don't live here anymore," Abby told her one day. "He used to, but he can't anymore. Mamma said."

"Did dat man hurt you, chile?"

"Yes ma'am. And I had to keep it a secret. But then, Mr. Buddy came to took him off to jail!"

"Well, I'll whup his skinny white ass if he sho up down here now. You be safe wid me, chile. I see to it." Maddie had her own room and toilet behind the kitchen and told Abby to come there at any time.

Everything had settled into a routine at the Inn, living quarters were all set, and business was good. But Uncle Boyd and Pearl argued for hours about whether or not the place needed another boat and a new captain, especially in the fall and winter.

"Now that Homer's gone and Matt is back in school, I

guess you're right. We need a captain. I just wish I knew this man," Pearl added. "Still, Boyd, I don't know."

Boyd ran his hand through his thin hair, frustrated with Pearl. "Well, my mind is made up. Captain Roar Dahl will bring his boat down next weekend, and his family will be down here soon enough to get their boys in school. They can live in the third house at The Row. So get the place ready!" Boyd had never been so pushy and direct with Pearl, but she held her tongue. Pearl knew how to pick her battles.

Pearl put little effort into the third house, making sure the children scrubbed the floors with Red Devil Lye, that furniture was placed and fresh sheets and towels provided. A few days passed when Captain Dahl showed up, just as Boyd said he would. Abby watched as the new family climbed out of an old car shaped much like her brother's. There was the tall sea captain, his little spit of a wife and two almost grown boys.

"Hello and welcome to the The Lighthouse Inn, Restaurant and, now marina, Captain and Mrs. Dahl," Pearl said in her most gracious and welcoming voice. She held out her hand to Mrs. Dahl and covered the lady's hand with her other hand. She did not touch the captain or acknowledge the boys. "Your house awaits you, but you'll need to get in your personal supplies."

"Abby, meet Captain and Mrs. Dahl and their boys. They will be staying here for a bit at Officer's Row." Abby caught Pearl's emphasis on *a bit*. "A storm is coming in," continued Pearl, "so let's get you folks settled."

The captain and his family did not acknowledge Abby, not even glancing her way when Pearl introduced her. Abby, however, looked them over good. The Captain did not have a dirty white sailor's cap. His hair was greasy, but Abby could tell he'd put pomade in it to slick it down and make it shine. The entire family spoke with very thick accents, almost like Mr. Peter. The Captain tipped his hat to Pearl whose outstretched arm showed them which house was theirs. Pearl unlocked the front door and dropped the keys into the Captain's hand. "We'll let y'all get settled in. Let me know if you need anything." With that, Pearl and Abby walked away, leaving the new family standing on the small porch of the residence.

Maddie Man called out of the front door of the Winter Inn, not yet open for the season but in preparation. "Miss Pearl," she yelled. "There a call for you!"

Pearl went back into the kitchen and picked up the phone. With a few words about how exciting it would be and of course there was always room at the Inn, warning that the weather might be a bit dicey, Pearl hung up. "Maddie, it looks like the Winter Inn is open for business, a few weeks early. We have a guest coming in tonight, so dream up something good to cook!" Pearl walked across the road to the marina store, where Matt was taking inventory, one more time. Things were definitely missing.

"Matt," Pearl said as she went into the store, "we've got a guest flying in tonight. We'll need to light the smudge pots."

"With this storm brewing? Who in their right mind would fly in a gale?" Matt wanted to know. "That's just crazy."

"Some important friend of Uncle Boyd's. Now, Mr. Pilot know-it-all, let's go light the smudge pots so the idiot can at least find the runway."

Abby, hanging around and listening, tried the word on her tongue. "Idiot," she said, and liked the way it sounded. She was still rolling the word around when she stepped into the kitchen.

Maddie stood in her kitchen, stirring up something that smelled good. There was a racket of wind, rain and lightning outside the kitchen window. Maddie looked up from her pot. She shook her head and kept stirring.

Outside, Matt covered in a plastic tarp, watched the little plane land safely, though its wings tilted from side to side on the approach. Matt anchored the plane quickly, so he could get himself and the guest out of the storm and inside the Inn. Once secured, Matt reached for the small side door to help the pilot down. "Good work, son," the man said to Matt, stooped under the wing.

"Yeah, thanks," Matt said. "Nice landing."

"Glad to be on the ground and not up there," he said, hooking his thumb toward the sky. "Let's make a run for it!" The two of them took off toward the inn. When Matt looked back, the plane was only visible when lightning lit up the stormy sky. The smudge pots were ablaze, spitting and sputtering against rain falling in waves. When the two of them made the Inn, they were soaked to the bone.

"Got the plane anchored," Matt said to his mother. "That's

a strong wind though. I'll have to check it now and then. Oh, Mamma, meet Mr. David Bolton."

"Welcome to the Winter Inn, Mr. Bolton. I'm sure that landing was a challenge. But Maddie Man has good soup in the pot that will warm you up. First, I'll show you to your room so you can change into dry clothes." Pearl was all smiles, but her fists clinched when she recognized this man as one from the secret meeting she disturbed at the marina not long ago. She knew she'd have to play her best part if she was to discover what the hell was going on. Her head was down, her lips tightly drawn as she led him down the first floor hall, an uneasy feeling growing. She glanced over her shoulder and smiled when they reached the first floor room, the one next to hers. "I'm afraid there is no private bath, but we'll move you into a suite in the big Inn tomorrow."

"This, right now, couldn't be better," he said. He looked Pearl up and down.

"Well, we are at your service, Mr. Bolton."

"Call me, David," the man said with an easy smile.

"Okay, David," Pearl returned his look, faking her sweetest smile. Her smile seemed to have him convinced and at ease. In no time, she'd be on to his game. She wondered if he remembered *her* from the secret meeting she'd interrupted at the marina.

Chickens in the Roost

Mornings after a storm always left a clear blue sky and clean smelling sea air. Mr. Axil's small office was a farther walk from Officer's Row, but Abby would walk a hundred miles to have her very own bedroom. She had a lot to tell Mr. Axil. She tapped on his door and let herself in.

"What fool flew in during that weather last night?" Mr. Axil asked Abby. He'd been waiting for her to come down.

"Mr. Axil. I have a lot to tell you. And could you please correct my English? I start school next week. Mamma says I sound like a swamp rat."

"Yes. We want you to sound as smart as you are," he smiled. "Now, what do you have to tell me? I'm all ears!"

"Well, McAllister is gone. I didn't even get to say good-bye. Then Maddie Man came. She used to help us over in Mobile and she's a good cook, too. Uncle Boyd and Mamma got in a real big fight, but Uncle Boyd won, and we have a new sea captain. I can't understand him. Maybe he's a Cajun." She paused and took a breath. "And best of all," she said, raising her voice, "I got to move to the house at Officer's Row. I have my very own bedroom and there is even a bathtub! Mamma thinks something's going on between the new captain and something else she found out. I ain't supposed to tell you or anyone." She decided not to tell him about Uncle Homer being arrested because she didn't want him to know why.

"Whoa, whoa, whoa," replied Mr. Axil. "Slow down, child. Catch your breath. That sure is a lot of new information! What did you say the new sea captain's name is?"

"I don't think I said, but he's Mr. Dahl, like doll."

"And the new guest?"

"The idiot that flew in during the storm is Mr. David Bolton."

"Well, well, well," Mr. Axil said, more to himself than to her. "All the chickens have come home to roost. Not good for your Mother."

"What does that mean?" Abby asked. She would need to gather as many facts as possible. Her mamma would be proud that she was able to get information, too.

"Bolton and Dahl are both Boyd men," Axil told the child. "Not good ones either. I knew your mother shouldn't be running around with that trash." Mr. Axil shook his head. "I tried to scare your mother away when you first came down here. I drug pipes and chains up and down those porches, hoping she'd think someone was breaking in."

"It was *you* making those strange noises?" Abby asked in disbelief. "That's why Mamma bought them two black poodles. She thought they would protect us."

"*Those*, not *them*," Mr. Axil interjected.

"Here, dear," Mr. Axil said, getting up from his desk and crossing the small museum. "There's something I've been saving for you. It's the skeleton of a horseshoe crab. Have you ever seen one?" He wanted to turn the conversation in a new direction.

"I saw part of one on the beach one day," Abby answered. "I wondered what it was."

"It's neither fish nor crab," he continued. "They are the oldest living creatures on earth and their blood is actually blue."

Abby carefully held the fragile shell that Mr. Axil handed her. She nested it in her lap and swung her legs back and forth under the chair.

"Can I tell my Mamma what you said?" Abby finally asked, trying to get back in spy service as she stood, taking note that Mr. Axil had headed toward his office door.

"I recommend you do," Mr. Axil said, showing her to the door. "And, Abby," he added. "It's important that you come a little more often to let me know what's going on." He closed the door behind her and flipped the sign over to read CLOSED. Abby waved and walked toward Officer's Row and her new bedroom.

Rainy Night Barge

The sun had set and stars were starting to peep out, barely visible against sky, by the time Abby got back to the Winter Inn. The house was quiet. The new captain's house next door was dark. Abby went straight to her room, wondering where everybody was. It was way too early to sleep, so she lay on her bed staring at the ceiling. She thought about everything she had heard today. She worried and wondered what, if anything, she should tell her mother Mr. Axil had told her. After all, her mother had told her not to talk to him.

I'm almost eight, Abby thought, in the twilight darkness and silence of her bedroom. I can figure out what to do to help Mamma. Or, I'll ask Matt. She liked that idea, and promptly rolled out of bed and walked through her tall French doors onto the porch, her arms folded over themselves. Thickening clouds slipped past the moonlight, first dark then light appearing on the porch, shadows moving toward the end of the floor boards. Abby, chilled, went back inside and slipped into some britches and a sweater. It was cold and windy but a stroll on the barge might help her figure out how much to say. Maybe Matt was down there, retying boats in the wind. She tiptoed quietly down the steps and out of the unlocked front door. She knew no one worried about where she was or when, but tonight felt different.

A misty rain started, and she realized she was very cold, her arms wrapped around her torso for as long as her arms would reach, and she wished she had put on socks. Maybe she was an idiot, she thought.

She'd been on the barge a few minutes and there was no sign of Matt. As she turned to go, she thought she heard a sound, like someone moaning. It was hard to tell with the rain, the wind and sail boat riggings clanging. She stopped and turned her head, trying to listen through the other noises. There. She heard it again. Where was it? She heard it again and inched over toward where she thought she heard the noise. She kept her feet flat on the slippery barge deck. Fish guts and oil made it hard to keep traction in the rain, which was falling harder.

"Oh no," Abby yelled, her scream lost on the wind. The sound was coming from one of the large holes in the barge! The big light up on the pole shown down on the marina and she could see that someone had pulled the boards off one of the holes, leaving a wide open trap. She forgot about slipping, and ran over to the gap and looked down. She expected to see a fisherman had fallen down in there.

She almost fell in herself when she saw her mother's body down in the space. The light went down in the gap at an angle, but there was no mistake. "Mamma! Mamma, you have to talk to me!" She stared in fear at her mother's slender figure balanced on the crisscrossed beams under the barges. Her mother's legs were dangling in the cold water, her dress up exposing her panties. Abby screamed, sure that her mother was dead. Pearl moved then, but only a little.

"Abby" Pearl pushed her voice to a coarse whisper, barely audible above the wind. Then she croaked loudly, "Get help. Hurry!"

Abby jumped back from the hole and looked around. She saw no one, no sign of life. Her brother must be down in the wash house, too far away. She was afraid to knock on the Captain's darkened door. Mary and Mags would be closest. She turned, ready to bolt down the barge and across the street to her sisters when she saw a small green and red flicker out on the water. It was a light, bouncing up and down, in and out of sight, but coming closer and heading right for the barge. She realized they were running lights from a boat.

"Help!" she screamed, running toward the end of the dock where the boat appeared to be headed.

"Hurry, Mister," she screamed as loud as she could. "Help! My Mamma's in a hole."

"What? What'd you say, little boy?" one of the fishermen screamed back.

"I ain't a boy! And my mamma fell in the hole in the barge. She's about to die. Hurry!"

Abby heard the motor speed up, as the boat spun around in a tight circle to tie up alongside the barge. The fishermen were scrambling as Abby screamed at them to hurry. "You have to get my mother out of the hole! Please!"

"What hole?" one man asked.

"Come on. Hurry. I'll show you" Abby answered, squalling, her stomach heaving.

The men ran, slipping on the slick deck. All three of them made it to the hole in the barge at the same time. "See?" yelled Abby. "Right down there."

"Damn!" One of them said, as the other one reached out his hand to his friend. They locked their hands around each other's wrists, and the smallest of the two men was helped down into the hole. He began talking to the woman there, whose body was bent over the beam. Abby watched the plankton twinkle in the churning water and worried about hammerhead sharks eating her mother's legs. The man lifted Pearl up to the other man who dragged her onto the barge deck, then hoisted himself out of the watery hole.

"Ma'am, you're damned lucky to be alive," the shorter man said. Pearl was coming around, but groggy and disoriented.

"Is my mamma gonna be okay?" Abby asked the taller of the two.

"Based on that goose egg, I think she hit her head on them crossbeams," the man answered.

"Can you take a deep breath?" the other one asked Pearl. She was able to fill her lungs. "Well, I b'lieve she ain't bad hurt."

"Stand me up," Pearl said.

"You sure?"

She nodded and one of the men put his hands around her waist while the other one put one of her arms over his shoulders. They gently stood her up. Within just a few minutes, Pearl was standing on her own two feet. One of the men had gotten her a blanket from the boat they came in. Pearl's nipples were visible through her wet dress and wet bra, and the men both took notice before draping her with the blanket.

"I am glad you three men were out tonight. I guess you might've saved my life."

"And me, Mamma! I helped, too," Abby insisted.

Pearl, as if nothing had happened, said, "Come on in. Let

me get you some hot coffee."

Abby followed the rescue party into the Officer Row house where lights seemed to come on at one time from all over the house. Mary dried Pearl off while Mags went to get Matt. Abby stood in her wet clothes in front of the open oven, which Maddie lit to dry Abby and the fishermen's clothes. Maddie put on coffee.

"I'm going to choke somebody," Pearl said, and her voice tightened. "Fishermen take those planks off all the time, swearing the best fishing is in those holes. I went out there to make sure the boats were secure," she offered, "then fell in the damned hole. I didn't even see it." She looked at her daughter, listening to every word. "Abby, thank God you found me."

Abby thought back and didn't remember seeing those planks removed or a fisherman fishing in the hole, for that matter. Just like she had promised Matt she would, she had checked the holes late this afternoon.

David Bolton

*Wh*en morning came, Abby ate scrambled eggs in the kitchen, answering Maddie Man's questions about the night before.

"Maddie, I checked those holes just yesterday," Abby said. "It's one of my important jobs I do for Matt. None of them holes was open."

"What do you reckon, chile? Somebody try to hurt yo mama? On purpose?" Maddie sat down with Abby, her coffee steaming.

"Mamma just laughed it off. Said fishermen probably pulled it off so they can catch whatever great fish they think lives under the barges. But if they did, take it off I mean, it had to be pretty late, because I had already checked it." Abby spread her favorite, apple butter, on the biscuit she had in her hand.

"Well, I thinks I just take a walk down there and see fo' myself," Maddie man said, sipping her hot coffee. "You wanna walk with me?"

When they reached the dock, they saw Matt busy nailing boards over the death trap hole, holding extra nails between his lips.

"Those look like new boards," Abby said.

"Yep. I couldn't find the old ones anywhere. Those fishermen must have tossed them overboard."

"Matt, they were here last night," Abby said. "I checked them, just like you told me to. I'm glad Mamma's okay." Matt just looked up at her, took one nail out of his mouth and continued hammering. "I'm putting down multiple boards, cross-hatching," he said through his lips closed around the nails. "I'm determined to secure them all. That way, it's not as easy as just taking up one big board."

Abby watched Matt hammer for a while but grew cold and

went inside. Maddie stayed out on the dock, talking with Matt. Once back inside, Abby saw Pearl for the first time that day and gasped as she looked at her mother, black, blue, bruised, and scraped. "Oh, Mamma! Don't you think you should go to the doctor?" Abby plead.

"No. Just a few bumps and bruises. Of course, I'm sore, but nothing is broken. Besides, I'm moving Mr. Bolton down to a suite in the big Inn." Pearl paused in front of the door next to her own and gave a gentle rap. "Mr. Bolton?"

"David. Please," came a man's voice from behind the closed door.

"David," Pearl said as cheerfully as possible through the door. "I thought I might move you down to the big Inn, where you may have a suite and spread out. Boyd indicated you would be staying a while."

The door swung open, revealing Mr. David Bolton dry and in the day light. "Good Lord, Pearl," he used her first name with ease. "What in the world happened to you?"

"Oh, just a careless accident. Now, let's get your things into larger quarters," she said as if she looked perfectly normal. Again, she wondered if he recognized her from the secret meeting. She wanted him out from under her roof as quickly as possible. "I'm afraid I'm short of man-folk around here at present, but we can put your bags in my wagon and go get you settled in. You pack up while I get you a cup of coffee. Cream? Sugar?"

"Yes. Both. That would be nice. It'll only take me a minute to get my things together." He closed the door and leaned against it, willing his face to stop smiling. It had not gone as he had planned, but maybe the broad would at least realize that her world was not as safe as she thought. Pushing off the door, he packed the only bag he had opened and set them out in the hall, as if a butler might appear by magic. Within the hour, David Bolton was settled into the largest suite available at the bigger Inn down the road. The lack of a telephone was his only disappointment.

Pearl went back to the Winter Inn and was quietly talking on the phone. As the day faded into dusk, Maddie had come back across the street and was busy peeling carrots and potatoes for the evening meal. Abby clung to the trim on the doorway into the kitchen, not trying to hide, but trying her best to hear what her mother was saying. She was talking to someone about a piece of land somewhere, but Abby just couldn't grasp the details.

"I've got a lot of things to do, Maddie. Make sure Matt takes a meal down to Mr. Bolton in case he doesn't come up here. I don't have anyone else on the books for dinner. Maddie, I have a weird feeling about this guy, so be careful what you say. If he asks you any questions, try to remember them so you can tell me." Pearl stacked up some papers and reached up in the top of one of the kitchen cupboards. She retrieved a long manila envelope and grabbed her keys and purse from the counter top. Pearl was going over a list in her mind and had not noticed Abby standing in the doorway.

"Where are we going, Mamma?" Abby asked.

"Abby, you scared the hell out of me. Don't sneak up on me like that!"

"Sorry. I'm not sneaking, Mamma. I'm going to stay with you in case that big goose egg makes you faint."

"A goose egg is a good sign, Abby," Pearl said. "I'm just going down to the big Inn to do some paperwork. You stay here with Maddie."

"Please, Mamma. It's getting dark and I want to go with you." Pearl didn't say no and Abby was not deterred. She stayed close to her mother as they walked down the darkening road.

They went into the Inn that was locked tight for winter closure. Pearl did not turn on any lights. She pushed open the swinging doors from the dining room into the kitchen and went straight to the fireplace in the back. Pearl threw in a few pieces of kindling that lay on the hearth and added in small pieces of wood, some wadded up newspaper, and lit a match. It took several matches before the paper and dried kindling caught fire, but it grew quickly once it started. Abby watched as the infant flickers of fire became larger and noticed the eerie light on her mother's face. She wondered what her own face looked like in the firelight. She was glad the fire added some light to the otherwise darkened building.

"Well, that's a nice little fire," Abby said, hoping to break the silence.

"It's big enough," Pearl answered, holding the stack of documents she'd gotten out of the kitchen cabinet. Abby noticed the papers were bound in blue paper on the outside. Pearl pulled each page away from the staple that held them together. Page by page, she tossed them in the fire, making sure each was totally burned before adding the next. Abby watched as pieces of burned, ashy paper drifted up the chimney. The last page Pearl burned was the blue one that had a stamp and some writing on the outside. "Let no good deed go unpunished," she said to Abby. Pearl smiled at her pun. They left the puny fire burning and walked back down to Officer's Row.

"Have you talked to Mr. Axil? Do you have any good spy news to report?" Pearl asked Abby as they walked.

"Not really. But he said something about roosting chickens and that Mr. Bolton and Mr. Dahl were not good men." Abby's mother was taking it all in, so Abby continued. "Mr. Axil thinks you need to take special care to watch those two," Abby added even though that wasn't exactly what Mr. Axil had told her. "How long is Mr. Bolton gonna be here, anyway?"

"He *won't* be here long, I can promise you that. We need the suite for other guests," Pearl answered with determination in her voice. "Keep your ears open for me. Visit with Mr. Axil when you can. I suspect he knows a lot more than he says. And thank you, Abby, for keeping me informed on what Mr. Axil thinks. I'm beginning to believe that old cuss knows a lot of stuff that I should know. Maybe I'll go call on him, myself," she said as they reached the house. "Now, scoot up to bed. Sleep tight!"

"Night, Mamma," Abby replied, lingering on the stairway, loving the undivided attention.

The next morning, on her way down to help Mr. Axil with the flags, Abby took a detour up to the porches past the front of the rooms at the Inn. When she passed Mr. Bolton's room, his blinds were wide open and he was lying on his bed naked! Abby scurried past the room as fast as she could, trying to be fast and quiet at the same time. She did not want him to know she was spying on him. Wait until she told her mother this!

The Liver Trail

Stonewall Jackson, Ole Stoney, was a beagle hound. He was the first of many beagles that Pearl bred at the Inn, all champion stock, and most of the dogs from Uncle Boyd's kennels. "I mean to keep the champion bloodlines clean and pure," Pearl told Abby. "The beagles from here will be like money in the bank!"

Back in the kitchen, Pearl announced to Maddie, "I think we need liver for dinner tonight. Nice and rare, sautéed in butter and onions." All of the children groaned. "It's good for you. Stop complaining."

"Yes'm," Maddie replied. "I know how you like it. You gonna eat it or feed it to the dawg?"

"I'm gonna eat it of course. And so are these persnickety children."

But after watching her children push the meat around, attempt to hide the rare liver under their potatoes, cut it into to fine bits, Pearl said, "Oh, the hell with it." The room was suddenly noisy as legs of chairs scraped on wood floors. "We'll use your left-overs to train the dog," Pearl added.

Pearl mustered her children in the dining room and brought Ole Stoney in first. He had been through this drill many times and didn't really need training, but Pearl liked to watch the dog work. She tied a small square of liver on a string and handed it to Abby. She then tied a handkerchief blindfold on the dog. He wagged his tail.

"Now give him a sniff, Abby. Then drag the meat around the floor, all over the place. Zigzag. Make him earn it." Pearl instructed, but Abby knew well what to do.

She gave Ole Stoney a long sniff, making sure his long and anxious tongue didn't pull the small piece out of her hand. She pulled the string with the liver tied to it all through the living room, dining room, kitchen and foyer.

After the trail was laid, Pearl removed the blindfold from the dog and with a command "Go get it, Stoney," she sent him to follow the scent. The beagle tracked as though he had watched every move Abby had made, his nose glued to the floor. Ole Stoney followed the path until its end, where he was rewarded with a juicy piece of liver.

"Just look at him!" exclaimed Pearl. "Best in Show, for sure. Now we'll bring out the new bitch and see how she does. Matt, go get me Lucy. She's the smallest one."

Lucy wagged and darted and tried to avoid the blindfold. She tried to gulp down the piece of liver shoved under her nose. With scolding and commands, soothing and cooing "good girl" from Pearl, she eventually settled down. Abby went through the routine again, doing exactly the opposite of what she had done with Stoney. Lucy twitched all over when the blindfold was removed, excited and eager to please and ready for the new game. Pearl held her back, then pushed her nose to the floor, right onto the liver smell. Off she went. Nose first, through the entire pattern, and back to the waiting treat, now in Pearl's hand.

"By God! I think that's the smartest dog I've ever seen! Have you ever seen one catch on at first try?" Pearl asked, not looking for an answer. "She is definitely ready for the hunt tomorrow!"

"What hunt, Mamma?" Abby was first to ask, though question marks lit up three other pairs of eyes.

"I'm taking you, too, Abby. We're going up north in the state to Uncle Boyd's plantation. He entertains a lot of important people up there and he wants me to see it. You can ride on the judge's horse with him if you're good!"

"I get a Roman Holiday already?" Abby asked. "I've only been in school a few weeks!"

"Roman Holiday, it is! Business is dead, and you've gone to school every day without complaining. They won't even miss you for one little ol' day. You are going to have fun running these beagles! Now go to bed early because I'll be getting you up long before day-light!"

Roman Holiday was Pearl's name for missing a day of school without being sick. Between opening the Summer Inn, the restaurant and the Winter Inn, the older children had had far too many absences from school and were relieved that they did not have to go to the plantation. Matt was particularly concerned because his high school grades and attendance were important now that he was thinking about college.

Plantation Hunt

Abby had barely awakened and was looking at the early morning light coming in the French doors, the sun not yet up. She heard her mother's boots clomping up the stairs, but rolled back over and quickly fell back asleep, forgetting she had to get up. The boots came stomping into her room, disturbing the dream she had just gone into.

"Wake up!" Pearl called, louder than necessary. She flipped on the overhead lights in Abby's quiet bedroom. "Time to rise and shine, sleepy head!" Pearl pulled back her covers.

Abby raised up on her elbows, her eyes squinting against the glaring light bulb. "What time is it, Mamma? Is it time for school?"

"No, silly. I'm taking you to run the hounds today. Remember? We're going up to Uncle Boyd's hunting lodge! Now get up, get clean and dress warmly. It will be chilly when we start but it will warm up later today. Wear your boots. Do you have any boots?"

"No ma'am. I don't have any boots. But I have tennie shoes."

"Well, I guess that'll have to do. You really should have boots around horses!" Pearl spoke as if Abby had forgotten to buy the right supplies.

The pre-dawn was breezy, the early morning sky a pale periwinkle. Pearl opened the car door and Abby crawled in. As she lay looking out the window, the sky was still dark enough for her to see the tail of the Milky Way. The beagles were in crates in the rear compartment. She wanted to stay awake and see the countryside up to the lodge, but her eyes were still heavy and soon she was sound asleep, laying in the back seat. The dogs had settled in for a nap, too. As the sun rose, the strong light of the morning sun beaming down into the back of the station wagon woke her and she sat up.

"Are we there yet, Mamma?" Abby asked. She looked around and saw nothing but pine forests with an occasional clearing of land where cows grazed on dewy grass.

"It's not far now," responded Pearl, her gloved hands gracefully draped over the narrow steering wheel. "We've been riding a couple of hours." She turned her head away from the road for a minute to look behind her at Abby. "Now Abby, it is absolutely imperative that you mind your manners. These are blue-blooded folks, with more money than we can count. Uncle Boyd is the real McCoy. I don't care what Mr. Axil says."

Pearl slowed the car and turned into a long driveway flanked by brick posts. Abby was struck silent. Before her was a beautiful white house with mammoth columns on the front. The driveway was edged with ancient oaks and crepe myrtles that looked like they were just planted. Mounds of pine straw encircled the new trees.

Pearl stopped at the closed gate, rolled down her window and with one gloved finger pushed a button on a box. The box talked back to her and the gate opened. "We're here!" Pearl squealed as the car pulled to a stop where other cars were parked. "Now, listen, there are a group of important politicians here for this hunt, so discretion is our word, right? And close your mouth, Abby! It's not like you've never seen a fine home before."

"Yes ma'am. But Mamma, it doesn't look like a hunting lodge!" Abby touched her hair. "I forgot my brush. Can I use your comb please?" The words were not out of her mouth when the comb flew over her head, and struck the far back window. Abby reached over, inched through the crates and retrieved the comb. She ran it quickly through her short locks and hoped she looked civilized. The part she had slept on stuck up like a rooster's tail.

"Mamma, I thought you could only hunt in the fall," Abby mused, proud of all the information she had learned from Mr. Axil.

"That's on public land," Pearl said. "On your own land, you can do what you damned well please."

Pearl raised the door of the back compartment and angled her head, signaling Abby to climb out that way. Abby crawled over into the rear compartment and jumped off the bumper onto the ground. A man in a formal suit appeared and took the crates of dogs out of the back of the station wagon.

"Mamma, how come they have that turkey tied up to that tree over there?" Abby asked.

"Shhh. Keep your voice low. Discretion remember?" Pearl looked over her shoulder. "It's so one of these damn fools who's never handled a gun will have a guaranteed kill. No hunting skills needed, but you didn't hear it from me!" Pearl handed the man a few dollars.

"Kind of like when we hook tarpons on those life jackets?"

Pearl ignored Abby.

The man refused the money from Pearl. "No ma'am" he said. "We don't get no tips, but thanks you anyway."

Uncle Boyd's round figure was standing in the tall doorway, his thumbs anchored behind each side of brightly striped suspenders. Over his dress slacks he wore a pair of cowboy boots.

"Welcome to White Springs!" Uncle Boyd rumbled. "The finest hunting lodge in the State. Hell, I'm glad you could come. You, too, little lady. Hell, we'll teach her to play poker tonight," he said looking at Pearl. "Hell yeah, we will do just that, we will." Boyd spread his arms wide. "Welcome to the Springs. Pretty place, ain't she? Pretty as a picture. No springs on the land though, so I'm thinking about renaming her. Grantham something. My man will get your bags. You just come on in for a cool drink." Abby stood still, a bit overcome. "Come on, little lady, you too. I'm sure we have something around here without alcohol." He laughed and made a slight bow as Pearl and Abby entered the foyer.

To the right, Abby saw a formal dining room with the longest table she had ever seen, freshly set and ready for a dinner party. To her left was a room with a dozen or so small tables, most of them occupied by men with cards in one hand and either a drink or a cigar in the other. This room was paneled in gleaming wood, the work of many hands over many years. Abby noticed she and her mother appeared to be the only females at the lodge.

"Jeremiah," Uncle Boyd said. "Please show the ladies to their room."

The man who unloaded the car and the dog crates grabbed their two small suitcases. Abby had not noticed them in the car.

"Are we spending the night?" Abby quietly asked Pearl.

"Of course we are. We'll chase the dogs all day, have a lovely dinner tonight, play a few rounds of poker, turn in early and head home tomorrow," Pearl said.

"But then I'll miss two days of school," Abby said, staring at her mother's beautiful red lips, just refreshed from the tube in her purse.

"You little worry wart. Two days will make it seem more likely that you were sick. I'll write a note. You know everything they're teaching anyway. I don't know why you're so worried. Your grades are perfect."

They followed the suited man upstairs into a big, beautiful bedroom. He sat their bags at the foot of the bed. Abby was relieved that she and Pearl were sharing a room and thrilled that the room had its own private bath. Pearl pulled her by the arm into the bathroom. She rubbed Abby's face, neck and hands with a cold wash cloth.

"Good God, Abby. You could grow potatoes in the row of dirt on your neck!"

Pearl opened a suitcase that had new clothes for Abby, clothes she had never seen before, including one pair of riding breeches that looked so tiny Abby wondered if she could get into them. Pearl threw them over to her, along with a white sweater, and ordered her to put them on. The breeches fit Abby well, and she felt very fancy, like the girls she had seen in pictures of horse magazines. She wished she had some boots.

Pearl opened her own suitcase and shook out a dress and a few blouses and hung them in the closet that smelled of fresh cedar. She then squeezed into a tight pair of breeches with a matching shirt and knee-high boots. Abby couldn't remember seeing her mother in pants, ever.

"Come on," she said to Abby, "the boys are waiting for us."

Pearl and Abby went down the stairs and into the room where everyone was playing cards. Abby recognized some of the men as having been guests at the fort. Uncle Ham was there, seated at the card table and seemingly unaware she was present. She silently vowed to keep her distance and stayed close to Pearl's side.

"Ladies and Gents!" Uncle Boyd resounded. Every head rose from the cards they studied in their hands. "It's time to get this show on the road, as they say. Yes, indeed. Burning daylight. Let's get these packs out and see who can outdo whom! We shall see today. We shall see!"

It was past coffee hour but not yet lunch time. Nonetheless, most of the men sitting at tables or standing, hanging over another's shoulders and talking, had cocktails in their hands.

Uncle Boyd saw Abby looking around. "Can I offer you a little bourbon and branch water, little lady? It'll warm you right up." Hands clasped in front of his belly, he laughed. Abby just shook her head. Pearl pinched the back of her arm.

"No, *sir*," Abby said, responding to the pinch. "But thank you for offering."

The group wandered outside, some tottering a little as they walked, others straight as sticks. Abby thought the men looked like they were dressed for a costume show, rather than a rabbit hunt. Ascots flying over tweed jackets, and tall black boots. The men lingered among the crates, gathering their own dogs. Two men mounted horses.

"Give me your hand, baby," one man said to Abby. "I'm Scotty King, one of the judges."

Abby put her hand up and he grabbed her, swinging her up on the back of his horse.

"Now, sit behind the saddle and put your legs up here, over mine. If you kick the horse in his flanks, he'll haul ass with both of us," Scotty said. "We'll be up front, chasing the dogs. The men, and your mother, will be behind us. When the dogs flush out a rabbit or a quail, they'll start barking and baying like hell. Every man back there knows just what his dog sounds like. Our job is to get there first so we can decide who the winner is."

Within seconds, the dogs were released from their leashes and Scotty kicked his horse, the abrupt start almost sending Abby to the ground. She wrapped her arms around Scotty and put her legs over his. As they charged through the woods, her legs were scratched by tree branches and tall vines and she was glad that she and her mother had on long pants.

Several runs were held. Old Stoney won one run, though Pearl said he was beyond his prime. Lucy acted like she had never been out of a crate before, running in circles like the poor rabbits they were chasing. A bell rang in the distance, signaling lunch. Scotty heeled his horse around sharply, again almost losing his passenger, and men called their dogs. It was time for a good meal and an afternoon nap.

Pearl stood near the door explaining to Abby the difference between breeches and britches, pointing to the additional panel of cloth inside their legs. Uncle Ham passed as Pearl bent over, her fine fanny shown at its best in the skin tight breeches, but he looked at Abby. She was familiar with that look. Abby drew close and tight to the seams of her mother's breeches. As more men came in from the hunt, they dispersed, some to play cards, some to dine, others for an afternoon nap. Abby remained aware and alert and avoided Ham.

"Come on, Abby. Let's you and me take a nap," Pearl said after a light lunch. Upstairs, on top of smooth, soft sheets with a soft wind blowing in the windows, curtains lightly flapping on the edges, they both fell asleep. When they awoke and went downstairs, an unruly game of poker was going on.

"Pearl," yelled a man's voice. "Come on in here and show these boys how it's done!"

Pearl beamed. She was still in the tight hunting breeches that showed off her perfect hour glass figure. She could poker the socks off of most of these men. Many a game had been played and lost to her on the screened porch at the summer Inn.

"Abby, stay right here with me," she said, glancing at Ham. "You can watch, but don't say a word that would give anyone a clue as to what cards I'm holding! If you get bored, I put some books in your suitcase and you can go up and read."

"Pearl," Uncle Boyd said, in a quieter voice than usual, "before you get started, come into my office. We got a little business to discuss."

"Abby, run on upstairs while Uncle Boyd and I talk. You can come back down later."

Uncle Boyd led Pearl to a room behind the kitchen in a part of a lodge she hadn't noticed earlier. His office, like the game room, was done in a deep wood with walls of bookcases, and soft down chairs. He pushed one of the chairs up close to his desk before walking around to the other side to his own chair. His hand pointed at the soft chair. Pearl sat and waited, wondering what was on Boyd's mind. She rubbed her hands together and licked her lips, suddenly uncomfortable with this man she had known for years.

"Pay day is a little light, don't you think?" Boyd got straight to it.

"What do you mean?" Pearl asked, trying to keep her voice smooth and buttery.

"The bag. Are you skimming money from the top? My man Bolton seems to think you and your son may be taking too much."

"Your *man*, Bolton, has parked himself in the most expensive suite we have and has yet to pay a dime in lodging, or for food or booze for that matter. Your other *man*, the captain, has yet to pay rent on his house and he uses as much diesel as he wants without payment." She leaned toward Boyd, her anxiety suddenly vanished. "*If* your bag is a little low, it's because your *men* are not paying their share!" Pearl's voice rose. "What makes you think you need to send spies down there anyway? Boyd, we've been in business, what three years at the fort alone? That doesn't even include all the work I did for you on that oil play in Citronelle. You trusted me then. Yet you feel a need to spy on me now? I'm insulted to the bone."

"Well, for one thing, you have yet to deliver my deed. I handed you a bag of cash to go buy that lot at Navy Cove because the folks wouldn't sell it to me directly. Politics and such. Have you done it? Do you have my deed?" Boyd's over-done southern gentleman's accent had vanished.

"What money? What land? What deed? What in the world are you talking about?" asked Pearl, smiling at Boyd with an innocent sweetness, trying to turn this into a game and trying her best not to squirm.

"You don't know who you're fucking with, do you woman?" Boyd spat.

"Now there's no need for vulgarity, Boyd. I just don't know what you're talking about. Please remind me." Again, she grinned, hoping he could find some amusement and calm down.

"You know damned well what money, what land, what deed. Homer said you sold that land to Bruce Ballentine."

"What in the hell would that worthless, white trash drunk know about our business or whether or not I sold anything to anyone? They locked him up, you know. That drunken slobbering fool doesn't know what goes on down there. I am not

189

stupid, Boyd. I like running the fort and I like the money we haul in. Why would I steal a piece of land from you of all people?" Pearl calmed her voice. "Why don't you just ask me what you want to know? Save yourself some money and take the assholes off your payroll."

"Okay. Where is my money or the deed? I'd be happy to have either."

"I have the money put away. There is no deed because nothing's been bought. When the seller decides to accept my offer, you get a deed to the land." She sat back and crossed her leg, looking straight at Boyd. She stroked the fabric of her pants down the length of her thigh. "You want to come to the Inn and see your money?" She smiled.

"Go play with your boys, Pearl. But be put on notice. I am watching every move you make and that deed or my money better show up in my hands before the sun sets on this month!" He got up and stormed out of the room. Pearl waited a moment, gathered herself and went to the game room. Boyd had put back on his jovial, card playing, dog-running face and was holding forth in the game room.

"Gentlemen, I'm afraid that my daughter has come down with some silly bug," Pearl said to the room of drunken men. "I'm going to have to take her home, but next time, I promise you a whipping you won't forget! By the way, somebody needs to untie that helpless turkey out there!" Pearl rubbed her hand through her hair and smiled.

"Hell, that's Paul's turkey, Pearl. You untie that bird and you untie any chance that fool has for shooting anything!" The room erupted into laughter.

Abby had followed her mother and stood outside of Uncle Boyd's office door, listening. She didn't hear all of what was said, but she heard enough. She had seen her mother burn the long papers in the blue wrapper. She knew her mother was in trouble. She dashed back up the stairs and hopped into bed with a book. Before long she heard Pearl's boots on the stairs.

"Abby, if anyone asks, you have a tummy ache. We need to leave. I forgot something important I need to do at the fort. I don't want Uncle Boyd or his gentlemen friends to think we don't appreciate the hospitality. I want you to act sick for me so we can go home. Can you do that?"

"Mamma, I wasn't feeling good anyway. It must be something I ate," Abby answered.

Pearl patted her on the head and pushed an ivory colored button next to the bedroom door. The man in the suit showed up. Pearl instructed him to get the crates and the bags in her wagon. This time she shoved a ten-dollar bill in his hand and he took it.

Pearl and Abby climbed into the station wagon. "Sit up front," Pearl said.

"It is a pretty place, Mamma," Abby said.

"Yes, it is. And full of ugly reptiles," Pearl answered back. She dropped the car into gear and they only slowed down for the big gate to open at the entrance.

The Bill Comes Due

It was pitch black night when Pearl drove the station wagon up in front of Officer's Row. She stopped the car and told Abby to get out and go to bed. Abby thought her mother was having a spell, one like she had not seen for a long time. She gladly fled the warmth of the car. When she got to her bedroom she got undressed and put on a cotton night gown. She was about to slip between her cool sheets, but curiosity got the best of her. Where was her mother going this time of night? Abby slipped through the French doors out onto the porch and watched her mother drive to the Summer Inn. The brake lights were all she could see from this distance. She went inside and quickly dressed, snuck down the steps and out into the night, headed for the Inn.

Abby hid behind the big oleander and watched Pearl tear straight to Mr. Bolton's suite. She banged on the door with both of her fists. "Wake your sorry ass up, David Bolton," Pearl yelled. She kept hammering on the door, one fisted, two fisted, then walked over to the window and peered in. She came back to the door and continued pounding. "Bolton, I know you're in there! Answer the damned door. I have the master key, you jackass, and I'll use it if I have to!"

Lights flickered on in the suite and a sleepy David Bolton opened the door. "What's wrong?" He asked in a panic. "Why all the ruckus?"

"Spying on me is what's wrong, Mister Never Pay Your Bill! Oh, yeah. Boyd told me all about you and your *position* down here. He and I go way back and if you think he'd trust you over me, you've got another think coming."

"Now, Miss Pearl, just calm down," he said as he pulled his house robe over his pajamas. "It's not as bad as you think. I was mainly down here to keep my eye on that skunk, Homer.

192

Now that he's gone, I'm just staying a little while until the captain gets his charters up and going."

Abby, hiding beneath the porch, watched her mother enter the suite and close the door behind her. Abby walked back up to the house and tried to go back to sleep, but her mind was busy thinking about what she'd overheard at the plantation and what her mother had screamed at Mr. Bolton. Finally, she drifted into a fitful sleep, every noise awakening her. At last, she heard the front door close and her mother's boots on the floor downstairs. She had no idea what time it was.

Abby awakened next morning to the sound of her mother's voice, screaming from downstairs. "What are you doing in my house? Who the hell are you and what do you think you're doing?"

Abby slid out from under her warm covers and hovered at the top of the stairs. Mags and Mary were already there. Squatting down and peering through the rails on the stairs, Abby could see Uncle Ham and a strange man who had a clip board in his hand. She tried to whisper the information to Mags, but Mags shook her head no.

"Lady, the only thing on this whole place that belongs to you will fit in your suitcase. Whatever you do NOT have a receipt for belongs to the Granthams." The man with the clip board looked at Ham. He stood by, licking his lips and it struck Abby that he looked like a lizard flicking his tongue.

"I will sue your pants off," yelled Pearl. "I have a ninety-nine-year lease on this peninsula, including this very house. You cannot barge in here and demand that I prove what I own!"

"Your so-called lease is verbal, is it not?" asked Ham. "Did Daddy actually sign anything with you, *Madam* Pearl?"

The house went whisper silent, the only sound was the wind whipping through oleander trees outside. The three girls barely breathed at the top of the steps, though Ham had spotted Abby when she stuck her head around the corner.

"Yep. That's what I thought," continued Ham. "Daddy did not give you a written lease on this place."

Pearl suddenly remembered she was only in a nightgown. "What the hell are you talking about?" Pearl was barely audible. The window was open and her new peach and white colored Persian kitten was playing with something in the window sill. She went and got the kitten and closed the window.

"Daddy says you've been stealing from him," Ham said. "He lent you a tidy sum of money out of the goodness of his heart so that you could run this place for him, and provide a decent living for you and for your children. But stealing from Daddy changes everything." His voice was controlled, but dripped with animosity. He spat out each word.

"I have not been stealing from your father," a calm and collected Pearl said. "Business has been slow this winter. And, like I told him, those deadbeats, Bolton and Dahl, are not paying for food, rent, or fuel for the boat. Not to mention the free-loading commissioner. They are the ones he should be mad with, not me. Or maybe you, Ham? I give the money to you most of the time. You stealing from your daddy?"

"You can keep everything you have a receipt for," Ham calmly repeated the words of the man with the clipboard. "We'll give you a couple of days to round up your paper work. In the meantime, I'd suggest you find your receipts and start packing."

"This is ridiculous!" Pearl screamed. "I'm going to call your father right now." She turned on her heel and headed for the kitchen where the phone was.

"Call away," dared Ham. "Call away! I'll come listen in. Make sure you get it right. I'll be right by your side, in case you need answers to go with your bullshit lies."

Pearl stopped by her room and grabbed a robe to put over her nightgown. Once in the kitchen, she dialed the familiar number. "This is Pearl Whitney calling for the congressman. Yes, yes, I am a friend of his." Ham laughed in her ear. She scowled at him. "Okay. Yes, ma'am. Just tell him I called and ask him to call me when you hear from him. It's urgent." Pearl turned to Ham, raising a hand to close her robe at the neck. "It seems your father is conveniently away on a junket. I am not doing a damn thing before I talk to him. You are a fool if you think I'll abandon a business I've worked hard to build."

"Two days. Get your receipts together," Ham repeated. The two men marched out of the kitchen. Pearl stood stock still staring at the door closing behind them.

The girls, lingering at the top of the stairs, heard their mother walk to the other room and sit down on her father's leather tufted couch and cry, soft sobbing floating up the stairs. They returned to their bedrooms without a word. The kitten pounced up the stairs following on Mags' heels.

Pearl stomped back to the kitchen and picked up the phone. "Bruce, you haven't filed that damned deed, have you? Good. Boyd's on to us. Just keep it locked away for a while longer." She hung up the phone with a clatter and flew upstairs to awaken the girls.

"Girls, Uncle Ham has lost his mind," Pearl told the girls who had lined up in the hall. "We have to get Matt to gather up his tools. You need to get your books and personal belongings. Until I can get in touch with Boyd, we are on precarious grounds. Don't panic, but be ready."

"Mother, what is going on?" Mary asked.

"Ham thinks we don't have a lease on this place and wants us out in a few days. Anything I can't produce evidence that I own, he says he will keep. I know Boyd is behind this, but he's lost his damned mind if he thinks I'll just sit back and take it."

"Mamma, remember? Mr. Axil said Uncle Boyd couldn't lease you this place because somebody else owned the lease?" Abby asked, though she stepped behind Mary in case her mother wasn't in the mood.

"Yes. I remember. But that's just not the case. In the State of Alabama, a verbal lease is just as binding as a written lease. I will not take this lying down, you can be rest assured."

"Mamma, will they take Leaner the Cleaner?" Abby pleaded.

"Not if you go get her and pack her in your suitcase with your clothes. I doubt we're going anywhere, but just in case I can't reach the bastard, or I can't get the sheriff to stop this nonsense, get your things ready. Mags, go tell Matt what's going on. Abby, keep your trap shut. Do not repeat any of this, especially to Axil. Do you understand? I don't know who we can trust." Pearl didn't wait for an answer or a nod. She swept back down the stairs, into the kitchen and started making phone calls. Boyd was still unavailable and she left a message for the sheriff to call her.

It wasn't long when the sheriff arrived, flashing lights going, everything official. He slowly climbed out of the car holding a fist full of papers.

"Thank, God, Hal. I'm glad you're here. I just left a message for you at your office. You will not believe what Ham is trying to pull in Boyd's absence!"

"Miss Pearl," Sheriff Cullman said hesitantly, glancing up at the three girls standing on the porch. "I have come to arrest you. Now let's do this quietly. Those pretty little girls don't need for this to get any worse."

"Arrest me? For what? Has the whole damned world lost its mind?" Pearl paced up and down in front of the house. "Girls, go inside. Except for you Mags. Go get Matt, NOW, and have him call Mr. Edmunds."

"Miss Pearl, you are under arrest for assault and pistol whipping one Homer Williams of Magnolia Springs, Alabama."

"Pistol whip? If I'd had a pistol that SOB would be dead and fed to the sharks. It was his good luck that the ABI agent showed up and arrested his sorry ass. He said I pistol whipped him? That lying son of a bitch hasn't even been down here except for some secret meeting I broke up."

"Now, Miss Pearl. Just come on with me. We've been friends a long time. You're going to bond right out. I could cuff you and put you in the car in front of your children or you can go gather your purse and keys and follow me to Foley in your own car. That way you can come straight home once you're bonded out. Probably ain't no judge available though, so you might have to spend the night," the sheriff said.

"Spend the night in jail? Me? Hal, you've got to be kidding!"

Matt came running up the road, Mags not far behind him. They were both out of breath. "Mamma, what in the world is going on?" he asked, his chest heaving.

"Well, it seems the sheriff is here to arrest me for supposedly pistol whipping Homer."

Matt opened his mouth, about to protest, when Pearl held her hand up. "Hold on, Matt. Let's not say anything just yet. Get in touch with Mr. Edmunds. He'll get this straightened out," Pearl said. "This bullshit will end in our favor. I guarantee it, by God. But it's got to play out a certain way. I will absolutely see to it that it goes *my* way and no other. You hear me?" Matt nodded. "You hear me, girls?" They nodded.

Pearl turned to the sheriff. "I did run that bastard off. And it didn't take a whipping to get his ass gone. But will you tell me, this, Hal? Just this, and I get in my car and follow you like a lamb." The sheriff nodded, waiting for her question. "Who

196

filed the complaint?"

"That's no problem, Miss Pearl. Homer Williams himself, along with one of Boyd Grantham's lawyers, filed the charges." He handed her the signed warrant.

Pearl turned to Matt. "I've got this figured out now." Pearl's eyes flashed their greenest. "Y'all get your stuff together. Load it into the station wagon and your car. Just the personal stuff for now. Don't worry, we'll see who gets what! These lunatic bastards don't know what kind of snake they have poked!" And she turned and marched to her car, taking control of even the sheriff. "Hell, let's go, Hal!" She rolled down the window.

Matt stayed that night at the Officer's Row house, nervously walking the floors and ordering the girls around. He left from time to time to go over to the marina, taking stock of what he could pack up. He gathered up as many tools as he could and stuffed them under his car seats. He took the back seat out of his rattletrap car and stashed tools beneath it. His very best tools wouldn't fit and he knew his mother had not saved a receipt for any of them. He watched for the headlights of the station wagon, hoping. He was worried that things would *not* go her way. Pearl did not show up that night. She spent the night in the county jail.

Mary, Mags, and Abby were upstairs, cramming as much as they could into small suitcases. Mags kept the kitten close at hand. "Damned if these thieving fools are getting my kitten," she announced to her sisters.

Pearl was released from jail the next morning and returned home, madder than she had ever been. She went straight to the telephone and made call after call. Her voice was strong, and her confidence became contagious. Matt and the girls moved about their business of stowing and hiding with renewed energy. True to his word, Hamilton Grantham and the man with the clipboard arrived the next day. The inventory began in the parlor. "This nice leather sofa, Pearl. May I see the receipt please?" Ham asked, the smile of a coyote in the hen house on his narrow face.

"I inherited that couch from my father. You know I don't have a receipt on it and I'll be damned if you're keeping it. Where is your father?" Pearl fired at him.

"Daddy is off doing the people's business," replied Ham. "He has asked me to personally handle this rather embarrassing situation."

Ham marked an 'X' on the tufted leather sofa with a piece of chalk he held in his hand. 'X' meant it belonged to him. There were X's everywhere, in every room, on almost everything. Even down at the marina. "The dogs belong to Daddy. We'll gather up the dogs later. And the dune buggy. And those two fine standard poodles. I like poodles, myself," he sneered.

"You damned well know that dune buggy belongs to Mary! And those poodles are mine, bought and paid for by me!" Pearl yelled, taking two steps in his direction.

"You got a receipt for those dogs or that dune buggy?" Ham smirked.

"I do not have receipts for either," Pearl surrendered. "My daughter saved her waitressing tips to buy the dune buggy." When Ham marked it with his chalk, it was like a boxer's winning punch to the head of his opponent. "What about my children's books, their toys? And Matt's tools?" asked Pearl.

"Of course you can take your personal belongings. Daddy is not being unreasonable, Miss Pearl. His money bought most of this stuff anyway, and yet he's allowing you to keep the station wagon and as many of your personal items as you can get in it. You have until sundown tomorrow to be gone or the sheriff will arrest you. Again."

"That car is in MY name," Pearl shouted at Ham who was standing with one knee bent holding the clipboard. "You couldn't take it if you wanted to, you bastard." Then she decided to turn things back her way. She swung with her best punch, thinking of Buddy and the possibility of additional investigations that might occur at the fort. She could trade away her threat later, to something of advantage with Boyd Grantham. She stepped right in front of Ham. "Well, if you and your sorry father think you're done with me, think again. What about that ABI Agent, Buddy? What about what he knows?" Pearl asked with an acid tone.

"Maybe you ought to keep a closer watch on your girls, Miss Pearl. Buddy's work has no effect on Daddy whatsoever. As a matter of fact, Daddy went to see Buddy's boss. Recommended him for an award, I believe. Good investigating and all that. I think Buddy's been sent over to Mississippi on some big case." Ham leered at Pearl and clapped his hands together. "Looks like I'm finished here." Hamilton Grantham and the man with the clipboard left.

By the next afternoon, a tow truck had arrived and was hauling off the dune buggy. Two men with a flatbed truck were taking the larger marina tools. Tears quietly slid down Matt's tanned face as he watched tools he had worked hard to pay for disappear onto the truck. Baying beagles were stuck in crates on the back of the flatbed. Suddenly, Abby plopped down in the sand, mindless of sand spurs and cactus, as she watched Ham put Mrs. Chi-Chi and Mr. BB into the back seat of the car they were riding in. She stood up and walked over to the car. As she neared the car, she heard Mr. BB snarl and watched the man with the clipboard back up, away from the dog.

"Maybe we ought to leave this one here," the man with the clipboard offered.

"Uncle Ham?" Abby plead, her bottom lip quivering. "Please don't take my dog, Mr. BB. He's the only thing I have that is truly mine. Please, Uncle Ham?" Abby's pride and anger had totally vanished as she inched as close as she could to the very man she was afraid of. "Please let me have my dog. You can have the fat one and breed her, too, if you want to."

Ham laughed, yet again. "Well, little girl, unless and until your mother can prove that she owns him, he belongs to me." Abby stepped back, heaving with sobs. "Don't you hear him growling? He's my personal watch dog and if you don't let him go, he's gonna bite you," Abby spat.

The man with the clipboard looked at Ham with a question in his eyes, moving farther away from the dog, praying the child would come fetch the snarling thing. "If he bites me, I'll bite him back," Ham looked at the child with devilish eyes. With that Ham and the leery sidekick climbed into the car, Mr. BB barking and snarling and jumping around the back seat until they were out of sight.

Matt came and wrapped his arms around an inconsolable Abby. "It'll be all right," Matt soothed her. "Mamma will get this straightened out. You'll get your dog back." Matt knew he was lying, but he couldn't bear to see his baby sister so heart broken.

Against her mother's warnings, Abby bolted from the yard and ran all the way down to Mr. Axil's office. He was startled when she burst through the door.

"Oh, Mr. Axil. You were right! Uncle Ham is making us move and Mamma can't find Uncle Boyd. Uncle Ham said she does not have a lease on the Inns!"

"I'm so sorry, my dear," he said as he hugged the crying child. "I was afraid something like this would happen. It's not the first time either. The last family who tried to make a go of this place were run off, too."

"The sheriff came and arrested Mamma for pistol whipping Uncle Homer, but she said she didn't do it. The sheriff didn't care! They took almost everything, including my brother's tools! Worst of all," she sobbed and tried to breathe, "they took Mr. BB!" Abby hugged Mr. Axil around his waist as she wailed. "Mamma says we'll empty out our cars and come back when they are gone and … "

"Oh, honey, I doubt she'll be able to come back if the sheriff is involved. All the law enforcement in the state is bought and paid for by Boyd Grantham. Attorneys, too. No one's going to risk their career for a lady and her four children. I wish I could help you." Mr. Axil kept rubbing the girl's short hair and patting her on the back.

"Mr. Axil? Is this the last time I'll see you?" Abby asked, looking up at his weathered old face.

"I imagine so, my dear. I imagine so."

Abby stayed as long as she could with Mr. Axil and then went to walk the rock wall. She sat down and said good bye to the wild cats and to her little hermit crabs. The porpoises went rolling by, blowing air as they broke the water's surface. She sat motionless on the wall. She did not cry any more, and at sunset she walked home to her first bedroom for the last time.

Last Ride

$\mathcal{P}$earl was up with the rising sun the next morning, rousing the children out of bed. Matt had stayed the night at the house on Officer's Row in case his mother needed protection. His heartbreak over losing his tools had turned into fury.

"Come on, Matt," Pearl said. "We've got things to do. Girls, get up and follow me," she yelled up the stairs. Abby had already stationed herself at Pearl's side.

Pearl and Matt strode over to the marina. Matt wanted to see what tools were left that he might be able to salvage. He headed out to the barge to check on the tied up boats, to make sure everything was safe and sound.

"To hell with that, Matt," Pearl said when she realized he was checking on the boats. "Those bastards are in charge now. Let them worry about *their* customers. But we do have a little boating to do." She smiled as she headed toward the *Mis Hap* with Abby right behind her. Matt picked up a few odds and ends of tools overlooked by yesterday's bandits and took them across the street. He opened his car door and jammed them in, smiling, thinking about the hidden booty under this car seats.

"Abby, go tell the girls to hurry up. I have a little job for them." Abby ran back across the street and went upstairs. The girls had long since been awake, stripping beds and carefully folding their heirloom sheets to pack.

"Mamma needs y'all over at the marina. She says to hurry up," Abby said. Abby slid down the banister, something she had been forbidden to do, but as near as she could tell, all bets were now off. Mags and Mary came along behind her.

By the time the girls arrived, the *Mis Hap* was started, the water swirling under the propellers. Matt was on board, but Pearl was at the wheel and fully in charge.

Abby hopped aboard, no longer afraid of the distance between the boat and the dock. "Can I come, Mamma, please? I'm scared to stay here," Abby pleaded.

"Abby, I had no intention of leaving you. Get a life jacket on. Mags and Mary, go get the wagon and meet me at Mimi's in Bon Secour." Pearl stood with confidence at the wheel of the boat. "Now, hop off and throw us the lines."

"I'd better go on the boat," said Matt. "Mags, can you handle the wagon?"

Mags stood with her hand on her hip and just looked at him. He nodded and smiled, remembering she could drive as well as he could.

"If we all leave now we should get there at nearly the same time," Pearl said.

Mags and Mary got into the station wagon. Pearl, Matt, and Abby were on the *Mis Hap*. Pearl backed her out of her slip with ease and headed north in Mobile Bay. Until that moment, Abby had not known that her mother could captain a boat as well as either man she had hired. She steered through Oyster Bay into the Bon Secour River. Matt sat there watching her every move, as amazed as Abby that she drove the boat like she had done it every day. Pearl stayed on course, but was a million miles away in her mind. Her dress flapped in the breeze. She had not said a word to Matt or Abby during the entire trip. She pulled up to a small pier in Bon Secour, clambered off the boat and talked with a man who had been waiting on her arrival at dockside. She stuffed a long white envelope into his hand. Abby and Matt jumped from the boat to the dock.

"Scuttle her," Pearl said quietly but firmly to the man. "Now."

"Yes Ma'am," he said, looking in the envelope and counting the money. "You sure? She's a nice boat. I could sell her for you."

"Sink the damn boat!" Pearl turned, walked off the weathered wharf and joined Matt and Abby. The three walked without speaking up a dirt lane until they came to an old, long closed restaurant named Mimi's. Mags and Mary were there and waiting in the car.

"Where's the *Mis Hap* going?" Matt asked.

"She's being parked where that bastard will never find her," Pearl said.

Once back at the house, a whirlwind of activity buzzed.

Maddie's son was there to load her things up and take her home. Pearl's station wagon was packed to the headliner with clothes, just enough room left for four people. Matt's car was stuffed, too.

"Maddie Man," cried Abby, "am I ever going to see you again?"

Maddie Man patted Abby's head and hugged her, her huge bosoms cradling her head. "Of course, we see each other soon. This ain't nothing but a minor setback for you mamma. I seen her in worse shape than this. She a survivor, baby girl."

Maddie and her son hugged everyone and slid into his old truck to leave Fort Morgan for good. Maddie waved at Abby and blew her a kiss. "Don't you be worryin'. Everything gone be all right. You see," Maddie said, her head hung out of the truck's window.

The sun was at the horizon, not yet melting into the bay, casting its bright yellow reflection across the water. Hamilton Grantham, followed by the sheriff arrived as expected, and was right on time. The wagon was packed and Pearl ordered everyone to get in. Abby lay on top of a huge stack of clothes, with the kitten curled up and sleeping beside her. Abby did not see Ole Stoney and guessed the bastards had taken him, too.

Pearl did not say one word to Ham or the sheriff. Hal, the sheriff, looked down at his feet, not wanting to look into the woman's eyes. She marched past them both, got into the station wagon, and started the motor. Abby looked out the back window at the flashing lights on the sheriff's car and the sun's last rays twinkling on the water. She heard the familiar thump-thump as they passed over the sea-wall. The sound had become comforting to Abby and she committed it to memory.

Abby was surprised when Pearl took a hard right into the sandy driveway of Uncle Ham's beach house. Abby sat up on her elbows, her head almost hitting the ceiling of the car. Pearl got out of the car, went under the stilted house and came out with Stonewall Jackson on a leather leash. Stoney walked through the sand, his tail wagging like a windshield wiper, and jumped in the car. He curled himself into a ball in the heap of clothes and settled down. Abby smiled. Her mamma sure was smart to hide Ole Stoney right under their noses. She wished she had hidden Mr. BB, too.

"Mamma, what are we going to do now? Where are we going?" Mary asked. Pearl looked in her rear view mirror to make sure Matt was right behind her in his packed car. She touched the brakes, and said, "Mags, I think you need to ride with Matt." Pearl pulled the wagon over on the sandy road side. "We're going to Jackson, Mississippi. I have some friends from the oil days up there who will help us get settled. I've got an opportunity at a job there. I'll go back to clearing titles as a land-man while I sue the britches off of each and every one of these bastards."

"Something wrong, Mother?" Matt asked as he pulled his car up next to the wagon.

"No. I just think someone needs to ride with you. We're going to Jackson, Mississippi and it'll take a while. You might need Mags to spell you driving." Mags scurried out of the wagon, inched her way past a mean cactus growing on the roadside, and went around and got inside Matt's car. After she closed her door, Pearl led the convoy up the road to Mississippi.

$\mathcal{Pup}$

$\mathcal{The}$ man stood in back of the courtroom, near the clerk-of-court window. He was finished with his case, just a few more papers and he would be leaving the courthouse for the day. He looked up as the judge read the case up next. Normally, cases that followed his were of no interest to him, but the man in the blue seersucker suit suddenly became very interested. He straightened his stance and tightened his tie. He looked at the defendant table, where the congressman and his army of lawyers were seated. Then at the plaintiff table, where a lovely woman stood alone behind a large wooden desk. He mopped his thin red hair with a white handkerchief, gathered his papers and turned to hear what was happening. It seemed to him the dull little court, that usually heard cases on the likes of car crashes and pig theft, was about to get really interesting.

"The court calls Case Number 127, Mrs. Pearl A. Whitney and her four minor children versus Boyd Grantham, Hamilton Grantham, Grantham Timber Company, Homer Williams, David Bolton and Roar Dahl. The parties have been sworn in, your honor," stated the clerk.

"Mrs. Whitney? Are you an attorney?" asked the judge.

"No, sir. I am not," answered Pearl.

"Do you have legal counsel?" the judge asked Pearl.

"No, your honor. None of the yellow bellied lawyers in this Great State of Alabama would take my case. If it pleases the court, your honor, I intend to represent myself."

The lawyer standing at the back of the courtroom looked at the woman and her four polished children sitting in the row behind her. She had the table before her spread out with papers and a shiny new leather briefcase. He noticed she was dressed exquisitely, with a hat accessorized with a tiny lace flap covering her eyes.

"Are you financially capable of paying an attorney?" asked the judge.

"I am perfectly capable of covering my own legal expenses. I just can't find an attorney who will take my case. Nobody wants to go up against this congressman," Pearl answered. "I am well-educated and well-equipped to handle these dogs myself."

A small commotion of laughter and snickers rolled across the courtroom as the judge gaveled the gallery into silence. An attorney, a tall man in an expensive suit, stood up at the defendant's table. Three other men, all well healed, chests puffed out, wore smiles of amusement.

"Your honor," he said as he rose, removing his glasses, "I am Sam Peterson, of Bryant, Petersen, Swartz and Cohn, attorneys for the defendant. We have tried to mediate with Mrs. Whitney to satisfy her ridiculous claims that wastes the time and would attempt to tarnish the reputation of my esteemed client, Congressman Boyd Grantham. She has been totally uncooperative. We will show that this is a frivolous suit brought by a woman in willful violation of the law. She is grandstanding and seeks nothing more than a pound of flesh from my client."

"Your Honor," interrupted Pearl, "the so-called *esteemed* congressman dispossessed me and my four minor children from an enterprise I was running for the congressman at Fort Morgan, Alabama. Without cause, I was unjustly hauled off to jail and told to leave the premises within forty-eight hours. He stole most of our personal belongings, including, but by no means limited to, my minor children's tools, toys, one dune buggy and two cherished family dogs. I had a verbal ninety-nine-year lease with the congressman which he now refuses to honor. Additionally, I have since learned his right to enter into a lease with me was fraudulent in that the congressman did not hold the original lease, as he led me to believe." Pearl shuffled through papers as she addressed the judge.

"Mrs. Whitney," the judge said in a stern, paternal voice. "This case may become one of high profile and detailed legal connotations. I strongly recommend that you seek and find counsel. This case will be continued for one week. We will meet back here, a week from today, next Tuesday at 1:30. Find yourself a lawyer, Mrs. Whitney." The judge continued the case with a bang of his gavel.

Conrad Adcock Byrne, III, quickly reached inside his jacket pocket and withdrew a business card. Conrad had been born with a silver spoon in his mouth, but his family was broke long before he entered his first year of law school. He owed it to his family name, indeed to the blue blood coursing through his veins, to try with this very case to win back some of his family pride, the most important thing a Southerner can possess other than land. This very defendant, the esteemed congressman himself, stole the mineral rights of his father's property in an oil play back in the fifties. But for that single blow, Conrad and family would still be in high cotton. Conrad had dreamed of a chance to right that wrong ever since he graduated from law school at Vanderbilt. This fine young woman and her poor minor children now knocked on his door with a ticket in their hands that could do the trick. All he needed was to punch the ticket.

Pearl sorted and stacked papers, carefully stuffing them into the new briefcase. The children sat stone still until Pearl turned around and nodded toward the door. She walked ahead, her children in single file behind her, out of the courtroom. Once in the corridor, Pearl could not remember which door they had come in and was looking around when a sweaty man rushed toward her. He sported a well-worn, wrinkled seersucker suit and round gold rimmed glasses propped on his nose. He pushed his hand through his thinning hair, as he stood right in front of Pearl. Pearl couldn't decide if he was in his thirties or his fifties. A solid, strong hand pressed a creased business card into her palm.

"Who are you?" she asked. She glanced at the business card in her hand. She read, aloud, "Conrad Adcock Byrne, III, Attorney-at-Law."

"I'm the lawyer who would like to represent you. Forgive my manners. I'm Conrad Byrne, the third, esquire. I am not yellow-bellied. There is precious little time to prepare. We must begin immediately bringing me up to speed on the suit," he said. His hand reached toward her waiting for a handshake, but it hung in thin air, the offered handshake ignored. "I prefer to be called Connie," he said, "but for the most part, people around here call me Pup. A long story I'll tell you sometime," he said smiling at the woman, slowly taking his hand out of the space between them, wiping it on the side of his slacks.

"Well, given you appear to be the *only* attorney willing to go against that bastard, I suppose I should take you up on that. But for the time being, I am going to represent myself. The evidence could not be any clearer. I will most definitely keep your card and maybe pay you an hourly rate for legal advice, if you have time for that." Pearl answered.

Pup's heart sank. "The judge might not look kindly upon you showing up next week without counsel, but yes, yes, of course. I will help you in any way I can. But I'm not cheap, fair warning," he said. His smile showed coffee stained teeth. He loosened his tie and unbuttoned his top shirt button. Pearl was comfortable in the heat, but the lawyer seemed to be melting. He swiped his forehead with the damp handkerchief again. "I'm not scared of any politician, especially that snake in the grass. Did you know he has several suits pending against him for fraud and other things?" Pearl just looked at him. "My office is just two blocks down there," Pup said, pointing his finger. "I stay pretty busy though, so do make an appointment." Pearl guessed he had almost no clients.

She was right. Pup mainly prepared divorces and wills or represented a wayward youth involved in some minor incident. He did some pro-bono work defending the indigent clientele the court threw his way. The other local lawyers saw him in the courthouse frequently, and that kept his peers guessing, at least.

"Thank you for your card, Mr. Byrne. Perhaps I'll be in touch soon. He'll put up a fight over $1.3 million dollars, I expect." Pups eyebrows shot up, but he pulled them back down, lest the potential client in front of him think that big cases were not his norm.

Pearl watched from the courthouse steps as Pup ambled over to his 1953 180D Mercedes Benz. The car was sun bleached beige with rust patches here and there, a few dents in the front fender. As he ground it to a start, thick billowing diesel smoke choked out of the tailpipe. She motioned for her kids, realizing she had followed the man out of the wrong door.

Pup was present in the courtroom the following Tuesday afternoon. Occasionally, he stepped over to the clerk's office to file something.

"Mrs. Whitney. I see you did not heed the court's suggestion that you get an attorney?" the judge asked looking over this thick black-rimmed glasses, his lips turned downward.

"No, your Honor. I took your wise advice to heart, but I have been unable to retain an attorney," Pearl answered. The judge shook his head, but called on Pearl to present her case against the congressman and the other named defendants. She flipped from subject to subject in less than an organized manner, further irritating the judge and lifting the mood at the table of the defendants. She often shuffled through the papers spread all over her desk, rarely finding what she needed. Pup sat in the very back of the courtroom watching and listening. Though the presentation was disjointed and hard to decipher, she presented enough material, that if it were true, sounded to Pup like she might have a good case. He also knew that this woman was merely bait for the sharks that sat across the aisle. He actually felt bad for her, reflecting that nervousness and fury are not a good combination when trying to present a case. The look on the judge's face suggested he had about as much as he was going to allow.

Pearl reached over the table, extending herself and suddenly fell sideways to the floor. Pearl's ankle bent as she fell off her high heels. It hurt so bad she was sure her ankle was sprained, if not broken. The judge, almost out of patience, continued the case until the next day.

"Lucky break for Miss Pearl" Pup said under his breath, laughing at his own joke. "Perfect timing." The judge looked like he was about to throw out the case and Pup wondered if she fell on purpose.

Pup rushed to the front of the court room and reached to help Pearl. She let him take her hand and steadied herself. The children were not sure if they should offer help or sit still. This was not a contingency they had covered. Pup asked Mrs. Whitney might he drive her to the closest doctor. "You must get that ankle looked at. Look," he said, "it's already swollen to twice its size."

Pearl agreed and looked back at her children. "Come on, kiddos," she cheerfully said as if she were in no pain. "Mr. Byrne, the third, here is going to take me to the doctor." She and the children climbed into the Mercedes and Pup took the family to the only doctor open in Bay Minette. The doctor said

her ankle was sprained, wrapped it tightly in gauze, and recommended she stay off of it for a few days.

"I can inform the judge of the doctor's opinion, Miss
Pearl," Pup said. "He will continue the case while you mend.
But I would have to be your attorney to move this in our fa-
vor."

"Why, you are such a kind, dear man," purred Pearl. "But
I will be there tomorrow and keep this case moving. Rest assured, I will send up a white flag if I need you."

In his mind, Pup could already see the newspaper head-
ings: *Attorney Conrad Adcock Byrne, III, Wins Suit Against Congressman Boyd Grantham.* Pup's society girlfriend, who fended
off his offers of marriage, would give in when he plopped a
huge diamond on her finger. His mother would hold coffee
caches and brag on her brilliant son. His late father would
smile down from Heaven, proud of his son for getting even
with that no account son of a bitch. The picture was so clear!
Why couldn't Pearl Whitney see how badly she needed his
services?

The next morning Pearl Whitney, beautifully dressed and
with a new hat, strolled up the aisle to her table, her over-
stuffed briefcase at her side. She did not limp nor grimace.
She had kept her foot elevated overnight and her fine narrow
ankle looked as dainty as ever, even if dark blue on close inspection. The children took their seat on the bench behind
their mother's table.

"Mrs. Whitney," said the judge, "you look none worse for
the wear. Are you prepared to continue?"

"Indeed I am, Your Honor." Pearl told about the verbal
lease that was binding in the state, had the defendant not
offered it fraudulently. A man of his status should certainly
be held accountable for that. She offered testimony and receipts, gave descriptions of chalk X's, told of the outrage of
men stealing her minor children's belongings. She was more
coherent than yesterday.

"Do you have any witnesses?" asked the judge.

"No sir. The defendant paid them all off," answered Pearl.

"Do you have any evidence to that affect?" asked the
judge.

"No sir. But it's pretty clear. The people who were my employees now sit on his side of the aisle," answered Pearl, her

frustration mounting.

The defendant's attorneys stepped up, taking turns. First one, then another, laid out their case clearly, providing solid arguments and precedents on matters of the law, wiping the courtroom floor with Pearl's sweat. Pearl continued to object. The judge overruled her each time. One by one, Homer, Ham, the new sea captain and the often-naked Mr. Bolton took the stand. Each sworn to upholding the defendant's case. Homer Williams added to his testimony that Mrs. Whitney had pistol whipped him. Abby was jumpy, seeing both Homer and Ham for the first time in a long time. She wanted to stand up and scream what they had done to her. That might help her mother's case, she thought.

"Objection!" Pearl jumped up. "I did not pistol whip that bastard, and I was unjustly jailed because of his lying."

"Mrs. Whitney. You are overruled. Please refrain from such outbursts." The judge pounded the gavel for emphasis.

By the end of the second laborious day, the judge ordered a short recess and ambled back into his chambers. Pearl watched as the congressman followed him. The congressman reentered the courtroom from a side door. The entire courtroom rose as the robed man returned to his large chair.

"Mrs. Whitney. After hearing and reviewing the information from witnesses and studying the facts presented by the defendant, against which I have only your word, amounting to hearsay without witnesses, without documentation, I declare this a frivolous trial and a waste of the court's time and the taxpayer's money. Ruling for the Defendant." The judge gaveled the case closed.

Pearl shot straight up out of her chair. "Your Honor! This man is guilty of fraud, of luring adolescent children into unthinkable things, of theft by taking—you can't be serious!"

"You, madam, are lucky you don't face more charges. I find you in gross contempt of court, Mrs. Whitney! In fact, it is my order that you are hereby and forthwith exiled from Baldwin County. Your choice is leave this county and do not return, or I will sentence you to the county jail. What shall it be?" He looked over his horn-rimmed glasses. The congressman's hands were propped on his belly as he smiled. "You'll be out of this county by five o'clock or you'll be in my jail-house. Now sit down and shut up. You're guilty!"

Matt, Mags, Mary, and Abby looked back and forth at each other. Pup Byrne was drooling. Pup didn't think that it was within the law to exile an American citizen. He'd never heard of such, not even in the annals of strange courtroom stories where plenty of crazy behavior was chronicled. Then, too, the fact that the congressman had been allowed in judge's chambers without his attorney, and a random dozen other details, all made a strong basis for appeal. And appeal he would file and win, by God, if Mrs. Whitney would only see the light and let him do so.

Pearl set her face against the embarrassment and the pain in her ankle. She packed her briefcase and headed to the back of the courtroom, straight to Pup. She held her chin up, kept her step light and even.

"Sic 'em!" Pearl said to Pup. "It's time for you to prove you're a full grown attack dog."

"Let's go to my office, Pearl," he answered. "I can absolutely get an appeal heard, and I will do everything in my power and the rule of law to overturn this verdict and win your original plea against the defendant and his lackeys. You will see. This judge has broken more rules than have been written. We'll take it to the Supreme Court if we have to. You can't exile someone, for God's sake."

Pearl said, "You mean my children and I don't have to leave?"

"No, until I get the law on our side, I highly recommend you leave the county as soon as we finish our meeting."

By nightfall Pearl and her children were out of Baldwin County.

Jackson, Mississippi

The ordeal in court was a few months behind her but a day didn't pass that Pearl didn't call Pup to check on the progress of the appeal. It had been granted, he told her, but a court date was not yet set. Pearl was busy doing title searches, which turned out to be a headache in Mississippi, had rented a small house and settled the children into school. Matt's grades had rendered him a partial scholarship and he had left for Auburn.

After the daily ritual of following the mosquito truck down the street at dusk, playing in the dense fog of mosquito repellent with her new friends, Abby came inside. The house was dark, not a lamp on. It was quiet and Mags and Mary's room was empty. Abby found Pearl curled up in their double bed, squalling into her pillow.

"What's wrong, Mamma?" Abby asked as she gently stroked her mother's arm. "Do you want me to cook you some scrambled eggs?" Food was the only comfort Abby could think of.

"He doesn't love me," Pearl cried, huge tears falling down her smooth cheeks. "He's going back to his wife!" Her squalls grew deeper, more violent, her entire body shaking.

"Who? Who doesn't love you?" Abby asked.

"Mr. Friendly. He fired me. He doesn't love me. He says he can't leave his wife because she's mentally ill." Pearl was still crying, only softer now, sitting up on the bedside, blowing her nose in a delicate blue hanky and smoothing her skirt down.

"The same Mr. Friendly who taught me to ride my bike?" Abby asked.

"One and the same." The question spun Pearl back into total desolate crying.

"Where are you gonna work now, Mamma? I can make coffee, too, if you want some."

"Oh, there's plenty of work," snuffled Pearl. "And Pup says that a court date will be set any day now."

Pearl got up, went into the small bath and splashed cold water on her face. She held a cold wash cloth against her eyes in hopes the lids didn't swell up like balloons. When she came out of the bath, the crying had stopped.

"I think I'll take you up on that cup of coffee," she said to Abby. "When did you learn to scramble eggs and make coffee?"

"Mags taught me. She also made me a puppet box so Judy and I can have puppet shows." Abby rambled on about odds and ends as it seemed to keep her mother's attention off of Mr. Friendly.

The doorbell rang.

"Oh, dear," said Pearl. "Who in the world is it now?"

"I'll get it, Mamma. Want me to tell them you are not receiving?" Abby was proud of the word she'd learned from Mary just yesterday.

"No. I'll get it," Pearl said. She smoothed down her hair first, then her skirt and hoped her eyes were not swollen.

There he stood. The old man from the fort who tried to make the dishwasher contraption. The old man who had proposed to her at least a dozen times. The old gentleman whose proposals she had regularly declined.

"Hello, my lovely Pearl," said the man's soft, deep voice. "I know I should've called first, but I simply couldn't find your number. I was hoping I could take you to dinner tonight."

"Oh, do come in! Your timing, as always, is impeccable," said Pearl, so quickly happy. "You remember my daughter, Abby, don't you? What in the world are you doing in Jackson, Mississippi?" she asked.

"On my way back to Montrose from visiting friends in Texas," he said.

"Well, visit with Abby while I pull myself together," chirped Pearl, using a voice Abby had heard many times when her mother was about to get her way.

That night at dinner, the old gentleman proposed again. That night, Pearl said yes. Pearl came in to inform Mary, Mags and Abby they were moving back to Baldwin County, but this time into a beautiful mansion on the bay. It was agreed that Mags could stay a short time with friends until she graduated.

Mary was more than eager to leave Jackson, the sooner the better. Abby had mixed feelings but was courteous.

"But, Mother," asked Mary in the privacy of her room. "What about the judge exiling us from the county?"

"I'll be entering under a new name. They won't even know I'm there until I come to collect my money. Pup thinks we have a very good chance of winning and now I'll have the funds to keep him, let's say, *encouraged*."

The old man spent the night in a local hotel, so the neighbors would have nothing to gossip about. He had been raised in a different era, one of elegance and properness. He had no intention of changing the rules by which he lived even though time continued to speed by him.

Pearl ripped through the little house, packing only personal belongings and a few cherished family heirlooms she had managed to slip off the fort. Just as she was double checking and crating up animals, the phone rang.

"Hello," a happy Pearl answered.

"Well, you sound chipper today," said Pup on the other end of the line.

"I am. I'm about to be a bride. Please don't tell me our appeal was denied or delayed," she said.

"Actually, out of the clear blue, the Congressman decided he did not want this case to go to an Appeals Court. He has agreed to all of your terms under the condition the settlement agreement remains confidential!" Pup was giddy. The terms may be private, but the case certainly was not. He could already see his picture on the front page. "Seems the old hard-ass has himself in too much trouble at the present," Pup gloated, "and with election time nearing, well, I guess he decided this one wasn't worth the type of publicity attached."

"Oh, Pup!" Pearl laughed. "We are both going to be rich and now you are famous! With attorneys in the State of Alabama thicker than the mosquitoes, you were the only one with enough guts to take this case on! I salute you, Sir!"

Pearl decided, for the time being, to keep this excellent news to herself. She looked back at the cottage, not an ounce of fondness or wistfulness about the leaving. This time, in a pink and white Chrysler Imperial with push button gears, they left town in broad day light, not under the cover of darkness. They stopped at the Big Boy and had a hamburger, Pearl dressed to the nines. After lunch, they dropped Mags off at her friend's house and hugged her good bye. It was less than a month until her graduation, and now they could talk about college plans for her as well.

"We'll have to get blood tests," the man said as he sped along. "But I have a friend in Lucedale and I know the judge. Old friend of the family. Shall I marry you before I bring you back into Baldwin County?" he chuckled.

"Oh, yes. Let's do!" said Pearl.

He was eighty-four years old. She was forty-two. The children were instructed to call him Poppa.

Pup strolled into his office the next morning, having deliberately hung around the coffee shop longer than usual, enjoying the pats on the back and kudos from his brethren lawyers. He had the Montgomery paper tucked under his arm as he strolled into his office, swearing he would now have his gilded name on the front window repainted immediately. He planned on sitting down at his desk, grading the quality of his picture that was on the front page and cutting out the article to have matted, framed and hung in his office.

On one side of his desk was the box with Pearl Whitney's case in it, the appeal paper open and on his desk. On the other side of his desk, he had the papers with all of the signatures from the mineral rights that had been stolen out from under his father. Now that he had kicked the big boy's ass but good the first time, he fully intended on proving his father's signature was forged and get back what rightfully belonged to his family. He glanced from Pearl's page with a huge smile on his face, then over to the page with his father's so called signature. He glanced back at Pearl's signature and back at the mineral rights deed. He felt his skin crawl. He couldn't be sure, but the signatures bore an uncanny similarity. The Montgomery paper had fallen to the floor.

"Gloria!" Pup screamed from his desk that was ten feet from his secretary's, causing her to jump and drop a stack of papers. "Do we know a handwriting analyst?"

Bayou Esperance, 2009

Pearl tried to stay focused on pulling weeds and prepping her garden for winter crops, but Doesie's call weighed on her mind. She stood up and rubbed the knot growing in her neck. She walked toward the leaning front porch and took a seat on one of the few smooth spots that offered a lesser chance of a splinter in her backside.

Her gray eyes stared at the creek as she beckoned long buried memories. "I'll never admit to one damned thing," she said to herself. "I did what I had to do and that's that. After all these years if she thinks she's going to just show up and make trouble, she's got another think coming."

To Pearl, it seemed as if she had been in battle all of her life. First, fights waged with her own family, a chicken farming clan from north of Mobile. Pearl sat there thinking and wondering how a mother, holding her newborn baby, with all fingers and toes present and accounted for, could simply declare that child different. Yet her mother had done just that when Pearl was born.

"You're a genius, that's what you are," her mother had griped constantly. "But if you don't get right with your Maker and stop shaking those skirts, the excelsior is going to get ripped right off your box. You can take that to the bank, young lady."

"Mother, why did you give your other children Biblical names, but named me after a piece of gritty sand stuck in an oyster's belly?" Pearl had asked her mother way back when.

"Your daddy thought you were the gem of the group. Your name was his big idea. The others always resented you for that."

Pearl smiled at the thought of her daddy, the only person she could think of who was ever actually proud of her or thought she was clever, funny, and smart. She had, much to her mother's dismay, grown into a beauty, shiny black hair with a slight curl, intense green eyes, high cheekbones and a crooked nose that hinted of a distant Cherokee background. Pearl stood six inches shorter than her six-foot father and six inches taller than her five-foot mother.

"Daddy, does she think I'm plain stupid? I know when she says I'm a genius she means I'm a liar," Pearl had said to her father.

Her father chuckled. "Honey, you have to admit, you tend to stretch the truth. You've done it all your life. Remember that story you used to tell about riding your horse under the cherry trees and catching the cherries in your mouth? That was a good one," he said. "No cherry trees growing in South Alabama." He laughed out loud at the memory and pulled his pipe out of the battered pocket of his shirt, tamping down the tobacco. "But you need to try harder to stick to the truth, honey. Then you don't have to remember what you said."

Pearl had grown up in a small town north of Mobile on a medium sized farm, dotted with long white chicken houses. Pearl's mother, in her later years, became an obnoxious, pious Christian, blushing each time Pearl swayed past in full skirts. But Pearl remembered stories about her mother running whiskey from her daddy's still down to the men at the shipyards in Mobile. In fact, back before she became a holy-roller, Pearl's mother had proudly told her that they came from a long line of sportin' women. Pearl was definitely a sporting woman.

Pearl's sisters sadly resembled red clay dirt clods, one indecipherable from the other. Their frizzy, un-tamable hair was the same color as their skin. It looked like the whole bunch of them had been rolling in the dusty orange-red Alabama sand clay that covered the county. As adults, they lived in identical houses on identical roads, each hen still clucking and scratching the same sand they had scratched as children.

Snapping out of her reverie, Pearl scooted off the porch and walked to the kitchen. She shuffled along, dragging her feet as she walked, almost as if burdened by the recollections of her girlhood and family.

She sat down inside, waiting for the coffee to brew, and another picture from her past came into focus. This one was at least happy and she smiled recalling when the Circuit

Chautauqua had come to Citronelle, the town closest to her parents' farm.

"Here, baby girl," her daddy had said, giving her the keys to his cherished 1934 Dodge truck. "There's a sight in town I think you wanna see." Pearl must have looked stunned. "If I didn't hand you my keys, you'd just steal them anyway, right?" He said it with a broad grin on his narrow, long face.

"Why, I wouldn't do that, Daddy!" Pearl beamed, batting her lashes at her father.

"Hmm. I seem to remember a time when you stole my truck? When your Mamma asked you where you'd been, you said *no where*. Then she went over and looked at the miles on the truck. She wanted to know where the extra miles had come from."

"And I told her there couldn't be more miles because I'd put it in reverse and backed all the way home!"

"Just up and told on yourself like she hoped you would!" Pearl recalled her father was in a full-out laugh at the thought. "That was a good one, baby girl."

Pearl had snatched the keys from her father, quickly dressed and headed for town. She couldn't wait to see what the Circuit Chautauqua was all about. As she passed her mother in the kitchen, she noticed the redness creep up her mother's neck. Her mother had turned back to stirring the chicken and dumplings without saying good bye.

"Boy, do I remember that day. The Troupe. The costumes. I snuck around behind the tents and saw it all." She leaned back in her chair, chatting up a storm with herself, as old folk living alone often do. "Thank you, Daddy," Pearl said, looking up to heaven where she knew, without doubt, he now lived. "That little peep into that tent changed my life forever. I knew right then and there I would not grow up to be a carbon-copied hen like my sisters."

Soon enough, Pearl had shaken her chicken farmer daughter's life simply out of existence, the long hard shake of a huge, wet dog fresh out of the river. From that day forward, Pearl began crafting herself into an entirely different person, beginning with books on manners, sewing, French, anything a properly healed young woman should know.

Devil Vines, 2009

Abby propped herself on the front porch banister, hanging over looking at the bushes beneath her, wondering if it was still hot from yesterday or already hot for today. Her garden clippers were in one hand and ice-cold tea in the other. Sweat beaded on her upper lip as she watched Joe rake leaves in the front yard.

Joe leaned on the rake and wiped his sweaty forehead with his gloved hand, leaving a brown smudge. His sweat soaked the neck and underarms of his old gray tee shirt.

"I'm going to die in this goddamned house," Joe said. He batted at a mosquito, or at least pretended he was being attacked. Abby wasn't sure. He stopped raking again and turned toward her. "And for the record, there are seventeen of your beloved magnolias. I've counted every damned one of them. And not a one of them under three inches in diameter."

"Joe, really. Don't be such a martyr. We can hire someone to clean up the yard, you know." He raked with more gusto.

"Do you want some tea or water?" she asked.

"Hell no!" he said, throwing the rake down. He plopped down on the porch steps, next to where she was now standing, and drank down what was left of her tea.

Abby pushed past him, past the broken spindles that were still sticking up. She was determined to continue her project of ridding this lovely yard of its dreaded devil vines. Abby had looked the things up in her big book of southern plants to learn that this devilish vine was called "Smilax or Sarsaparilla," The book informed the reader there was only one way to win a battle against the thorny vines with heart shaped leaves, the leaves that danced in the breeze and taunted her. You had to find the mother tuber, hidden and huge, somewhere deep in the ground and kill it, dig it up, chop it up. When she first started, she was confident she'd be victorious. But after a few weeks of chopping and digging, she declared defeat. She would settle for cutting the vines off at ground level. Out of sight and out of mind. The irony of the task of killing the devil vine and the risk of killing the beautiful bushes under which they grew did not go unnoticed. She risked the same if she attempted to dig the truth from her mother's manure-filled earth.

"So," Joe asked, startling her, her rump sticking out from under an old azalea bush. "When are you going to see the old girl?"

"Were you reading my mind?" She looked at him, the afternoon sun reflecting from her sea green eyes, his blue eyes shielded by sunshades. "I was just thinking about Mamma. Well, I was thinking about getting rid of these vines, which brought Mamma to mind, oddly enough. I haven't even called her. I'm not even sure she knows I'm here."

"Isn't that the real reason we're down here?" he asked.

"Of course not. It's only a part of the reason," she answered.

"I don't understand. I have never understood why you want a relationship with her at all," Joe said. "If I were you, I'd never speak to her, at all, ever, period."

Abby didn't resent his position, given her mother's history. She'd made excuses for this woman her entire life. She knew they were limp, weak. But if this place was to become their Garden of Eden, there was a snake she must deal with. She guessed there must be a snake in every Garden of Eden.

Abby put her clippers aside and burrowed in her jeans pockets for the crushed pack of cigarettes. She lit one and started toward the house, her shoulders slumped. She looked at her fingernails, at the dirt that would not wash away even with a scrub from a brush. She was weary of chopping vines, of trying to make Joe feel at home, but mostly of her wishy-washy thoughts about what she was going to do about her mother. Abby regarded herself a woman of decision and action. This uncertainty did not suit her.

Abby stopped and crushed out the cigarette. She turned around to face her husband.

"I will call her in the morning. First thing," she said, and went inside, closing the door.

The Visit: 2009

"Mamma, I'm not *investigating* a thing. After traipsing all over the country for the last twenty-odd years, Joe retired. We decided to move home. Or I did. Joe decided to come along."

"Oh, bullshit, Abby. I know you've been asking around, sticking your nose where it doesn't belong. I still have lots of friends, you know. They've told me who all you've talked to. For God's sake, Abby. Can you leave the past in the past and what's left of my reputation alone?" Pearl was seething.

As she looked at her mother, Abby wondered if she still had the "spells" she had when Abby was a child. Back then, Abby had come to believe she had two mammas. One mother was relatively normal, except for constant lying. The other mother, without rhyme or reason, would go into rages, stomping so hard the dishes rattled in the cabinets.

As a child Abby dreamed of her turn for walking through the gardens at Ecor Rouge or the woods at Bayou Esperance with her good mamma. The mamma who knew everything there was to know about every living plant and everything that flew. During these magical walks with the Good Mother, Abby hung on to every word of Pearl's stories as she spun fantasies fit for fairy tale books. Tales of when she'd been a spy, hush-hush stuff. Or discourse about getting one of her *two* PhD's, one in psychology and one in horticulture. "The psychology was a waste," Pearl had said, explaining that people always lied and therefore you couldn't help them. These were precious times, listening to her mother spin endless tales. Back then Abby believed every word. Then, without warning, these enchanting walks with captivating talks would simply evaporate and out of nowhere the Bad Mother would show up. Screaming, grabbing Abby by her long blonde hair, swinging her as if on a rope, dragging her to the ground, accusing her of misconduct that had not been committed.

Back then, Pearl assumed an air of sophistication with ease, and yet kept an earthy depth in her eyes that drew men to her like magnets. She dazzled men and women alike with her wild stories of trips and oohed her guests with a table always perfectly set. She read palms and people exclaimed amazement for her accuracy. Pearl read people like they were recipes in a cookbook. All her wile and cunning and skills were ready made for her eventual role of grand dame at Ecor Rouge.

Pearl's icy voice snapped Abby out of her daydream. Suddenly, Abby was back in the shack with Pearl who continued her rant about Abby's so-called investigation. "So what the hell do you want to know, Abby? I was a single woman raising four children, doing the best I could. What else is there to know?" Pearl was stewing. "Gossip flew because people back then did not believe that a single woman could possibly make a living, and a damned good one I might add, without something nefarious going on. Well there wasn't!"

"There's a lot I want to know, Mamma. The truth would be a good place to start." Abby had stopped breathing and reminded herself to inhale. She sipped her coffee politely, as if she had not just insinuated her mother was a full-blown liar to her face. The next step in their typical conversations would be to change the subject altogether, the routine when uncomfortable subjects were being discussed. Just one question, then she would take the expected detour and ask about the garden. "Mom, I'm a grown woman now. I can handle anything you want to share with me. I'm not as pure as the driven snow, you know."

"Now you're calling me a liar and a whore?" screeched Pearl, spit flying out of her mouth and into Abby's face.

"I am not calling you a whore," Abby said, carefully avoiding the liar part. "I'm just saying that some things you did may have been justifiable."

"That's it, Abby. Get out of my house and do NOT come back until you can mind your manners. And don't you dare wear dungarees in this house again."

Abby stood, gathered what little she brought in and held back her tears. Pearl slapped her hat on her head and fled to her dear garden. Abby's hands shook as she climbed into her car and lit a cigarette. The meeting had gone a little worse than she had planned. Abby was ashen and feeling guilt for something she couldn't identify. She took the long, scenic route home, giving herself time to calm down. She lit another cigarette and took a long, deep drag.

Abby thought, *Joe is right. Pearl is right. Why am I back down here? What are my real motives? God knows, I'll never get the truth out of her. I'm going to have to piece this together myself. I doubt I'll ever understand her intentions, even if she did tell me.*

Prior to returning to the south, Abby had dreamed of, yearned for, hot sticky nights and summer bug noises, frogs squawking, windows open while the rain beat down on big leafed plants. She yearned for an apology from her mother, at least an acknowledgment, or maybe the truth. Things Joe would never understand and things that Pearl wouldn't give a damn about.

As she drove toward her new home, she started the thought process, yet again. "Let's see," Abby began her list of why she wanted to be here, trying to take her mind off of the confrontation she had just had with her mother. "Iced tea in the South is not seasonal, as it is in New England. People here know that trucks tump over, rather than turn or dump over. Southerners know what "Idn't" means. They know that juke joints are just smoky bars where you have more fun than where they serve cocktails. Fish are to be eaten with hot, peppery, and buttered grits. Crawdads are bait, not dinner. Southerners know that Louisiana is pronounced Luzianna and that chicory, in the right amount, makes a good cup of coffee great."

Abby felt the wind blow through her hair as she sped along Scenic Route 1, the top down on her little car. She day-dreamed and questioned herself, her judgment, her life. Years of therapy had not put this to bed. She was on her own. "Kid-do," she said to herself, "it's just you and me. Maybe I'll go by Ecor Rouge."

Abby's saner-self thought it an unlikely stop over. Joe would just grunt at the idea. He was so tired of hearing about Ecor Rouge. As usual, her less than sane side won. She turned left, rattled over the cattle trap at the brick and wrought iron fence and drove down the long driveway past the monkey puzzle tree.

"I do hope the new owners are nice. Damn, I grow more like her every day." She stubbed her cigarette out, put on a smile and opened the car door.

Guilty of Everything: 2009

Abby sighed with relief as she pulled into her own driveway. The house was shaping up. Big white rocking chairs, just as she had long pictured them, donned the porch and huge ferns hung between each column. She smiled entering the front door, glad to be home.

"Well," Joe asked. "Did the ol' girl come clean? Did you learn anything you didn't already know?"

"Things went *just* as you predicted, Joe." Abby sighed. She had been emotionally battered and did not need his sarcasm. "Joe, I was *in* that courtroom, dammit! Granted, I was young, but I was there. The judge yelled at mother 'Sit down, shut up, you're guilty!' Guilty of what? She refuses to talk about anything. No, I did *not* get what I went for."

"Guilty of everything, not what," Joe answered. "What she did to you children was and is unforgivable. She's a sociopath, by the book. Look it up. She's not crazy but is willing to do anything it takes to get what she wants. No compunction. No conscience. And, Abby, this is America. There is no way you were exiled from Baldwin County. This is not Russia and judges can't go around exiling people."

"Joe, this is where you can help. You know your way around courthouses and old documents. Let's go to the courthouse tomorrow and find the case. You weren't known as the Idea Man for nothing in your working days."

"Abby, I'll go and help you. But don't get your hopes up. I'm telling you now. There is nothing to find. Even if, and I mean IF, such a case existed, it won't be in writing. She was dealing with the congressman of the district and the Governor of the State, for God's sake. I can assure you no stenographer was present. There will not be a sign that a trial ever took place."

"I was there, Joe. It *did* happen. Maybe we can find some shred of evidence. You're an investigator. Investigate, please!" Abby was exhausted from the day and Joe seemed her last, best hope. He had been one helluva investigator in his day and they both knew it.

"You plan on calling your sisters and brother anytime soon?" Joe asked. "They were older. Maybe they can shed some light on this for you."

"No, I haven't called yet. I'll call Matt, but I'm not ready to hear all the girls' glittered-covered bullshit yet. Do you want some tea?"

"No, thank you," Joe replied. He was right at the good part in his book and though trying to be empathetic, he really wanted to get back to the story which lay open on his stomach.

Abby poured herself a tall glass of tea, dumped it out, and made a pot of coffee. She picked up the phone and called Matt.

"Well, hello, Baby Sister," Matt said, somewhat caustically. "It's about time you remembered you had a brother. How long you been here now?"

"A few months," Abby replied. "It took a while to get everything unpacked and get Joe used to the mosquitoes, the humidity, the South! God, it's good to hear your voice. I went to see Mamma today."

"Yep, that word is already on the wires," he said laughingly. "I understand you called her a liar and a whore!"

Abby listened to his laughter on the other end of the line. Matt parted ways with Pearl just after college and had seen her as little as possible since then, though he lived just across the bay in Mobile. He didn't trust anyone who trusted Pearl but had admiration for his little sister as she stood up to her.

"Matt," Abby said, "I didn't call her a whore or a liar. I'm just trying to put together what went on down at the fort and why. Why was I simply given to Uncle Homer? What mother in her right mind would hand off a child to a toothless, old drunk?"

"Because she doesn't give a damn about anyone but herself," he replied. "I don't want to talk on the phone about this, but since you're here now, maybe we could come over, see the new house and I can fill in some blanks."

"Oh that would be fantastic. Joe doesn't believe for one

minute that we were exiled from the county. You were there. You were old enough to remember."

"Joe would be wrong. I guess he's never seen how a kangaroo court in Alabama works. We were exiled. I was there. I know."

"What did she do?" Abby queried.

"Everything you remember and then some. We'll get together soon and compare notes," Matt said.

"Joe says if Pearl's lips are moving she's lying," Abby interjected with a small laugh.

"He's mostly right. There is some truth in there, but ciphering it is the tough part. I don't see her and I don't tell Mary or Mags a thing about my life because I don't want Pearl to know where I live, where my children are or anything else about my life. If you and I talk, it will be under the same provisions."

"Matt, I have to see her. I have to glean what I can from her. Besides, she's ancient now. I promise not to breathe a word about us meeting or anything we say. I was going to call the girls and let them know I'm back."

"Suit yourself. They know you're back. You won't get any information out of them. They are all sunshine and roses, neither wanting to look at the past at all. And, if we meet, I don't want them to know either. I don't trust the whole damn bunch. You have no idea what we've been through, thanks to that gang, since you've been gone. Give me your number and I'll get back with you." The conversation was over. She hung up the phone and walked back into the den.

"Joe, I talked to Matt."

"Well, how is he doing?" Joe asked. "He's the only one I trust."

"He's thinking about coming over, but I guess a lot has happened in my absence. He wants to talk it over with Jane and he'll let me know. He did confirm we were exiled from the county, Joe. He's older than me and was definitely old enough to remember."

"I'm telling you. None of you were old enough to understand how the court system works. We'll go up to Bay Minette tomorrow and go through the log books. Maybe we can find a case number or some hint of a trial, a starting place maybe, and get to the bottom of this," Joe said as he turned his attention back to his book. "I sure would like to see some court transcripts." he added, peering over his book, "but honey, don't get excited. I'm pretty sure they do not exist."

"I went by Ecor Rouge today," Abby said. Joe gave up and laid his book back down on his chest. "The new owners are nice."

"Abby, really? Do we have to talk about that damned house incessantly? I know. It was a grand house. It was on the bay. You had a horse. Your beloved Poppa was there. Pearl let it go for a song, yet one more of her brilliant moves. You really need to let that go. I don't think it's healthy for you to dwell in the past. We have a good life, Abby. Why can't you just enjoy it and leave the past in the past?"

"God, you sound just like Mamma! I have to get some answers, Joe. Then I can let it go." Abby turned sharply and went into their bedroom. She saw the days' paper on the floor, the usual graveyard for Joe's read papers. She had long since given up arguing with him about throwing them away. She bent over to pick it up when a headline on page four caught her attention. It boasted, "When the Money Came to Town," an article about the Citronelle oil play back in the fifties. "It was a scandal," the article started out, "even those being robbed blind had no idea they were signing away their futures and their grand-children's futures." Abby scanned the article quickly at first, checking to see if her mother's name, or any other name she knew, was in the article. Grateful that she saw none of the names she should have seen, she sat on the edge of the bed and read how the poor folks of backwoods Citronelle had signed away their mineral rights for a paltry sum, and those wells just kept pumping to this day. She thought back on her mother, the land-man, all those years ago. The most successful land-man. **The** land-man everybody wanted to hire. The late hours. She inhaled deeply, trying to breathe at all. She carefully folded up the article and placed it in the bottom drawer of her night stand. Yet another lead to follow. She knew this scam had Pearl's fingerprints all over it. She wondered if there was a statute of limitations. She wondered if that's why Pearl kept herself hidden away down in those swamps.

What Appeal? 2010

Christmas had come and gone without the family celebration Abby had hoped for. Joe's bitching and fussing about a holiday family get together at their new house had been too much. She had not invited anyone. Good to his word, Matt and Jane came over and Joe was at least partially convinced that there was a slight chance they may have been run out of the county.

"You ready?" Abby called into the bedroom.

"Yep," Joe answered. "Let's go the courthouse and see what we can find." Joe seemed to be in a good mood.

As they got into the car for the forty-five-minute ride to the county seat, Abby said, "Oh, I do hope we can find something. Any little thing that can give you a place to start. Joe, you're such a good investigator. Do you still have contacts that can help should we find anything?"

Throughout his career, Joe had been given awards because he was the investigator that thought outside the box. Other agents had had him review their cases, knowing if a stone had been left unturned, Joe would be the one to find it.

"To be honest, I'm having a difficult time adjusting to retirement, anyway. This could be an interesting case," he said. "I still have all of my contacts. Problem is, the law. You can't just go dig out information on someone without a reason, an investigation, a case. Private investigations don't count."

"I'm sorry," Abby responded. "I have been so wrapped up in my own probe, Joe, it never occurred to me that you were bored or having a hard time."

"Oh, I'm not bored, thanks to that damned house. Abby, have the bathtub moved to the bathroom and please, think about selling this house. It is much too much house for us in the first place and that GD yard is going to be the death of me," Joe said.

"I didn't realize that you still hated it. I thought we had settled in nicely," she said.

"It's not that I still hate it, Abby. I've always hated it. I never stopped hating it. I still don't know what you were thinking when you bought it."

"Okay" she said. "I'll call a contractor this week and get the bath renovated. We might be able to break even at this point if you want to sell, but we might lose money."

"I don't give a damn. Just find us a manageable house with a small yard. And no damned magnolia trees," he answered.

They reached Bay Minette, parked in front of the records building of the courthouse and took the elevator to the second floor.

"May I help you?" a nondescript and disinterested woman asked.

"We're looking for a case number on a lawsuit from back in the early 1960's. Do you keep records that far back? Microfiche, anything?" Joe asked.

"About all we have are the case log books," the woman answered. "I'll go dig out the ones from that time period." She disappeared behind the glass enclosure in which she worked and exited through a back door marked employee's only. The woman returned to her protective glass office hauling enormous books with more effort than it actually took. She came out of the cage and plopped three long books on a nearby table. "There you have it. That's all we got."

Joe showed Abby how the books worked and what they were looking for. Abby looked at the old, marbled binders and the swirly handwritten notes within the books. Some writing was barely legible. After only an hour or so Joe spouted "Eureka! There's a case number, but it looks like an appeal number. Keep looking to see if we can find the original case number."

Abby excitedly went over to Joe's book and discovery. There it was, in beautiful hand, "Pearl A. Whitney vs. Grantham Timber Company, Boyd Grantham, Hamilton Grantham, Homer Williams, and David Bolton, 127-61-A."

"Oh my God!" Abby whispered in a hushed voice that seemed required in this quiet, musty place. "You've found it!" She threw her arms around Joe's neck.

"This appears to be an appeal number. She must have lost

and appealed the case. At least it gives us a starting place, but it is not the actual case number, so there's no document number for the clerk to find. Keep looking." Joe smiled. He felt like he was back at work and his wife was elated. It was a good day.

Between the two, they managed to go through all three books but did not come up with a case number under Pearl, Boyd's, or the timber company's name.

Joe went up to the glass wall and asked the clerk, who glanced at the clock on the wall before acknowledging him. "Do you have more books?"

"Hon, those books cover from 1950-1970. If there was a cased filed here, it would be in there."

"We found an appeal number but not the case number," Joe responded.

The clerk sighed and glanced up at the wall clock again. "Run down to the Archives Building real quick before they close. We close at four. They might have it down there."

Frustrated and in a hurry, having found the car and gotten accurate directions, Joe whipped into the parking lot of the building that read "Archives."

In total opposition to the name "Archives" this building was fairly new and nicely appointed. The receptionist was sitting in a smaller glass box at the entry, but at least it wasn't hot and musty. *Boxing in employees is a sad sign of the times*, Abby thought.

"May I help you?" asked the young and attractive blonde behind the glass. She casually glanced at the clock on her desk as she asked.

"We are looking for an original case or case number," Joe said. "It occurred in the time period of 1959-1961. The Records Department thought it might be here."

"Well, let's see what cha got," the young clerk answered. She spat her chewing gum into the palm of her hand and dropped it in the trash basket next to her desk as Joe handed over a small note pad. She read over the notes Joe had hastily jotted down back at the Records department. "You got any names or anything else?"

"Yes. Yes, they're right there," Joe answered, pointing to the small note pad.

"Oh. I see. I couldn't read your writin."

Joe spelled out each name for her and suddenly, her sullen, disinterested attitude evaporated. "Y'all wait right here. Let me go see what I can find." She looked at Abby with deep, sympathetic brown eyes.

The clerk disappeared behind yet another door, marked employee's only and Abby said to Joe, "Wonder what that was about?"

"What?" replied Joe.

"That look she just gave me. It's like she thought my cat just died or something."

"Sorry, I didn't notice," Joe said. He had noticed it and had the feeling the young blonde at least knew of the case but didn't want to admit it to Abby just yet.

After quite a period of time and well past the four o'clock number the blonde had been waiting for, the employees only door slapped open and the small blonde appeared.

"Y'all, I am so sorry. I just can't find anything that relates to this appeal number or these names, which is kinda surprising." She sounded genuinely sorry. "Maybe the Records Department will have it."

Joe sighed, trying to be patient. "The Records Department sent us here."

"Oh, that's right. Well, we don't have a thing with this number or related to any of these names. I just looked."

Joe knew the clerk was lying. There was a certain tone in her voice he had heard a hundred times during his career. Disheartened, Abby strolled out of the Archives Building, now well past four o'clock with nowhere else to rush.

"Don't worry, honey. I'll call Jim Snyder down in New Orleans. I think that's where the Mobile and Baldwin Counties appeals would likely go. I'll see if he can shed some light on where to look next."

Joe arose early the next morning and called Jim Snyder over in New Orleans. Jim looked up the appeal case number.

"Joe," Jim said. "This should be in our appeal district, but for some reason, it went to the Atlanta District Court. Let me call somebody up there and see what I can find. I'll call you back."

That call was made before Abby woke up. Joe's interest and curiosity were piqued and he was still busy on the phone when she poured her first cup of coffee. "Joe," Jim said into the phone. "This is really weird. The appeal *did* wind up in

Atlanta. As you know, they only keep these files for a period. It seems your case has been shipped off to the Federal Records Repository in St. Louis. I've got someone in Atlanta trying to find the ascension, box, and shelf numbers for you."

Joe laughed. "Wouldn't our lives be easier if they could just file it under a name, like the rest of the world? Thanks, Jim. I know some people in St. Louis. I'll see what I can find, too. Thanks for you help."

"Joe," Jim asked. "You've got me curious now. Let me know what you find."

Joe would sit on this information, for a while. He did not want to get her hopes up, though his were starting to sky-rocket.

The phone was barely back on the receiver when it rang. It was Mags. She needed to talk to Abby. Now.

"Baby sister, even though you've certainly kept a low profile, I wanted to let you know that Mom took a bad spill in the garden yesterday," Mags said, as if they had talked every day since Abby had been back.

"Oh, no, Mags. I just saw her a few days ago."

"So I heard," Mags said mockingly.

"Is she seriously hurt?"

"No. They have to do an MRI to make sure her brain is okay, but it seems that she is just bruised. Nothing's broken, but I'm going to move her to my house so I can keep an eye on her for a bit," Mags answered.

"Sounds like fun." Mags knew Abby was trying to be funny, her normal reaction to bad news. "She will fight you all the way home, you know."

"Yeah. The old girl does like her independence, but she's been stumbling and falling a lot lately. She needs to be here."

"I'll help where I can," Abby responded before hanging up.

The Case Is Not Closed

Pearl never fully recovered from her nasty spill in the garden, though on some days she felt well enough to leave her hospital bed that was in Mag's sun room, and have coffee at the table, usually wearing a colorful dress or blouse that Mags had struggled to get on her.

Abby made an effort to visit more often, though Mags and Mary had everything under control. Abby watched the dance of the two sisters attending their mother. It seemed like a well-choreographed ballet, fish swimming in a school, or birds in flight that managed to never even bump each other. Abby felt like an invisible intruder, a voyeur watching a private party.

At times, Pearl's mind was as sharp as a tack, willing and ready to discuss politics or religion, her two favorite topics. At other times, she seemed to be in another place, gazing out at non-existent horses and crooning how lovely they were. Hospice care had been ordered by Pearl's doctor, the end imminent, he said.

When she and Abby were alone, Pearl was vivid and vicious. Abby wondered if her dementia was a skillful ruse. Each time, Abby left with some vile comment still ringing in her ear. Each time, Abby swore she would not be back.

"Who are you?" Pearl asked Abby one day. Abby had been at her bedside for at least an hour, busy changing the old woman's diapers and putting lotion on her scrawny hands and arms.

"I'm Abby. Your youngest daughter," Abby replied.

"Well, no. No you are not. Abigail never comes around. But you sure are pretty, whoever you are. Where's my son?" Pearl smiled sweetly, staring Abby right in the eyes.

Pearl's body continued to melt like butter in the hot sun.

Her mind followed. Still, Pearl lay in her hospice bed for well over a year. A blessing, Abby thought, that her mind was weak. She couldn't imagine what kind of hell it would be, otherwise, for this once active, attractive and vibrant woman to be stuck on her back staring at the ceiling.

Abby's sisters huddled and cuddled, circled, brushed, clipped, bathed, changed sheets and changed diapers. Abby watched the elegant, slow dance of Pearl's death, as refined in death as she had been in life. Abby was amazed, as she sat and watched her mother dying, that not one emotion tweaked her heart. After her long morning shift, Abby went home.

The next morning, Christmas Day, with Mags and Mary by her side, Pearl smiled at her daughters and died.

Abby's phone rang. "Abby, this is Mags. Mother died this morning," she said without a hint of sadness, as if she was merely reporting an upcoming storm. "She died about an hour ago. Mary and I sang her favorite hymns to her and she looked up and smiled at us. Then she closed her eyes and was gone."

Tears poured from Abby. "Did it occur to you to call me *before* she died? I would have liked to help sing her to the other side," she said as gently as she could. "You called Mary to be there?"

"Well, yes. I did call Mary. I didn't think you would want to come," said Mags. "Mary fixed her hair, oiled her entire body, and put her in a pretty night gown. Hospice has been here and the ambulance should be along soon. She donated her body to the local university, you know."

"What I know is I could give two hoots in hell that she's dead, but I wanted to be with you and Mary."

"We didn't think..." Mags began. Abby hung the phone up, mid-sentence.

Abby turned to Joe and in a rather matter of fact tone, stated, "Pearl is dead."

Abby walked out of the back door, into her studio, into her refuge. She plunged down in the pink and white chair, spattered with paint of every color. After lying on her back for over a year, Pearl's death was a relief to Abby and her sisters. Abby, however, was devastated that it never entered her sisters' minds that she might have wanted to be with them, to feel, just once, like she was part of their sisterhood. She cried over her sisters, not her mother.

The University of South Alabama picked up the body and that was that. Her doctor said it was noble for Pearl to donate her body. *Just like her*, thought Abby. *Don't just die and get buried. Do something 'noble.'* Since her death was on Christmas Day, Mags and Mary delayed the memorial a month into the new year.

The First Part of My Life

Abby stood in the vestibule of the chapel and watched the slide show her cousin put together in honor of Pearl. The pictures flickered in a laudatory tribute, suggesting the deceased had lived her life with a unique spirit and limitless kindness.

Abby looked around at friends and family, many of whom she had not seen in years and most of whom did not know that she had moved back to Alabama. Mary caught her eye and eased toward Abby. The black dress Mary wore shimmered slightly and looked rather worn.

Abby asked, "What are you wearing?"

"Mother's dress. Don't you think it's pretty?"

Abby opened her mouth to answer just as the preacher, dressed in a long white robe with purple sashes, put his hands together as in prayer, and said to the crowd, "Let us walk to the chapel and begin the service."

The group followed the preacher into a small chapel that gave the impression the funeral was well attended. Abby sat motionless and quiet. She felt nothing. Nothing at all.

After the service, people meandered into the reception hall, chatting with people they hadn't seen since the last funeral. Her cousin's memorial slide show had been moved to the reception hall and continued to flicker photos of the apparently well accomplished woman.

Joe looked at his wife. "Abby," he said taking her elbow gently in his hand. "How about we ride down to the fort? This seems like the perfect day to say good-bye to that place once and for all. Why hang around and hear how wonderful a woman she was when everyone here knows otherwise?"

"I think that's a plan. I can't shake another hand, any-way. Joe, when the preacher asked everyone to think of a good moment spent with Pearl, I couldn't come up with even one pleasant memory."

"Well, I didn't even try," Joe said.

Joe cranked the old Mercedes and they discreetly left the church. They rode in silence a long time, each lost in their own thoughts, Abby noticing how much the scenery had changed on the way to the fort.

"Now that I'm away from the chapel and the unwanted hugs," Abby finally whispered, "I can think of a few things."

Joe looked at her, puzzled, and asked, "What things? What are you talking about?"

"When the preacher asked us to think of a good memory with her," Abby barely croaked, her voice lost somewhere in-side. "I can think of a few."

"I'd like to hear those, Abby."

"Well, first, she ate only the hearts of watermelons, re-gardless if we could even afford a watermelon." Abby smiled. "She knew that a cold, salted cantaloupe served properly and beautifully, would remain in the mind of a child forever. At the reception, my niece told me that was her memory. She knew that fresh flowers in the house would cure any malaise." Abby stopped and actually laughed. "Once, she choked down scrambled eggs I had made for her. Ewww, Joe, those eggs were floating in butter, but she ate them anyway. Folding your napkin, in fact manners in general, was imperative. She be-lieved in nature walks, with her offspring and their offspring, to point out pitcher plants, hidden wild orchids. She taught us to taste, touch, smell, and enjoy everything, especially na-ture."

"Well, that's quite a picture you paint. Maybe you should have given the eulogy," he said as he reached over and took her hand.

"One thing's for sure. She was never bored and never bor-ing."

"Abby, I'm amazed you can find a good word to say about her," Joe responded. "After what she did to you, I just don't know how you do it."

"She stole the first part of my life. She can't have the rest of it," Abigail said. "At least she didn't go to hell on a technicality." Abby and Joe both laughed. "And, don't worry, Pearl will not become a saint in my mind for merely passing out of this world."

By this time, they had reached the fort. Abby heard the familiar "thump-thump" of the seawall beneath the tires as they entered the compound. They passed the area where the hotel and restaurant had been. There were no buildings there now. None at all. The paved landing strip was cracked and weedy, its use a thing of long ago. Abby was somewhat dismayed when Joe parked the car on the recently paved parking lot that curved around a newer and larger building where Mr. Axil once sat and wrote his books. She smiled at the seven flags proudly flying over the mouth of the fort. She and Joe walked into the larger museum and spoke with an old gentleman at the counter.

"Why, yes, we all remember Axil," he said smiling, his eyes deep in memory, answering Abby's question. "Been dead for years now. I'm told he's buried down here somewhere, but I couldn't tell you where."

"What about the old inn that used to be down here? There seems to be nothing left to even prove it existed," Abby asked. "It's like it was a mirage."

"From what I hear, those buildings burned to the ground back in the sixties. Folks said you could see the flames all the way in Mobile. But we don't maintain any history of it at all," he added, seemingly confused about that detail.

Joe and Abby, hands locked together, went and inspected the old pilings, the only remnants of the pier on which she once played and slept in a summer sun, nodding off in a beer-soaked sleep.

"Abby," Joe said gently, gazing out at the waters in the bay. "Not all is lost on the case, if you still want to find it."

"What? You found something?" Abby dropped Joe's hand and stepped back, looking straight into eyes she knew were hidden behind the reflective shades he always wore.

"Well, after a few dozen calls, I located a very old man at the Federal Records Repository in St. Louis, the final resting grounds for all old cases. He remembered that any case that occurred prior to 1980 was still cataloged the old fashioned way, on cards. He was able to find the numbers I needed in order to have the actual appeal pulled. I had him pull it for me."

"Joe, are you serious? You're just now telling me this? How long have you known?" Abby felt like she was six again, ready to run up the dunes and scream her head off. The feeling of another secret hidden from her billowed through her mind. She felt the bile rise in her throat. "What did he find? What does it say? Why haven't you told me?" The mixed emotions of relief of possibly finding her truth and the rising rage that Joe had sat on this information for who knew how long, was turning into nausea. Abby pulled off her stockings and put her toes in the sand at the tip of Mobile Point. She had always grounded herself in this sand. She was determined to do so now.

"Abby, digging up this case is much akin to those damned Devil Vines you keep trying to kill. Getting to the mother tuber took a long time. I haven't been keeping it from you. I just didn't get all the information until a few days after Christmas. Given the death of your mother, I just thought I'd wait to tell you."

"Joe. I understand. I just wish I had known sooner. That old bat," Abby spat. "She knew I would get to the bottom of it. The least she could have done was to have given me a hint, left me a letter, something." Abby skid her bare feet against the sand, creating the expected squeak. She noticed the sting rays swimming toward the beach, toward the noise of the sand. She didn't know whether to laugh or cry.

"The old geezer who pulled out the file read the important part to me. He was as speechless as I was, that on a Federal Appeals document, the language actually said a woman and her family were exiled from Baldwin County. He, nor I, can believe the word 'exile' exists on a Federal Appeal document. But it does! The full document is in the mail as we speak. This case is not closed. There's a chance we can now trace it back to the original case and maybe, maybe, find out what really happened."

"Sit down, shut up, you're guilty," Abby murmured to herself. She hooked her arm in Joe's elbow and they watched a giant cargo ship make its way through the channel. "Well, Joe. The real killing of the real devil vine now starts. We will dig up the mother tuber and eradicate it, once and for all. You realize, of course, the esteemed congressman probably had the documents sealed or destroyed or sanitized in some way." Joe smiled. Now Abby was starting to think like an investigator.

"I want to go to Citronelle, too," she continued. "I want to find out how many deeds, how many signatures, she actually forged in order to become the best land-man in the county."

They turned, looked back at the sun twinkling on the Mobile Bay, and slowly made their way back to the car. Abby left her hose on the beach.

The End

Faith Anderson Kaiser was raised in coastal Alabama. After years away, she has resettled in Alabama with her husband and eldest daughter. She has two grown daughters and a beloved grandson. Faith enjoys painting and pottery when she is not writing. She had an article published in an international pottery magazine, but this is her first novel.

Printed and bound by PG in the USA